MATED TO *my ex*

kate prior

Also by Kate Prior:

The Claws and Cubicles Series:

(1) Love, Laugh, Lich

(2) The Orc from the Office

(3) The Gargoyle from General Management

Meet Me at the Anvil

Short Stories:

And They Were Broommates

Only One Bedroll

ISBN: 979-8-3303-5405-4
Imprint: Independently published

Cover design and stepback art by: Kate Prior

Reader, be forewarned:

This book contains parent death mentions, sibling death mentions, divorce, religious trauma elements, brief body image struggles, difficult family dynamics, blood (clawing/biting flesh), brief descriptions of gore, animal gore, alcohol, light drug use, full monster/human oral and penetrative sex, and some Catholicism.

0

Elise

Word of advice: if a guy ever refers to your tit-jobs as "mystical," don't be swayed by it. He's just gonna ghost you the way the guys who don't wax poetic after sex do.

Don't get all enamored with the tiny picture of him in the text chat bubble. Don't develop a Pavlovian butterfly-in-stomach response to the little *buzz-buzz* of your phone's notifications, hoping it's another message from him, even after he drops off the edge of the earth, again.

Don't forgive him when he comes back. Don't be so happy that you don't even care what the explanation is.

Don't spend so many nights at his apartment that all your clothes are in every load of laundry, and you might as well live there, really.

Don't marry him because no one else has ever made you feel this way.

Don't love every moment of it when it's good. Don't pretend the red flags aren't there.

Don't be surprised when it crumbles.

Really, you shouldn't have kissed him the first time you met, when you stepped into the street, and he pulled you back onto the curb before that car went roaring past. It doesn't matter that both your hearts were pounding, it was the first of many bad decisions. Maybe it would have been fine if it hadn't led to said tit-job that evening.

Here's what you do after your dizzy whirlwind romance drops and shatters you on the ground: you pick up all the pieces.

Move. Cut your hair. Listen to Fleetwood Mac's "The Chain" until the lyrics are burned into your heart. If he can't love you now, he will never love you again.

Cut your hair again. Move to some ass-end of nowhere town. Change yourself and your address as many times as it takes to scrub the memory of that idiot girl you used to be out of existence.

She wouldn't recognize me today. Letting my roots grow all the way out, the nails I stopped biting, the absolute puddle of mustard-colored sweaters I wrap myself in these days.

She would have hoped I knew better by now.

1

Elise

I don't have the energy of a go-for-a-morning-hike person, I just wish I did. I push myself out of bed the fourth time my bladder wakes me up in the night and put on just enough clothes that I'm not shivering my ass off, never mind how goofy the resulting outfit is.

That's how I wind up outside in the woods when it's still o'dark-thirty, my hands jammed in my near-nonexistent pockets, because I grabbed the wrong pants.

It's more than a little foggy out. Sometimes it seems like clouds come down and rest on the mountain for a while, the dim morning light casting the trails in a hazy blue lens.

In three years, I've never run into anyone one out here. I've spooked deer and raccoons on occasion, but for the most part, the world is still entirely asleep. Hell, I'm pretty much asleep. Sometimes when the trail is straight and level, I walk with my eyes closed for a few paces, like it'll add up to a little more sleep.

I yawn as a flutter of birds take off some distance away, cawing like they're mad about something. I don't think anything of it until I hear a noise, vicious and animal.

Mid-step, I freeze.

My heart is climbing into my throat one thud after another as I turn my head in the slightest amounts, scanning my surroundings much more intently than I had been before.

I don't know what it is, but I catch something out of the corner of my eye. Even with minimal detail, I can tell it's a hulking figure of an animal, dark fur.

I swallow and peek over my other shoulder. The trail back is long and winding. I can cut through the woods and get back to the house sooner.

A low growl thrums through the woods and raises all the hair on the back of my neck.

I'm off at a sprint, leaving behind everything I probably should have learned in Scouts about not giving chase to predator animals.

For several seconds, I'm nothing but one harried foot hitting the ground after another, nearly slipping on wet leaves and who knows what else. I'm covering more distance than I thought I would; I can see my backyard in the distance.

There's a hint of a self-congratulatory feeling that I'm going to be able to get back into my apartment before anything catches up with me.

But the woods are not as kind as the main trail.

My foot slips out from under me, and I sprawl through a mound of leaves and pine needles.

Oof.

The points of my body that hit the ground hardest are still ringing with the impact. Not the worst fall I've had in the woods, but still dizzying.

I start to pull myself up, but I glimpse through my hair the large paws stepping through the leaf-covered ground, circling me. I still. I'm simultaneously wishing for a hair tie, and that I had never gone out for a hike.

My heart is quivering like a rabbit in my chest. Maybe if I remain motionless, it won't see me.

But I doubt my neon-green yoga pants will blend in with the ground.

I can feel its breath puff against my ankle, feel the graze of whiskers move up my body until it's sniffing loudly by my ear.

Not biting, just smelling. I dare to look at it through the tangle of my hair across my vision.

Maybe not a wolf, I realize. Something else. Maybe wolf-like, but the shape of it is somewhat wrong.

Maybe I just don't really know what a wolf looks like, I start to think, but that can't be it. There's something too lanky about the beast's limbs. Tail, ears, fur, muzzle, but an arch to its back that looks unnatural, its head not angled in the way a wolf's would be.

I squeeze my eyes shut again as it sniffs, trailing down my neck. An involuntary breath escapes me, a hitch in my voice carried on it.

The beast moves back an inch, startled by the sound I made.

And like, that's fair. Same here.

I peek at the figure looming over me. I'm more convinced it's not a wolf the more I look. Wolves don't have . . . abs?

But at the same time, I don't know how else to describe what I'm seeing.

The creature watches a moment, before carefully resuming its inspection. Its hot breath clouds in the cool morning air, as its nose grazes my skin.

Smell me all you want, just don't bite me, I think.

Bit by bit, I shift onto my side, and slowly push myself up to sit, instead of being face down in the leaves. The beast hasn't eaten me yet, at least, but I don't feel like I can get up and go on my way either.

Maybe in ten minutes I'll be able to stand and back away. Worst comes to worst, I'll walk home with this thing following me, scoot inside the back door, lock it, and search the local Parks and Rec number.

I manage to angle my head so that my hair isn't entirely in my face anymore, and the canine creature stops sniffing me. I hold still again and look carefully at it.

Brown eyes. I've seen a lot of brown eyes before. But there's something striking and familiar about the shape, and I can't fathom why.

I've never seen this wolf before. I've never seen *a wolf* before, not in person. Not this close.

By all means, I should be more afraid of this wolf. But I'm not. Maybe fear just doesn't feel the way I thought it would. Maybe my sense of fight or flight is just kinda fucked. My skin feels heated, my pulse pounding throughout my entire body. I'm not one hundred percent certain, but I think my nipples feel . . . peaky.

Oh god, I'm hot for this beast. What the hell?

We eye each other for a long moment, and suddenly, it's my turn to inspect. I'm searching its face, looking for something I know is there, but I don't know how to find it, or even what I'm looking for.

Don't I know you?

I'm not sure why I think that, or where the thought comes from. I don't think I said it out loud, but the beast reacts as if I did, lowering its head as if to pounce, a snarl wrinkling its snout as it bares its teeth.

It lets out a growl that moves through me, low and rumbling.

The sound does something to me that it should not. All the heart thumping, blood rushing heat under my skin takes direction, and my knees press together involuntarily. The beast's growl summons the attention of my clit in a way I'm utterly unprepared for.

I let out a full-bodied moan and roll out of bed.

2

The number of times you wake up naked outside should really start decreasing after you hit thirty. Realistically, it should drop after you hit twenty-five. When your knees start to creak, at least. Which, because of a semi-hereditary hypermobile joint problem, really started around twenty-three.

Coincidentally, the number of times you get blackout-drunk should also start going down as you get older. The two might be related, but I haven't checked the statistics.

This is an excellent way to die of exposure, and really, I should stop enabling this. This is also a fantastic way to get ticks in really hard to reach places.

I blink a few times before I realize I have leaves sticking to my face. I sit up and realize I've rolled a few feet from my campsite. It doesn't look like much of one, just the smoldered remains of my fire, a bedroll and a completely unzipped sleeping bag, and a mostly empty bottle of Jack.

I pick myself up and, scrubbing a hand over my face, drag myself over to the bottle. I pick it up and swirl the little aconite petals floating in the bottom around, contemplating it.

It's an old family trick, for restless nights.

Casting a look around for my clothes however, I'm starting to think it didn't work. I thought I'd put more than enough of the flower in, but I suppose not when I find that my shirt, jeans, and boxers are all torn one way or another. I pause to count the flowers, swirling them around. Usually this is enough to assure a much quieter night for this phase of the moon, a mere quarter of it barely visible in the sky between the tree branches.

Luckily, I am a firm believer in bringing a change of clothes with you, no matter where you go. If that means folding them like Marie Kondo says until they can fit into a fanny pack, then that's what it takes.

I go down to the river to rinse some of the dead leaf bits from my face. I pull on the shirt I took out of my pack and dry my face on the inside of the collar. It's a morning of gnashing teeth and grumbling to the empty air. Best to get the grievances out before I actually get home.

Home.

I wonder how much it'll be like before I left—if anything will have changed about the place. Mom was still rebuilding the front porch then, and in eight years, I doubt either of my brothers will have found the impetus to move out. I wonder if they'll have turned my old room into a reading nook like they always said they would.

I kind of wonder if they'll have decorations up for my brother's wedding. Mom was always big into decorating for every holiday, I wouldn't think she'd pass up the occasion.

Then again, she kind of did when it was mine.

There's some sort of irony that what brings me home is the same thing that kept me from it all these years.

It's hard not to be at least a little bitter about coming home for my brother's wedding when I couldn't get any of them to come to mine. Then again, he didn't pick the wrong girl the way I did.

If you really loved her, you wouldn't have lost her, ya dingus.

My youngest brother's words come back to me in the early morning. I'm repacking my backpack, watching the sun rise through the clearing. It's time to break camp and get back on the trail. It was one hell of an "I told you so," and it's crossed my mind more than once to say some similar shit to him every time he goes through a breakup.

I pause and rub the heel of my palm into my eye. I just know it's a conversation that's going to come up at dinner.

3

I lay perfectly still for several moments, inspecting the grainy, wooden floorboards my nose is hovering over, the fraying woven rug, and then a surprising amount of dust accumulated under my bed. How long has that been there?

I push myself off the ground and climb back into my bed, rubbing my head. My alarm went off an hour ago, but my phone is under my pillow, muffling the sound.

Weird dream. Weird, very horny dream. I've had unusual horniness-driven dreams before. I just don't think they've ever felt that real.

It's one of those dreams I can't really shake the memory of, leaving me a little perturbed. What is my subconscious thinking—sex outside? Where I can get ticks? I'm sorry, I was a little traumatized by that one episode of *House MD* where the girl had a tick up her vagina. I could never. My pussy is an indoor kitty.

And it's a little easier to focus on the thought of getting ticks in unsavory places than to confront the other part of my dream, at least before coffee.

Pulse still thrumming between my legs, I don't really know what else to do except grab my vibrator and finish the job. The battery is low and it's not actually all that satisfying.

Whatever. I glance at the clock, and it's already too late to get to work on time.

I'm really happy to be here. This is honestly my dream job. Ok, it's a compromise on my dream job. I think my catering business really only stays afloat because of the partnership with Aconite Ales. And I have been low-key renovating a rundown little cottage in western Massachusetts, and yeah, technically, I'm renting it right now, but I've been talking to the landlord about buying it when I can afford the down payment. It doesn't sound like a dream house, but really, I wasn't going to be able to break into the housing market for anything less than nearly condemned.

If I'd asked myself ten years ago what I'd be doing now, never in my wildest dreams would I be living as good as this. Or at least, I thought my wildest dreams would involve something other than a sexually charged chase through the woods.

Most Wednesdays, I head over to Aconite Ales with a number of trays full of prepped food. Mystic Falls has some small tourist industry, and both tourists and locals like to visit the front end of the brewery where they hold little wine tastings, and I make a bunch of hors d'oeuvres that pair with the different alcohols. Sometimes, when there're bigger events, I get to cater company lunches or engagement parties. It pays to be local, though not a lot. But I'm proud of my small business, no matter how many business cards I put up on the front desk that guests always take and never call.

Today though, my boss, Deanna, has another contract for me. One of her sons is getting married, and she wants me to cater it. We had a phone call about it, and we're going to start planning everything today.

My car shudders as it crests over the big hill, and the Hayes House comes into view. I have to remind myself not to just drive past it to get to the brewery, which is just a few miles further up the hill, with some woods separating them. I've heard the kids in town tell spooky stories about it, but there's nothing to it.

Honestly, I feel a little weird every time I pass by this place. Very briefly, my last name was also Hayes, though that was very quickly reverted back to Barrons after the divorce. I guess it's a common enough name to show up in plenty of places, but it still bugs me at the back of my mind.

Whatever. I've left that life behind and moved on. I'm a new, different person.

Aiden catches sight of me backing my car up the long, winding driveway and jogs out to meet me by the time I get out. He's a bit younger than me and about as gym-bro-y as I've ever seen a person be. I always come in this way because it's closer to the kitchen.

"Need a hand?" he asks, already popping open my trunk.

He always helps me unload when I show up at the brewery, so I'm not surprised. In a way, this is our secret handshake: he lifts up the tin foil lids on my covered trays to sneak a taste and I have to slap his hand away.

Some days, like today, he's actually quick enough to grab a homemade mini-quiche and pop it wholesale and cold into his mouth before I can say anything.

"One of these days, I'm going to bring something raw that you can't just eat." I sigh and roll my eyes. I can't hold back my grin when I let him know these are actually leftovers from the last brewery event I brought over just for him. I'm only here to do the recipe planning today.

"I'd survive it," he scoffs, hefting the sample food trays out of my trunk, heading away for the kitchen. "I've eaten gross things. You can't even imagine."

"You don't even eat leftovers," I scoff as I pass by Aiden's brother, Logan, on my way in, following behind with the last of the trays.

"Hey, man, congrats on your engagement! I had literally no idea," I start to say, fully intending to tease him a little. I'd consider the brothers my friends at this point, or at least work friends.

Logan shoots me a glare that I've seen people wither after receiving. I don't think I've been on this end of it before, and I nearly drop the two trays I'm holding.

I don't have time to really process the evil eye he threw my way before the Aconite Ales' owner strolls down the hall, looking for me.

Deanna Hayes greets me with a perfect, red-lipped smile, her dark-brown hair pulled back into a graceful bun with fine, silver streaks through it. "Morning, Elise. This way."

"Morning, Mrs. Hayes, Deanna, I mean," I stammer, clutching my stack of trays.

She plucks the pair of them from my arms like they're nothing. It's hard not to be a little formal with her, she's just so put together.

"Um, is Logan doing ok? Thought he was gonna bite my head off."

She waves a hand. "There was some issue with a supplier he's been dealing with at the brewery. It's been a topic all week. But! That's not for you to worry about; we have more important things to discuss."

Once I've shaken Logan's glare off, it's hard not to marvel at how lovely their home is. It's like stepping into a magazine every time. She leads me into their kitchen, where she has her coffee and newspaper set out like she usually does.

It appears Aiden has left my other trays stacked on the stainless-steel counter, though none of the lids have survived his curiosity. Of course.

"Oh! Before I forget, I wanted to let you know. Since the brewery isn't hosting events next week, I went ahead and put the clam delivery on hold."

"Oh, good you remembered that."

"Right? I swear I had a premonition about it last Friday. I woke up in a cold sweat after a nightmare that we got the delivery and didn't have enough cold storage."

"We would have too. I've been so buried in this I didn't even think about our regular vendors."

Buried is an understatement. Deanna has been all over the wedding preparations. Over the weekend, every couple of hours she sent me another recipe from the *NY Times* to ask if I thought it would go with the menu we have planned for the dinner.

She sits down on one of the industrial barstools and takes another sip of her coffee before pushing some printed-out recipes at me out from under her newspaper. She lays out three different sets of pages that still have the ads from the website interrupting the recipes on them.

"I know we've already been discussing the menu, and I hate to bring this up so last minute. I had wanted to get a local bakery to do the cake," she starts to tell me, then wrinkles her nose in disappointment. "But I wasn't all that impressed with the selections we tried from them. And before I start driving two hours away to look for a place I like better, I thought I'd ask—"

"I would love to. I'm a great baker," I tell her quickly, and she smiles.

She pats the recipes. "Let's start with these and see how they turn out."

I nod, excited. I've never done a wedding cake before. It's bittersweet, honestly. I don't really believe in getting attached to your employers or business partners, but I've worked here a few years now, and I've become fond of the family's dynamic. Sometimes I feel like a part of it.

Deanna starts to pack up her newspaper and coffee to go back to her office, when it occurs to me that in the years I've worked here, I've never even seen Logan date anyone. I've seen his younger brother flirt with anything that moves.

"Did, um, his fiancée pick out the flavors or recipes? What's her name, anyway?" I duck my head a little lower and whisper, "I didn't even know he was dating anyone!"

Deanna pauses for a long moment, a little bit too long to recall someone's name. At least, someone who I would hope she would know somewhat well by now.

"Celina Carrington, she lives in Boston," she says. "Neither of them are much for party planning, so it's going to be a small, private event. But I wanted to make it nice, so they have some pretty photos to look back on."

That does make sense. Logan often goes out on deliveries; he probably visits her when he does.

I guess I'm not surprised that I haven't met his fiancée before. He's the more introverted of her sons, and tight lipped over anything resembling a personal question. But he's been polite enough and compliments my recipes, so I just kind of accept that he's a little on the shy side.

I begin clearing the long countertop to begin the task Deanna set before me, when I see a glimpse of the front page of the local newspaper. Something about wolf sightings in the area.

My cheeks flare red and my heart slams in my chest when I remember the dream I had this morning. I'd all but put it out of my head.

She pauses as if she heard my heart rate spike, a concerned expression already on her face. "Something wrong?"

"Oh, it's just that, uh, the newspaper," I stammer, and try to come up with something that isn't my really weird dream. "Do you think hiking is unsafe if there's been wolves around?"

"Don't worry dear, I'm sure it's just hikers who don't know what a coyote looks like."

I nod as she leaves and get to work. I'd nearly forgotten that dream. Things are too busy to linger over it. I don't really have time to confront the fact that my subconscious was totally ready to bone a wolf-thing.

4

Shawn

It's nearly eleven a.m. when I finally get back on the road. I've been dragging my feet, taking the long way back home, kind of hoping I'll get lost.

I brush off most of the leaves before I get in the car. It's a rental because I've simply forgone the headache of trying to find parking consistently in Boston. In the last decade, I haven't needed one to make the drive to Mystic Falls in the far corner of western Massachusetts, because I've also forgone going home until now.

I could have stopped at a motel for the night instead of sleeping on the ground, but it's better that I didn't. There're less damages to pay after scratching the hell out of some trees instead of walls.

And because I'm procrastinating the last couple miles to my childhood home, I take the route through the middle of historic Mystic Falls. I could kill a couple hours at the local diner. The last few times I've made a rest stop, there were the Aconite Ales bottles starting to creep up in the refrigerator cases behind gas station counters, along with all the other small-batch labels. There were a lot of other little breweries or distilleries dotted along the mountain. Mystic Falls doesn't see a ton of tourism, but Aconite's label has started to spread.

The bell clings as soon as I open the door, and there's only a few seconds before I feel too many eyes on me. Eight years and still all the same regulars at the Circle E, and none of them have learned to mind their own business since then either.

Sliding into the diner seat, the leathery plastic squeaks beneath me. I've got that wild mushroom omelet they used to make on my mind when I feel someone hovering at the table's edge.

I look up and it's Laura with the little waitress apron slung around her waist, and in the next moment she's plopping down in the booth opposite me. Her hair is twice as big as I remember it, but she's still wearing just as much makeup as she did in high school.

"Oh my god, I didn't think you were gonna show up," she says, eyes wide, post abandoned for the foreseeable future. I glance over the back of the seat, and it looks like she was the only one taking orders.

"Hello to you too," I return, sighing. It's hard not to smile when I see her though. Guess I can forget about breakfast. But I'm glad to run into her. A temperature check with my cousin was probably a good idea. Laura was always good for saying the quiet part out loud.

"Shawn," she says, with more urgency in her voice than a greeting really calls for. She ducks her head, but barely lowers her voice. "Were you even invited?"

Hardly a welcome home, but still warmer than the greetings I'm expecting.

I meant to call my mom or text one of my brothers. Every time I passed a rest stop, I meant to pull over, get gas, and let them know I'd be coming home. Before I knew it, I was at my exit, and I hadn't found the stones to even pull their contact info up.

"You really think they wouldn't make room on the seating chart for me?" I ask, and her eyes dip down as she bites her lip.

Jeez, I didn't think that'd actually be on the table.

I turn in the booth, propping a foot up on the seat beside me. "So. What's she like?"

Laura shrugs simply. "Never met her."

My gaze narrows on her. Laura knows everyone and everything. She convinces you to let her practice her beauty-school-dropout hair cutting skills on you and ends up wheedling out everything you didn't want anyone to know while she makes you regret your decision.

I prop my head up in my hand, watching her carefully as she examines her nails.

"Has *he* met her?"

A smirk crosses her face, and I can tell by the way she rolls her eyes as she turns to me, revealing her teeth as her smile widens, that I've stumbled on her most recent favorite topic.

"You mean did the family pick someone out for him?" she asks, voice actually hushed, so that the others in the diner can't hear us. "Someone . . . appropriate?"

"Did they?"

She rolls her eyes and looks out the window. "I mean, I don't doubt it. You've been gone. Some of the cousins have moved away. Family's getting small."

"It happens. People move away when they grow up. It's expected."

"Other people do."

She pauses, and the bell by the door chimes as someone else comes into the diner, flannel shirts dusted with the beginnings of rain.

Laura sighs and scoots out of the booth, stretching and pulling her notepad out of her apron pocket. She waves the customers to sit wherever they want but stops to lean over my shoulder with some final words.

"And there's been rumors around town about some animal attacks. Wolf sightings."

My heart catches in my throat at that, a stab of panic in my chest.

Laura shrugs like she said nothing important at all, like she didn't make me start to sweat. Twirling one of her wild curls around her finger she adds, "I wouldn't be surprised if the family started getting superstitious."

For the first time, I feel truly guilty about not being home. Maybe I should have been there this whole time. Maybe I was wrong to leave.

She walks off to bring a pot of coffee and some thick ceramic mugs over to the other table, and I get up. Forget breakfast, I need to get home.

I cut through some service roads that weave through the woods to get there, the rain never letting up. The urgency in my chest doesn't ease up until I'm passing the wide stretches of my old neighbors' farm acreage, and I'm at the start of the long driveway up to the house.

Home, when it hasn't been home in so, so long.

The house looks the same as it ever did, maybe the porch finally looks fixed. I don't recognize all the cars out front, there's some new flowers planted in the garden beds.

My youngest brother is in the driveway, taking out the trash when I start to crest the hill. It takes a moment to recognize him, the way he's filled out his scrawny bones, the fact that he's cut his hair short. He still dresses like a kid though, with his superhero T-shirts and fuzzy pajama pants in the middle of the day.

A smile breaks out across his face when he sees me, and that eases my hackles a little.

"DUDE," Aiden booms, jogging across the gravel drive to meet me.

I'm barely out of the car when he leaps into my arms like he half-meant to tackle me, and I drop my bag to the ground with him. It's messy and a little awkward, but the heart is there. At least someone is happy I'm here.

"How is everyone?" I ask, clapping a hand against his shoulder.

"They're all inside," he says, not quite the question I asked. "We're still doing all the wedding prep stuff, and I'm, uh—"

"You were hiding out here," I finish for him, and he gives a bashful laugh, nodding.

"We should go in—oh, wipe your feet out here, Mom will go postal if we track dirt inside again. She's been, well, you know. She's Mom."

He wrinkles his nose, giving me a knowing look. I can only imagine what it's been like to share a roof with her while she fusses over planning and preparation. Homesickness twists in my chest with that hint of bitterness.

He grabs my backpack up off the ground, and I follow him inside.

"GUESS WHO'S HERE," Aiden bellows as he throws open the front door, kicking his shoes off on the welcome mat; flecks of muddy water still make it onto the polished tile.

The light that hangs from the high ceiling sways a little at the sheer volume of his entrance, the only response.

It looks the same as it always did, but cleaner. The front hall is empty, but the hardwood floors are shiny, and the room is overpowered by the scent of lemony cleaning products.

"That's a little disappointing."

"Pssh. Mom'll go nuts once you see her."

I hang my bag up with the rest of the raincoats, since it's wet. The same way I did for years and years. It's strangely easy to just come home. Like the last eight years was nothing at all.

"Where is Mom?"

The further I step into the house, the more it smells like home, but there's something warmer about it. Like cinnamon and nutmeg, and something unplaceable. It's familiar, but it makes me feel a little on edge. My heart's still hammering in my chest, the tension winding tighter when it should be easing up.

"I think they're all still in the dining room." Aiden shrugs, and heads that way,

"Everyone?" I repeat, because the word gives me pause as I follow him. "Hey, when am I going to meet Logan's fiancée—"

I cut myself off, the breath knocked out me when my eyes fall on her. My heart stops short, like it knew ahead of me that I was about to go over a cliff.

There, in the dining room with the rest of my family, is my wife.

5

I've thought a lot about how I wanted things to go if I ever ran into my ex-husband again. A lot of the scenarios I cooked up involved being forty pounds lighter and wearing some kick-ass heels so I could step on his self-worth with them.

When I went to some therapy, I decided I didn't care, actually. Because I wasn't ever going to see him, never, ever again. I didn't need to make him know what he missed out on, to grovel and tell me how he was wrong and full of regrets. I don't need that, and, more importantly, I don't *want* that anymore. I don't even like wearing heels.

All the blood draining from his face when he looks at me feels pretty damn good though.

Except that a moment later, I realize we're still standing in the dining room. I'm at a job. I have half an urge to tell him to go away because he shouldn't be here, like this is just some non-sequitur in a work-stress-dream.

Deanna was just telling me about all her plans for Logan's wedding, the various hors d'oeuvres she wants served while guests arrive at the reception, what tables we'll need to set out, how she's going to arrange furniture best for that. I was so excited to show her how good of a cake I can make; I talked her into letting me use her kitchen to try the recipes out. The first two of the three cake recipes are in the oven, and the vanilla-bourbon recipe smells amazing. We're making plans while they bake for how the kitchen will be stocked to accommodate all the extra food.

"Dude," Aiden says, the youngest of the two brothers, as I look around to him, Logan, and Deanna. I've always been able to see the resemblance when they stand in the same room, the way they all have the same angular nose and divoted chin, but it's a little too present right now.

Slowly, it clicks into place.

This must be what it feels like to have a stroke or an aneurysm, I think. I've had nightmares kinder than this. I swivel my gaze to each of them, and land on Deanna. My boss looks as puzzled as I feel.

That's his mom. *Holy shit.*

"Shawn?" Deanna looks at her son with a face full of concern, glancing back at me. "What are you doing here?"

I stare back at Deanna, looking at her with new eyes.

A moment ago, she was just a woman who I met at my first catered event when I first moved here. She stepped into the kitchen as the event was winding down and I was cleaning up. Sometimes guests come into the back to ask for recipes. Often enough those conversations turn into new jobs, and Deanna had been thrilled to learn I lived nearby, and wouldn't I love to partner with a small, local brewery for regular events?

And now she was the woman who would have disowned her son for having married me.

"You two know each other?" Logan supplies as the silence in the room stretches uncomfortably long; that is the understatement of the century.

My mouth opens to try to form some kind of answer, but words don't work.

I swallow. My heart is thundering in my chest. I don't know how to answer that question.

I know every freckle on that man's ass. I know he thinks he doesn't snore when he sleeps, but he does, and he gives himself the hiccups if he tries to rush through his morning routine, and if you tickle the spot just above his left hip, he will drop whatever he's holding.

With every growing second, I feel like the floor is dropping out beneath me and hope it will just swallow me up and get me out of here. Simultaneously I'm sweaty, hot, cold, and clammy.

I meet Shawn's eyes, and mentally beg him, pleading with my eyes, *do not, do not, DO NOT tell them. I live here. I need this job. I need everything to stay as it is.*

He has never been particularly good at receiving my messages.

"That's—" he stammers, his voice coming out a little strangled, "Elise."

Deanna's brow wrinkles in confusion. "Yes, this is Elise."

"She works at the brewery," Aiden puts in, unhelpfully.

"Partners with," I correct, almost out of rote memory. "I cater some events."

"She makes these AMAZING stuffed mushrooms bites—" Aiden starts to say, because he has eaten entire trays of those, when Logan cuts him off with a hand on his shoulder.

Shawn takes in a sharp breath, his shoulders relaxing the slightest bit. What did he think I was doing here?

It only digs in a little that apparently his mother doesn't even remember my name from when he tried to introduce me to the family all those years ago. Then again, why would she?

But wouldn't Deanna remember me? She remembers everything when she talks to me.

After the amount of hurt these people caused me, the hours of therapy I spent sobbing over the fact that somehow, without meeting me, they had decided I wasn't good enough for them.

It made me pick myself apart, looking for what was so wrong with me—I couldn't just suddenly reconcile it all with the completely normal and nice and warm people I'd been cooking for and working with for years.

A sort of numb apathy rolls over me. I want so badly to exit this moment that I decide actually, yeah, I'm just going to leave.

"I left my oven on at home," I say to no one in particular, and I don't care that it's obviously a lie. As if I'd come back after they're all done realizing who we are to each other.

I take a few steps out of the kitchen, brushing past all of them with as little eye contact as possible.

The moment I'm out of sight I break into a jog, the anxious awkwardness seeping into my every movement, especially when I hear raised voices escape the dining room.

I push out the front door and down the long driveway, past my car, and I'm down the street. I can't stop. I wave my arms around like it can burn off the sheer amount of ick I'm feeling. I make some truly bizarre noises trying to let that awfulness out of my chest—something between hysterical laughter and choked horror.

I think I would take being chased by a wolf over this, honestly. Now that I think about it, that dream was not nearly as bad as this.

There's the sound of a door slamming and when I look back, there he is again, back to haunt me. Like the first time I saw him today wasn't enough.

"Elise! Elise, wait," Shawn calls after me, and my entire body stiffens.

I hold still, not for him, but the sound of his breathing, shaky and hard, reaches me before he does. I close my eyes. Even if I hadn't seen him in the house, I would know him by the sound of his breathing, even a decade unheard. I can pick it out from anyone else's by the barest trace of voice that rides in each breath.

I turn around and look at Shawn. Really look at him.

Time has really done a number on my memory of him, turned him shorter and scrawnier and just . . . less. Because I couldn't have married a man that dreamy, that just didn't seem realistic. But he's tall with a head full of chin-length dark curls; those round tortoiseshell glasses don't make him look nearly as dorky as I remember.

Maybe my memory didn't do me the injustice of remembering just how stupidly gorgeous the guy who divorced me was, but it's staring me in the face right now, making me feel like an absolute mess. His hair is even doing that gorgeous thing where it falls just right around his face.

At the same time, he seems like a stranger. Maybe it's in the way he's aged or how he's holding himself. There's just enough there that's different.

I realize my teeth are gnashing through my inner cheek after glaring at him too long.

I don't know what words will unsolder my jaw. What do I even have to say to him now? I don't want to dig up all that pain.

It would be all too easy to fall into old patterns, to shout at him, *"You know, maybe this was going to be the consequence all along of never introducing me to your family. That your mom could meet me one day and hire me to cater a wedding. You really should have seen this coming, Shawn."*

"Elise, slow down, just hang on, can we, can we—"

He fumbles through half-posed questions that sound like he was going to say "talk" or "start over," and I'm not ok with either of those options.

I'm seized by this terrible déjà vu. The tangled, raw mess that the end of us was. Conversations that were unproductive and led nowhere. Solutions picked apart until they were just as bad as their original problems. All the things I held back because I couldn't bring myself to ask for better from him.

I can't be here. I need to get out of here.

"No. Shut up," I say, because my brain has nothing kinder in the bank.

He actually does, blinking at me in surprise.

I take in a deep breath, and then let it out. I look at him for a beat. I was kind of hoping something else would just happen to come out on the exhale, and when it didn't, I have to try again.

"I'm leaving. Don't call me," I tell him, even though I'm pretty sure he does not have my number anymore. Or that I blocked him years ago. I probably should have just said that I need space to breathe and think, but I don't have the capacity.

I don't feel like providing any answers. His mom can sure as hell explain to him how I ended up in that house for the last two years, and I'm sure he can figure out the rest from there.

To his credit, he takes a step back, and slowly nods. He crams his hands into his pockets.

I don't flee.

I turn around, telling myself that I'm not shaking either, when I get my keys out of my pocket and struggle to find the right one.

I get in the car, and I want to just drive. I don't know where I would go. Do I just run out on this job? Deanna and Aiden and Logan? Do I pack my things and move the fuck away again? I could use the downpayment I had nearly all saved up for my cottage, but I'd have to start my catering business somewhere else and that would eat into my savings again.

No, that was desperate, deranged thinking. I can't just throw away everything I've built because Shawn showed up, can I?

Not to mention, I've never abandoned a job in the middle of the day before. The cakes are still in the oven, I still have to wash the stand mixer bowl and implements before I head to the brewery for today's house brews tastings.

What tasting? How am I going to wander back inside and get the cakes out of the oven and dodge questions that will most certainly rip the whole life I've built to shreds?

It stings to think about abandoning the brewery's catering contract when the Hayes have been so good to me. Like when I got sick right after Thanksgiving and was stuck in bed for a couple days and couldn't fulfill my end of the agreement that weekend. The memory overwhelms me, thinking about the stack of movies Aiden brought over with Logan in tow, carrying a quart of wonton soup, and later Deanna dropped off a box of herbal tea so fancy I still can't bring myself to open the packaging.

No, no, don't think about it.

The feelings start to reach my eyes, and I know I can't be here. Not when it feels like an asteroid of emotional damage is headed my way, and I need to get out of its path.

So, I drive. I get on the road and leave down the lonely, winding road from the house. I glance only once in the rearview mirror, watching my ex-husband's posture wilt.

I don't know what makes me stop. Exhaustion sweeps through me, and my hands feel shaky on the steering wheel. I don't really think about putting the car in park—it just happens.

I don't know what I need. Maybe someone else to drive, to take the wheel on this whole situation. I dig into my jeans' back pocket and thankfully find my phone. Now that I'm looking around, it looks like I left my bag at the Hayes House, and I'm not going back for it right now.

Whatever. Right now, I just need a moment to be a baby and call my mom and cry.

It rings, and it rings. And it rings.

And then it stops.

I hesitate a moment before I call my stepdad, if only to tell him to put my mom on the phone, but it seems like his phone is off. The call doesn't even go through.

I call my dad, also no pick up. I hang up before it asks me to leave a message. I'm not sure I can explain what just happened coherently. I nearly chew through my lower lip trying to figure out if it's worth it to call my half-siblings or stepmother, to get stuck trying to catch them up on history.

I give it a try, and it cuts off after the second ring.

At first, I think the call dropped, and try the number again, watching the screen. But it barely makes it through one ring before *CALL REJECTED* flashes briefly across the screen.

Of course. None of them have time for me. Why would they?

A wave of feeling so potent it borders on dizzying moves through me. I drop my phone in the passenger seat and just lean my head against the steering wheel until it passes.

Shawn is still waiting outside, when I look up; he's moved closer, actually, and somehow it still looks like he's holding himself back. He's not quite pressing his face to my car door window, just peering in a little too close. I can't decide if that's restraint from him or not.

I steel myself, ready to be angry with him for following me specifically when I said not to. But I'm so tired from the last ten minutes, I can't bring myself to go through the emotions.

Once upon a time, I'd been charmed by the slight Boston accent and gray sweatpants always hanging off his hip bones. Now I'd lived in Massachusetts long enough that it didn't have as much of an effect on me. Hopefully.

His eyebrows go through a number of reactions as I sigh and roll down the window. We're going to have to talk eventually. He's literally the last person on the planet I want to be near right now, but somehow, he's the only person waiting to hear what I have to say.

I stare at him, rain dripping down his face like some kind of sad kicked puppy. "Hi."

"Hey."

"You look . . . healthy?"

Feeling uncharitable, I reply, "That bad, huh?"

He startles back a step trying to recover from that conversational landmine. "No! No I just meant, like, I didn't know if saying you looked good was ok or not, but I didn't want it to sound like I didn't think you—"

He rambles himself into a corner, gesturing with his hands until he decides to just stop talking and put his hands back in his pockets.

"It's, uh. It's been a while," he tries again.

"Yeah."

"Do you need to borrow a phone? Maybe we've got different providers if you need to call someone—"

"No, they were all busy."

He crouches down, probably kneeling on the wet asphalt to get down to my car's level. His chin still hangs just over the edge of the car door.

"Listen. I wasn't actually invited back here for the wedding. I can leave. If that would make things better—"

I shake my head, unable to come up with the words. I don't care. Him actually being present isn't what I'm most upset about. It's what it means. Instantly, the last few years I've lived here feel like a lie.

"I just . . . can't believe you're working for them. Of all places to find you . . ." He trails off, looking still somewhat shaken.

"It's not like I realized this was your family when I took the job." I sigh. "I mean, for fuck's sake, they invite me to movie nights. They were my friends before they were your brothers."

He looks incredulous. "That's literally not how that works."

"That's not the point. It's . . . my employer is now also your mom. And I don't know how we're going to come back from that little revelation."

I end on a tired look that feels too familiar for these conversations. Now I have to figure myself out of this one. I look at him, expecting the same helpless expression he always wore when we got into serious conversations. I always had to clean up the disasters.

He shakes his head though, and something feels different. "We don't have to. I didn't tell them. I mean, they know we know each other clearly, because you ran out when I showed up. But we can keep that to ourselves. You can keep your job as long as you need."

"I don't need you to fix this," I tell him pointedly. "Just stay away from me. I'll figure it out from there."

He's quiet for a long moment. I can't fully blame him for ruining things, or showing up, but I want to. And I think he knows how much I want to blame him for ruining everything all over again.

"Alright. I won't fix things, but I don't want to make them worse," he offers quietly, and I have a hard time holding back a comment that he most likely will. He watches me carefully. "I just want to stay for my brother's wedding. I'll stay away from you, and I won't tell them about us."

Us.

The word makes me grit my teeth.

6

Elise, here. Here, like actually here. I still don't believe it.

The shock of seeing her again and watching her leave, *again*, has worn off, but I've still yet to process it.

She looked so different I didn't even realize it was her at first. But at the same time, all the familiar things about her reveal themselves. The way she chews her lip while she's thinking, the scattering of freckles, the flit of her dark eyelashes when her eyes look up into mine.

I wouldn't have thought it possible to dread going back into the house more than I have been while getting here the last couple days. I really just thought the whole ex-wife thing was going to be ignored for a while, then come up as an uncomfortable conversation during dinner or something.

Never in a million years did I think I'd find her in the fucking dining room.

The house is quiet when I step back inside, practically haunted by Elise's scent. I don't know how I didn't recognize it before. It conjures memories of her that I haven't thought about in years, suddenly fresh as the day they were made.

I'm so lost in thought, I barely notice Aiden come into the room I'm sitting in, until he tumbles over the back of the

couch, shoulder checking me on the way down. It's just
occurring to me now that I shouldn't be sitting on the couch
after standing in the rain for several minutes. Mom
might . . . ground me? Can she still do that?

"I did say Mom was going to go nuts when she saw you."
Aiden hums, sounding all too pleased with himself for the
accuracy of his prediction.

I slouch down in the cushions, scrubbing my hands over
my face. "I don't think you can take credit for predicting all of
that. If you could do that, you should have warned me or
something."

"I would have thought Elise would have seen it coming.
She's convinced she's psychic or whatever, but I guess not."
He nods, and I can feel his stare on me. "When do we get the
explanation?"

I glance to the hallway, where it seems empty, but that's
not something that can necessarily be trusted in this house.
"Never."

"Come oooooon."

"It's none of your business."

"Dude. It's obvious she's an ex-girlfriend or whatever.
We all have eyes; it wasn't hard to figure that much out. I just
want to know the rest of the story."

I guess that much would be transparent.

It's a lot harder than I thought it would be to just not tell
Aiden everything. He's always been the easiest to talk to and,
out of all my family members, probably the most
understanding.

I shrug and sigh. "Ok. I'll tell you right after you tell Mom it was you that peed in the baptism water—"

His eyes widen and he claps a hand over my mouth before I can get out the whole threat. It's a memory so old, I don't actually remember if that had been my idea or not.

That is the moment my mom chooses to step back into the foyer, however.

There's something incredibly nostalgic about my mom appearing at the exact moment one of my brothers is trying to force me into a headlock while I try to twist his arm around the wrong way.

It almost feels like things have gone back to normal for a second.

"What did you do? Do you know her?" our mother demands, looking reproachfully at me.

Aiden releases me, falling back on the couch, pretending he wasn't just wrestling in a room that it's forbidden in.

"Glad to be home," I deadpan, not withholding any bitterness from my tone. The urge to just shake all the rain off over the polished tile floors rises in me, and I just barely hold it back.

She scoffs and acts like I'm the aggressor here. Home at last, only to assume my rightful mantle as the problem child. I don't know why I thought it would be any different, really.

"Where is she going?" Aiden interrupts, leaning to peer out the window like there's a chance Elise's car will turn around in the next few minutes. "Did she say she was heading to the brewery or going home?"

"I don't know," I snap over my shoulder. Aiden mutters something about just wondering, and slumps against the window.

I sigh and scrub a hand over my face. He didn't deserve that from me. "I'm sorry, man. I think we all just need a minute."

"We all need a minute," my mother echoes, clearly in disagreement. She turns her glare on me, hands on her hips, and asks the question I've been dreading. "I want to know why you scared her off. I mean, what are you even doing here?"

My jaw tightens. Keeping my promise to Elise is already being tested, and I doubt my family is going to stop until they're satisfied.

"I heard about the wedding. Laura posted about it," I say, kind of casually. I wince as my mom's perfectly plucked, thin eyebrows narrow.

"Laura told you?"

"No, Mom, she posted a picture of the wedding prep online."

"I need to have a word with her," Mom sighs. She puts her head in her hand, careful not to disturb her makeup or hair as she does. After a long moment, she simply says, "Well, we don't have you in the seating chart."

It's as close to a direct statement that I'm not actually welcome here as I'll probably get

Logan materializes in the room in that sneak-up-on-you way he has, holding a few slices of cake that look like they've been in the oven too long, just on the edge of burning.

"I don't know if Elise was planning to put icing on these, but I like the rum raisin one," he says, his tone pretty indifferent to the situation. I know that asshole is enjoying this. "But I know not everyone likes raisins, and I could go with the other one if she has a good icing flavor pairing for it."

It's so weird to hear him talk about my ex-wife like he knows her. He'd been on our parents' side when Dad said he'd disown me if I brought home a human girl. How can he talk like he respects her opinions?

My mom barely looks at Logan. She's too busy being disappointed in me, and after being gone for eight years, I guess we've got a lot of time to make up.

After a few more thoughtful chews in the utter silence of the family meeting in the foyer, Logan offers, "I'll call her in a bit, then."

He would be the one to try to do damage control. He was always the good son. Of course, he would also be the one to get married to someone our mom picked out.

"I heard there's been wolf sightings, Mom. Animal attacks," I say, trying to stress the urgency that news made me feel. She looks on at me, unmoved, like I said nothing at all.

I glance at Aiden and Logan, the weight of that statement falling over them, at least. Their faces darken.

I'm not about to outright accuse one of them of going feral and attacking people. The pack code has always been not to expose outsiders to our curse, but going feral tends to make a wolf forget about upholding the code.

My mother, an alpha in her own right, purses her lips and deigns not to make eye contact with any of us. I know what she thinks. If I'm going to open this other whole can of worms and imply one of them has been losing themselves in their wolf form, it'll have been my fault for leaving the pack in the first place.

I sigh and back off. "I was worried about you all. That's it."

"There have been no wolf sightings," she says resolutely, and, for a moment, I doubt myself. I haven't been here, maybe she knows better than I do.

But I can't disregard what Laura told me.

I scoop up the newspaper from the table, holding it up for her to see. "What do you call this?"

"It's nothing! We're fine, we are as strong a family as we've ever been," she insists.

She hasn't changed, I realize. Eight years and not one shred of remorse, or reconsideration. She holds my stare with her arms crossed over her chest, determined to simply put her foot down. Deny, deny, deny, until the world follows suit and agrees with her.

I look her in the eyes, searching for any reprieve.

"Well, then. I see I was wrong to come here," I say, grabbing my bag from the hook and heading back towards the door. There's a little too much bite in my voice for talking to my mother.

I can see her wince at the snarl in my words, and it pierces my chest to see that I'm hurting her. I want it to stop, but I need her to stop fighting me too.

The door slams behind me. I drop my bag on the front porch and pull the fanny pack with a tightly bundled change of clothes in it out. I'm not quite ready to leave, but giving everyone some space to process what happened seems like the best thing that I can do. And I need to give my wolf the chance to burn all the energy from these feelings off. I strip down from my wet clothes and sling the fanny pack around my chest.

I stretch into my shift, rolling my neck and twisting my body as the bones slide into place, the thick fur pushing through my skin. It only hurts for a moment, and it's only about as bad for you as cracking your knuckles.

My paws hit the muddy ground, and I find her scent immediately. I know it well, and I recognize it for what it is now: that cinnamon and nutmeg, and under it, just her, all her, sweeter than I remember.

Even with the rain, I can pick it out better than anything else.

7

I've never just run away from a job like that. It doesn't even register that it's raining harder, and I'm just wearing a sweater as I lean against my car and think about the nearly-saved-up-for down payment for a house that I put in my rearview mirror without a second thought.

Usually in town I just go and get groceries, but there's a small diner I stop in often, and I go in automatically, without really thinking.

The diner's mostly empty, and it almost feels like a good idea to bury my welling-up feelings under a pile of crinkle-cut fries. And a milkshake. Nothing will heal a damaged heart like a chocolate milkshake.

When you're within spitting distance of Vermont yet somehow still in Massachusetts, every other place has a little corner of "Vermont Genuine Maple Syrup" sold all in the same exact maple-leaf-shaped bottle. The further up the mountain you go, everything is priced for ski-bro tourists too, because if you're rich enough to have this stupid, expensive hobby, then you probably can afford a second home in the mountains to summer in, or whatever it is rich people do. Winter, maybe. I don't fucking know how to use seasons as a verb.

The bell on the door rings as I push it open. There's maybe one waitress left in the place, sitting at the counter—big hair, dark curls, acrylic nails, and red lipstick.

On one hand, Laura is just the friend I need right now, but the wound today opened is still fresh and raw, and for half a second, I think maybe I shouldn't talk to her. She's Logan and Aiden's cousin. That makes her Shawn's cousin too. And maybe she doesn't have anything to do with this, but I can't help but be wary.

She raises an eyebrow at me, concern drawing down her face, and I wonder if I look as pathetic as I feel, drenched to the bone.

"Honey, what happened?" Laura asks, dropping her pen.

"Bad day at work," I mumble, sitting down at the diner bar. The seat squelches underneath me. "Put in a chocolate shake and fries for me?"

She nods and waves a hand at the line cook reading in the back. It seems like he heard.

Laura settles in on the other side of the counter. "Aunt Deanna driving you crazy with the wedding prep?"

"I saw my ex-husband for the first time in years today."

The words make it real, and I feel woozy just saying them.

It's like clutching my hand over a bad cut, maybe it won't be as big and gross as I fear it is, but I won't know until I open my hand to rinse out the blood and examine it. Right now, all I see is the gore; I don't know if a bandage will do, or if I need someone to drive me to get stitches.

"Oh my god," Laura says, hushed, awed, wowed, an interest in drama lighting her eyes. "Today is just the day for it, my cousin came through here earlier and let me tell you—"

She stops mid-sentence, something I don't think I've ever seen her do, the color draining from her face. Her excitement falls away for a quiet horror to match mine.

"It can't be—Shawn, was it? Oh my god. Girl, no."

I look up at her, tearing my attention away from the emotional wound I'm trying to clean out. Fuck. Not ten minutes after I told Shawn not to say a word.

My hands grip the counter at first to ensure I don't fall out of my seat, but then my head feels like it's spinning. I don't know how I'm going to do this.

"You can't tell anyone. I don't think I can deal with people knowing."

"I won't. I promise. Oh, girl," she says, twisting a napkin nervously between her hands, shredding it to pieces as she stares at me.

I can see that she knows what happened without even asking. She had heard the story of my divorce from me many times over a glass of wine in the cottage, but I could never bring myself to say his name.

"I always thought what they did to her—um, you—was unfair," Laura offers quietly after a moment. She swallows hard, apology deepening the lines in her face.

For a moment, I don't know that I can stand to look at her, even though she wasn't really complicit in it. She's their cousin, this whole damn town might as well be theirs.

Laura covers my hand with hers and squeezes. She has always been a good friend. It's sad I won't know her for longer. I honestly don't know if I can go back there, not now. I might be packing up my things tonight.

My first thought is to miss Deanna and the boys. I've grown close enough to them that I care more about them than just clients.

But the anger I've been nursing these last many years wants to throw that all aside. I can't bring myself to care. Fuck him. Fuck the people who hurt me without another thought.

"Wait," she says, glancing up at me with a strange look. "That would mean he's the ex in all those stories you told me about? Whirlwind romance, mystical tit-jobs, donut proposal, and shotgun wedding?"

I didn't realize the tears were starting to creep down my cheeks until I shudder out a laugh.

"Oh my god. I thought he would have known better than that. Donut proposal, really? He should have gotten you a real ring! We know the funds are there. Ugh, and I'm gonna give him so much shit for the mystical tit-jobs thing."

Unwillingly, I smile a little at that. I can't believe I doubted that talking to her was the right thing, even for a second.

She looks at me then, sizing me up briefly and wrinkling her nose. "Ew, girl. You gave my cousin tit-jobs, and I know for a fact he never deserved them."

I can't help but giggle in response. Even if she's just trying to cheer me up, I needed to hear that kind of thing from someone who actually knows him.

Talking to Laura always feels like a masterclass in active listening, her expression attentive and her body language wrapped up in total focus— eyes wide, gnashing into her acrylic nails. I probably wouldn't have opened up to her so much, and kept going, if she hadn't been hanging on my every word, urging me to say more every time I nearly finish a story.

It does for me a lot of what I thought therapy would do, except that no therapist has enthusiastically nodded, saying, "What a piece of shit!" to my ranting. My last one could learn a lot from her.

After an hour, I still feel like my chest has been cracked open, but at least all the debris has been cleared out. The wound is clean, and it still stings and burns and aches, but maybe one day it'll heal.

My milkshake is empty and there's just a smear of ranch left of the fries. My stomach is gurgling with an intolerant storm.

Laura's nearly gnawed the acrylic tip off her ring finger in the last ten minutes. "And you don't know why they never wanted to meet you?"

I shake my head. And then pause. "Do you?"

She shrugs a little, her attention in the glass of ice cubes she swirls a straw around in.

"I believe there were some, uh, specific qualities they were looking for," she says. For my benefit, she doesn't repeat them.

"It's probably because then I was working my way through college and here he is from some WASP-ass family and a stupid, big house and, y'know what, they probably paid for his student loans. I bet he never actually had student loans," I ramble, a little drunk on emotion.

"I don't think you can be Catholic *and* white-Anglo-Saxon-Protestant," Laura puts in quietly, and I can't resist the eyeroll that takes me.

"WASC, then. Whatever."

I vaguely remember there being some concern about me not being Catholic enough for his dad, but that didn't seem like enough of a thing to disown family over. At least, not in this day and age.

"I'm sorry it didn't work out. Maybe things could have been different if they hadn't put you through that," Laura offers, and I sober instantly.

"Yeah, well. I'm not. I'm happier without him."

She opens her mouth to respond, but there's a thud outside against the diner's back wall; I can see how a picture frame shakes with it. Laura looks a little alarmed and goes to the back to see what it was.

I finish off the last, too-warm dregs of my milkshake. Laura returns, shrugs it off, and totals the check. I dig through my coat pockets for cash. When I check my phone, there's a few missed calls.

My gut twists, in a non-food sensitive way. For a second, I'm not sure who I want a call from less—Shawn or my mom.

But it's Deanna's phone number. I hadn't expected it to be her. Guilt and ten other conflicting feelings sit uneasily with the milkshake and fries.

I look at my empty plate and glass and sigh. I should probably figure out what I'm going to do soon. I sure as hell can't stay in this diner forever.

"I should go," I tell Laura after a bit. "I have to deal with the fallout."

"You don't need to go back yet. I mean, if you need to be around people, you can stay at my apartment, I've got a couch—"

I shake my head. I know her terrible pull-out couch from our movie nights, but it's sweet of her to offer. "I'll let you know if I need it."

The drive back to Aconite Ales Brewery is more automatic than I would like. My head is in such an emotional fog; I'm so used to driving back and forth for endless last-minute grocery trips that I barely register most of it. I pull into the back loading bay like I usually do and turn off the engine, but that's as far as my body carries me. I clutch the steering wheel. What am I going to do?

Sit in the car for several minutes, apparently. I don't have the courage or recklessness to say fuck it and just get things over with.

It's strange to not be greeted by Aiden when I go into the brewery. Instead, I have to carry in a half-dozen trays of prepped food myself. It leaves me feeling off kilter.

I grit my teeth just to hold it together. I'm emotionally raw. It would be so easy to just fall back into what our dynamic was before, just friendly clients and caterer. But I can't just gloss over the fact that she was the woman who haunted my marriage, the mother-in-law who hated the thought of me.

On the one hand, I'm sure it's no easier being on her side of the phone, not knowing why any of that happened. On the other, I take some relish in knowing our true relationship, when she doesn't. I never got any closure for why she disapproved of me.

Feeling seizes in my chest. As much as I hate who she is, I can't ignore that I genuinely liked her. I liked that she thought my recipes were creative, that she praised my cooking, and that we could chat for a while. She likes me in the way I wanted someone my mother's age to like me. She thought I was a cool young person with genuine talent, instead of mildly disappointing.

And as for Aiden and Logan, they'd been like what I always imagined having brothers would have been. I felt safe around them and like they would look out for me.

Maybe that's a weird relationship to have with your clients. It just kind of happened.

Someone must have brought over the trays Aiden took into the Hayes's kitchen this morning, a cool condensation on the counter around them, indicating they're still cold. Somehow it feels like it happened a year ago.

It's hard not to notice there's also a bonus check left for me on the clean, stainless-steel kitchen island.

"For the wedding catering. It wasn't part of your original contract. I wouldn't want you to go uncompensated," Deanna says from the doorway while I was eyeing the extra zero.

She's always been generous, but I imagine today's offstage drama affected her decision while writing it.

I doubt she would have put it here if she'd known I was her ex-daughter-in-law.

I stare at the check, wondering if it's worth staying here, to slip back into that life of having it held over my head that I just wasn't worth it to him. I doubt I'll find the answers I wanted eight years ago, but maybe it'll be worth it just to watch Shawn squirm.

Closure is a well-paying dish, it seems.

8

Shawn

I'm not eavesdropping. I'm really not.

The thing is, you can't *not* eavesdrop in this house. At least, none of the wolves can avoid it. It wouldn't matter if I was up in the attic, I'd still hear every word exchanged between my mother and my ex-wife.

Despite everything that went down the other day, Elise is still going to work for my mother and cater my brother's wedding, it seems. And despite all the growling and snapping at each other we did, when I circled back to grab my things and figure out how to get to Laura's apartment, my mom had come downstairs and handed me a folded set of sheets and a pillow with a glance towards the living room couch. It wasn't an olive branch, but a silent offer to keep the peace until after the wedding.

For the first hour or so of Elise's car being parked in our driveway, I've done a really great job of keeping my promise that I would stay away.

Leaning in the hallway near the kitchen isn't the most subtle of choices for not-eavesdropping, but it's the only one where I can catch Elise's expressions, reflected in the stainless-steel refrigerator door. She's got her arms crossed around herself, and she shifts her weight every so often, her face dipping in and out of view.

"You can tell me what the matter is. I'd sooner put him up in a hotel then make you uncomfortable," my mom is saying, in a tone gentler than anything I've ever heard from her before.

I nearly scoff out loud. Of course that would be the answer. It's not like I'm family or anything.

Elise shifts back on her heel, putting just a few more inches between her and Deanna, her reflection coming back into view. I can see the uneasy tension in her cheek. "I don't really want to get into it, but that's not necessary."

"Are you sure? He doesn't have to be here."

"It's fine, really. I'm sorry I had a little freak out, but I would just really like to get back to work and pretend it didn't happen."

Even without seeing it, I can imagine the tightness in my mother's jaw. The number of times I'd tried to place a boundary and watched my mother clasp her hands and nod like she was agreeing to respect it. I can't imagine how long this is going to last.

I should have come up with a cover story with Elise. My family is all going to want to know. And they're all just going to keep asking until one of them pries the answer out of us.

It's strange. I never would have thought I'd see this come to pass. Elise and my mom talking like they're close. Unthinkable.

The urge to say "I told you so" is almost overwhelming. *Of course* she'd like Elise.

I knew that from the moment I met her. She's smart and organized and driven, she's had a successful small business since college. But I have to keep that to myself, at least until the wedding is over. Elise wouldn't take it well, and I already feel bad that I've disrupted her life. If only it were as easy as backing away and letting things resume as normal, but I guess she wouldn't want to stay here now that she knows who she's working for.

That particular wonderful moment, Elise chooses to appear, ducking out of the kitchen to glare at me for a change. It does seem like there always needs to be someone on duty for that.

Since when can't I go anywhere without running into her? I avoided her marvelously for the last few years.

Her scent is different today. There's less anger. When our eyes meet, I see only her annoyance, but I can taste the warmth of her casual mood on the air. Interesting.

She's absolutely swallowed up by a huge yellow sweater, just a peek of her jean cutoff-shorts visible. She's got a pair of leggings underneath them, outlining the shape of her thighs. I've had this dream before, where she's close enough that I could just dig my hands into the softness of her thighs.

After a few seconds of just drinking the image of her in, I realize I've started just leaning on the doorframe for support.

"Shawn," she snaps, her voice like a whip.

The hypnosis her legs have on me breaks. I look up and jam my hands in my pockets, and nod at her. "I was just leaving."

Yeah, I should go, but it's just so easy to get under her skin. I'd be lying if I said I didn't miss it.

She nods, and I'm working on leaving in any direction when Aiden thunders down the stairs, stopping the moment he sees us.

"Hey, E," Aiden chirps, looking a little too obviously excited that he has front-row, standing room only tickets to this moment. "Still on wedding prep duty?"

She shrugs, and says, "Yeah, I need someone to lick the beaters when I'm done with the third cake recipe."

"Yeah, sure, I'll lick anything you tell me to."

The first thought falls out of my mouth before I can really process it, but as soon as I hear it, I close my eyes and immediately wish I was anywhere else, anyone else, even.

Good god, man. Get a grip.

Aiden's face looks somewhere between horrified that he had to hear me say that, and a little bit like I just handed him a bucket of popcorn for the show.

"I will see myself out." I sigh, turning on my heel. I make it down the hallway to the foyer before I hear Aiden let out the snicker he was clearly holding onto.

"Wow. That was . . . wow. Yikes, dude," he says after he fails to find the adjective he wants.

"Yikes doesn't even cover half of it," she sighs as I head out the front door. "Also, not telling you."

"Come on! You too? I mean, don't feel obligated to hold back just because he's my brother. Feel free to bitch about him."

"Really, I'd like to keep it private," she says, and the moment I'm out the door, I'm digging through my backpack in search of anything else I can occupy myself with to avoid hearing them.

Work will have to do.

I move into the living room, sink into one of the armchairs and open my laptop up on my knees. Freelance audio editing, in addition to being a career path my dad would have hated, has really flexible hours, which is great when you need to travel.

Noise-canceling headphones help cut Elise and Aiden's voices out a little, but I can only turn the sound on the audio tracks up so high before it hurts, and I can replay the same clip only so many times before it starts losing meaning, and the ADR work I'm doing feels off.

Staring at the much-smaller screen in the dark has been getting to me. Still haven't adjusted to having one screen instead of three to spread different programs and folders out across.

Not quite sure why it's such a manual process when it's called Automatic Dialogue Replacement. My attention easily drifts from the lines the actress reads in every time I have to hunt for a different window to find the right file. Even when they stop talking in the kitchen, every sound Elise makes finds its way to me. The way she sighs, or her footsteps, the way she drums her fingers on the countertop when she's thinking.

It's so familiar it aches, carving out the spaces in me that she used to inhabit.

The end of us was . . . quick. I'd never had to mentally put her on a do not touch list. *Hands to yourself*, a refrain that has been ringing in my ears since I was a kid. Don't touch the museum exhibits, don't pick up strange cats, and now, don't grab your ex-wife's ass. Tempting as it is.

No, I can do this. We've been divorced eight years, and I haven't even once drunk dialed her or emailed her telling her she still haunts my dreams sometimes.

Eventually, I give up on trying to get work done and close the laptop. It's dark, and Elise's car is gone from the driveway, but the smell of her skin lingers in the house.

I head outside without even putting shoes on. In the woods, I discard my clothes and shift into my wolf form. I run so that I don't have to think.

For a solid half of the month, between the last quarter moon and the first, my wolf has almost no power over me. But every night after the first quarter, as the moon waxes, its influence grows until I can't contain it, and the transformation reaches its peak.

Between drinking aconite-infused liquor and exhausting myself, I usually can calm the fervor of it some.

Shifting has felt different lately. It's more frantic, less controlled than it used to be. Probably why I got so worried when I thought the pack had started going feral. Maybe it's just a part of getting older and I've been concerned over nothing.

It's getting to be morning by the time my mind finally clears as my wolf recedes.

The sky is a moody teal, the moon a pale orange against it. The woods and the grassy hills are a near-black outline cutting through the sky, and the house nestles into all of it almost invisibly. Only the scattered rectangles of yellow light spilling out from the windows carve its presence in the hillside, and the brewery further down the hill. I get dressed in yesterday's clothes when I find them, only partly damp from the morning dew.

It's ass-crack of dawn early, but Logan's already there when I slip through the back door, his keys and coat sitting on the counter nearby.

He's in Dad's old office when I find him, looking less haggard by tonight's quarter moon than I feel. Then again, he probably spent the night locked in the cellar under the brewery.

The brewery has a cellar; yes, it is creepy. I didn't go down there often, even when I did live here. It's the safest option, those rooms being specifically built to contain us at our worst.

Logan glances up at me, frowning instinctually the moment he sees me standing in his doorway. His long, dark hair is reminiscent of our mother's, especially with the cold, detached air he holds himself with. If he has an issue with me running the hills instead of staying locked in all night, he doesn't say anything about it off the bat.

We haven't taken the time to catch up since I showed up, and by the less than enthusiastic looks he's been giving me, I don't really think he wants to. He's always taken our parents' side on the whole marrying a human thing.

I'll keep this brief, then.

"I'm running out of aconite buds," I tell him instead of a greeting.

"You should have stocked up before you came here," he sighs, nonetheless pushing back from Dad's big desk. Logan's things are lined across the top, including a number of wedding well-wishes cards, likely from other wolf families our parents used to attend church with.

The family photos where he and I were barely more than toddlers sitting on our parents' laps, the ones that used to sit on Dad's desk, are up on the fireplace mantle facing across from him, alongside an urn.

Can't say I'm too bothered by our dad not being here. I finished mourning whatever respect I had for him a long time ago. What did it matter that he was actually dead now?

I scoop up a ratty, old baseball cap sitting beside it, the one he wore whenever he went outside, alongside a thick smear of sunscreen on his nose. The hat smells more of dust than sweat and grass now. I turn it inside out and hang it on the urn's lid, just because I know it would irritate him if his ghost is watching from heaven. I don't think he deserved to get in, but I'm sure he could have blustered his way in there.

I turn my attention back to Logan as he pushes a framed photo of the brewery some forty years ago on its hinge to reveal one of those little wall safes. His code's changed since I last was here, I note as he punches it in.

"I did," I insist. "I've just been running through my supply faster than I thought I would."

My little trick with them hasn't been working so well these last couple nights. Maybe it's the stress of all the recent drama with my family and Elise that has my wolf riled up and restless. It's only going to get worse the closer it gets to the full moon.

The safe beeps and he pulls a liquor bottle with a minimal label out. It's sealed with dark-red wax, the Aconite Ales brand stamped into the glass.

"Don't drink it all at once."

Dropping a couple petals into any wine is good for a quick fix, to calm the wolf and put it to sleep, but my dad's side of the family has been brewing a much more potent cocktail for at least a century. While Aconite Ales brews plenty of blends of floral meads for human consumption, we've always had a special reserve for our extended family, and a few neighboring wolf packs.

"Y'know, I am careful about some things," I reply, because I can't *not* rise to it. "Then again, maybe I wouldn't have to be if you didn't schedule your nuptials for the full moon. Hell of an idea."

"It is traditional," he says plainly, putting the bottle in my hand and turning away.

It would be, to allow for a proper mating. Werewolf society could be positively medieval with the way arrangements were made between different families. But I suppose the way werewolf weddings end, expecting the newlywed couple to run off into the woods together to mate as wolves, tie a different knot and mark each other with a bite, isn't too different from tying a bunch of cans to the back of the car for a human couple leaving for their honeymoon.

"You should use the shower before Aiden wastes the rest of the hot water," he says as he gets back to his desk, and that's as close to a heartfelt sentiment as I'll get out of him. "Some of your old clothes are down there too."

Aw, he does care.

A hot shower is the closest thing to a balm I can manage, short of a barrel of IcyHot.

My muscles burn from shifting back to my human form. It's too much like the all-over body ache I get every time I think I should sign up for a 5K. It wasn't as bad when I was younger, but now my body has a harder time going from the exertion in my wolf form. My knees fucking crack in the morning too. Supernatural abilities notwithstanding, everything gets harder with age.

Partly an effect of the aconite, my shift back is slower, achingly drawn out across my morning. When I peel off yesterday's dirty clothes for a shower in the brewery's basement, it's clear the hair stays just a little too thick on my arms and chest, nails like claws, the arches of my feet lingering as the bones figure out where they're supposed to go.

And the uh . . . wolf dick.

I hadn't really noticed that when I got dressed in the woods before.

It's thicker and longer than my human counterpart's, with distinctive veining. I'm sure I had the thought in my early twenties that it'd be great if I could keep the wolf dick around while human. Younger me definitely thought no one would notice anything other than its girth and length and that it would just be abstractly better for my dating game.

I've never had my wolf dick get hard though, now that I think about it. The sensation is a little different, radiating the need to be touched up my veins.

The entirety of the sex talk I got from my dad was that masturbation was a sin. I still cringe remembering him saying that the point of the knot was to never waste a drop of semen. Not that I really wanted more of that conversation with him—I wasn't about to explain how many times I wiped the history of "creampie" searches from our family computer history.

The haze of my transformation clouds whatever reason I was aroused in my wolf form. It's not uncommon that I don't fully remember what happens when I shift. What happens is often more instincts than conscious thought, and they're harder to recall.

I've never jerked off in wolf form before. Mostly because of the claws.

There's something extra-sensitive about my wolf cock that makes me audibly hiss and groan when I start to stroke my hard length. I'm thankful for how loud the water is in here. The kind of pleasure I'm feeling just getting started would be enough to make me come in moments normally.

I continue stroking, sure that I won't last long. But it keeps going, like I'm not putting enough effort in.

I doubt my phone is waterproof enough to search up something to watch as I lean back against the steamy shower wall. My hands work faster with the shower water falling against my chest.

God, the way Elise's thighs looked in her denim cut offs. So thick you could smother yourself between them.

A zing of pleasure arcs through my cock, up my stomach.

Fuck, Jesus. I can't be thinking about my ex-wife like this. She'll kill me, for one.

But it's hard to keep myself from reminiscing. We were wild for each other. Before long, I'm thinking about one of our picnics where she wore a sundress and just those lacey panties underneath, tracing the design until it was wet, while she fed me grapes and tugged the neckline of her dress down. Her soft breasts under dappled sunlight, licking her nipples until they were red, the way they moved above my face as she straddled and rode me right in the grass.

Thinking about her makes my cock feel on the edge of something too big for me to handle, like I've never climaxed before. I haven't. Not like this.

As precum starts to bead at the head, I go to palm my balls when I graze against a shape I'm unfamiliar with, a rounded swell near the base of my cock.

Holy fuck. This is a knot. My knot.

That would mean I've met my mate.

9

In the morning, there are fresh scratch marks on my cottage door.

I don't remember any scratching sounds during the night though. It makes me think briefly of the wolf sightings, but maybe I'm just anxious and ready to leap to conclusions. Maybe I'm just paranoid.

Briefly, it makes me think about whether I'll still get my damage deposit back on the cottage, since technically I'm still renting. It'd be nice to be able to keep that when I move on from Mystic Falls. Admittedly, I've been dealing with my anxiety over this whole situation with an excess of preparation, reaching out to as many people as I could think of. I've put a couple feelers out into moving somewhere else, working in a restaurant for my old culinary school friends, or being a private chef for old clients again. Anything that will help me hit the ground running in a week.

I don't really know what I'm more scared of: the idea of running into a wolf, like I keep hearing about, or my ex.

I'd rather be hiding in my cottage through all of this, but I think if I choose to do that, then one of the Hayes boys will sense that my drama with Shawn is too big to be in the same room as him and too easy to guess.

I haven't seen Shawn at all since our little chat the other day. We didn't lay down any ground rules for how we'd be getting through the next week or so until the wedding, and I'm going to be around a fair bit. I can hope he understood implicitly that I want to see as little of him as possible, but one can never know.

I also don't really know how he got to Mystic Falls. He hasn't got a car in the driveway at the Hayes House. There isn't exactly a bus route around here, so I can't imagine what other options there are. But I'm not about to go ask him.

My mom still hasn't called me back either. I keep thinking about calling her again, and trying to tell her everything that happened, crying like a child that's discovering the hell of stubbing one's toes. If nothing else, she should be able to empathize with the horror of running into your ex-husband in public after years of not seeing him.

I'm determined not to let any of it bother me. I'm going to do my job as efficiently as I can, and then in my spare time, I'm going to get ready to pack up and move away.

Until then, I've been burying myself under frosting.

"So, these are all buttercream bases. We've got lemon buttercream, vanilla buttercream, coconut, toasted marshmallow, cinnamon brown sugar—"

I pause for a glance at Logan, who hasn't said a word since he greeted me at the front door, now lurking in the Hayes' kitchen while I set things up.

And honestly, that's fine.

Of all the Hayes family, he's probably the one I can deal with the most right now. Even if he wasn't all that happy that I dragged him out of his office for this first thing in the morning, I wanted to get it out of the way before I got started on the food prep for the brewery. There's a bunch of stuff I had been preparing at the Hayes' kitchen pre-Shawn's return that I need to get ready to move to the brewery.

For the wedding cake icing flavors, I've taken a little shortcut, and just made a regular batch of buttercream and a batch of meringue in the stand mixer and then sectioned it out and stirred in a few different flavor extracts.

"If you want Swiss meringue, we've got the same flavors added to little cups of a batch of that. I am going to draw the line at making multiple types of meringues," I tell him, because I still have to figure out what to use all the separated egg yolks in. I think I'm going to have to make pasta from scratch and I don't love the thought of having to dig my pasta roller out.

This whole cake thing has been kinda last minute, and it's not my usual thing. In my mind, this is cutting corners. Usually, I want clients to have a wide variety of options, not two options disguised as ten.

"You made a lot of icing." Logan nods.

"I made a couple batches of icing." I shrug. "*Buuuuuut*, I also got out some jams I had on hand, and we can make permutations of jams and icings for the cake filling, and then with some of the cakes from yesterday. So now there's even more options, when you think about it."

Logan moves further into the kitchen, and stares at the array of little cups and paper slips denoting which icing is which, the pile of spoons for tasting them. He reminds me of a Borzoi sometimes, a face a little too long, with even longer hair.

Instead of tasting anything I've prepared, he looks at me and says, "You don't want Deanna to decide this?"

He rarely calls her "Mom," especially when talking to me. Maybe it's a holdover from the work he does at the brewery. Can't very well call her that to most people.

I hold still for the first time maybe this whole morning, and it puts a crack in the dam in my chest. I don't know that I could withstand a whole icing and cake taste testing with her right now. I don't want to be in the same room as her, talking about wedding things, and start marinating on how she never bothered to attend mine.

"Dude, it's your wedding," I tell him, and that information doesn't seem to make much of an impact. "You are required to make some decisions."

Logan nods once and continues to stare at the icings like they're a puzzle I've laid out for him. Usually, I credit him as being a little more on-the-ball than Aiden, but he seems at a loss for what to do.

"We can toss out the jams part of this if that's throwing you off," I suggest weakly. I have a vague feeling that isn't the problem, though.

Logan turns then, glancing to the doorway, right before Shawn walks by. A little jolt of anxiety moves through me. I don't know why I didn't think he'd bother showing up here.

I steel myself against looking at Shawn again. This time may be without the pouring rain to make him look sad and pathetic, but it's no use. His hair is still that shoulder length, frizzy, curly mess, but you know it's the softest thing you'll ever touch. He's wearing a faded shirt that fits just a little too snug around his biceps and, oh my god, when did his arms get like that? And of course, he's always got this stupid look on his face like he's been enjoying a nice day and seeing you made it even better. I see it when his eyes catch Logan's.

"Hey, man, just wanted to catch you on my way out," Shawn says, coming into the room and knocking shoulders with Logan.

Without a doubt, he is the most intensely physical person I've ever met. Every time he comes into a room, he has to go hug someone or lean on them or pick them up and haul them over his shoulder.

Even Logan leans into it. "Right, well. Stay out of trouble."

It almost sounds like he means it humorously, but not quite. A beat goes by before the pair of them look at me just as my heart pinches uncomfortably. I keep eye contact with Logan because it's easier, but I can see the silent question that he's been sidestepping, and that Aiden has asked me roughly one hundred times. *What's the deal with you and him?*

I have to look away to avoid it.

Something like muscle memory makes me turn to Shawn, somewhat expecting to have to go through the motion of saying hello. But the space between us feels hollowed out when he stands ten feet back. I can see how he's crossed his arms over his chest, less like he's mad and more like he's stopping himself.

And for once, he's looking at me like his day just got a little worse.

"We're, um, figuring out the icing and cake combinations, for the big day," I say, wondering what will make him leave.

Shawn nods, and eyes the marble island with my makeshift buffet. "Is this for everyone to try?"

"Well, I made enough because I figured Aiden and Deanna would also want a taste, but we're not voting on which ones are best. Ultimately, it's up to Logan."

"Bride-to-be doesn't get a say?" Shawn asks, directly dipping a finger into the first icing cup, and pulling out a dollop.

He's tasting it just as I round the marble island and start putting the spoons into each of the cups, because apparently it wasn't clear enough what they were for. I'm not quite fast enough, and he does stick the same finger he just licked in another cup before I can finish putting the spoons in all of them.

I can't wait for Logan to leave so I can kick Shawn in the shins.

Logan continues to stand far enough back to watch this whole little vaudeville act, not commenting, also not intervening.

"I imagine normally his fiancée would do taste testing with us, but I wanted to get this out of the way, so I know whether I need to order a bunch of eggs or a bunch of butter for the frosting."

"Have you met her?" Shawn directs at me.

"No . . . but I'm sure she's lovely," I say, glancing sideways at Logan. He keeps pretty much everything private, so it's not odd to me that he's never brought her up before.

Maybe they've been a long-distance couple. I don't know for sure that he's got a computer setup in his room, but I imagine that's what keeps him up there, and they probably play a lot of online games together.

"Is she?" he asks, and Logan's gaze drops to the floor.

"You remember Celine." Logan shrugs, his body language a little too tense.

"I remember her mother always trying to get us to hang out with her."

Shawn doesn't seem fazed by this. I'm trying not to let my jaw hit the ground. They're acting like it's normal. I'm glancing between the two of them rapidly, waiting for one of them to give me a hint on how to react.

". . . Is this an arranged marriage? Is this like a weird rich people thing?" I ask before I can stop myself.

"I don't know? I mean, maybe," Logan says, struggling between talking to me and glaring at Shawn. And for what, revealing this weird little factoid?

His posture tightens, his shoulders raise up a little, his arms cross over his chest.

"I don't really want to get into it," Logan mutters. Now he's pointedly looking away.

Aw, shit. I sigh. "I just meant . . . I mean, it's ok. You don't have to. I can ask Deanna about the icings, if you prefer."

He gives a brief nod and pretends to glance out into the hall like he heard someone calling him. "I should probably get going, I've got some things to do."

"Oh, well can't let nonspecific things wait," Shawn starts to say, but Logan is gone down the hallway before he can finish his sentence.

I may have lived here a while, but clearly there was something missing from the picture. There's some weird dynamic here that I only got a glimpse of from the other side when we were married. Those two years we lived together felt like enough to really know him, but they weren't.

I don't really know what to make of it, now that I'm starting to see what goes on from this side. Maybe I don't know enough about how arranged marriages are supposed to work in the modern day to judge, but my heart goes out to Logan, whatever he's going through.

I wait until I hear Logan's footsteps disappear before I turn around and glare at Shawn.

"You knew that was private. I wasn't supposed to know that, was I?" I narrow my eyes at him. "How did you know?"

"Because I know my family."

There's just a hint of bitterness in his tone.

"Whatever. I need to get working on the hors d'oeuvres for this evening." I make a shooing motion at Shawn and start gathering some veggies out of the fridge.

I knew Shawn's mother was the main reason I never met his family, that she opposed us being together, but he never gave me a real reason why. I've never thought of the Hayes family I've come to know through working together as particularly cryptic. It's hard to reconcile what I know with the scant details Shawn gave me back then.

"You need help?"

"No, I don't, you can go—"

"It's fine to need help, y'know, it sounds like your workload has increased, and you could use an extra hand."

Staring at Shawn, I realize something has changed. I haven't seen this side of him before, a defiant streak that didn't really exist when we met.

He wanders around the kitchen island, finding the sink piled high with the aftermath of my efforts. He glances at the comically long rubber gloves that are dripping from the dish towel hooks. I'm waiting for them to dry out again before I tackle the sink.

"I don't need you to help me wash dishes," I say preemptively, but he's already pulling open the drawer with all of the dishtowels, laying them out on the counter for when he's done.

"Isn't that what I'm here for?" he says over his shoulder, then with a smooth, sardonic tone, "I know how you love to snap the latex on."

I don't really approve of wearing gloves for cooking, but I can't stand washing dishes barehanded. I don't like touching dishes with food scraps that have been soaking for the last hour, making a terrible soup in the sink.

"I thought you were here to annoy me," I say over my shoulder, checking the fridge door shut with my hip.

"Well, that too. Maybe I wish I'd had more time doing dishes with you, alright?"

"Let's be clear, you are doing them by yourself, voluntarily."

"Sure, boss."

I set the bowl of focaccia dough and veggies out on the part of the kitchen island that isn't set up for icing flavor combinations and turn back around to root around for a knife and a cutting board.

"I just wanted a chance to talk a bit. We haven't talked in . . ."

I pull the cutting board out. "Eight years."

He flinches.

I turn away and take out the olive oil and a carton of cherry tomatoes. "What was there to talk about? Our lives untangled pretty easily."

"You think I don't want to know how you've been?"

I make a gesture to our surroundings, the palatial kitchen that I spend most of my time in. "What's there to tell? I've been working with the brewery, *and with your mom,* for a few years. Clearly, I didn't realize that when my business partnered with Aconite Ales."

His eyebrows raise in surprise. "Years?"

I nod. "Yeah, it's consistent work. I was enjoying a bit of job security, there isn't always much of that in the catering industry."

"I'm sorry," he says after a moment, and I can see in his face that he means it.

Whatever that's worth.

I fold my arms together and hold them close against my chest, weighing his apology. "Well, thank you. I appreciate that you apologized."

"Yeah, I . . . didn't always think to do that," he says, then winces, and I wonder what specific things he's remembering.

I'm not gratified by that. I squash whatever sense of peace I feel at thinking he regrets how he behaved during our relationship. I still hate him, on principle. But I can't pretend I haven't wondered what he's been up to as well, how the years have treated him, what he's like now.

He takes a cautious glance at me, apparently thinking along the same lines when he asks, "How's your family doing? Or, families, in your case."

I feel my expression sour reflexively, like taking a straight bite of lemon.

Shawn looks like he swallows a laugh at my expression. "That bad, huh?"

I huff out a breath. "No, they're fine. Both my stepsiblings graduated high school last year."

And neither of my parents thought to invite me to either ceremony. They forgot I exist, again.

I clench my teeth at the thought. It's been so long since I've talked to either of them, that I honestly don't know why I care anymore. I can get along fine on my own.

Deep in thought, I'm watching Shawn roll up his sleeves, not bothering with the big rubber gloves. He easily lifts the large ceramic mixing bowl that's been soaking, and I can't help but watch the lean lines of his wrists, the tension in his forearms as he works dried batter off the bowl's rim with a sponge.

But I still want him to leave.

It dawns on me after a few minutes, that I'm really just staring at his arms. He's always had amazing arms. I mean, I'm sure there's always been some definition there, but it toes a line between a sort of natural muscley-ness and a guy who actually works out. I kind of wonder then, if he could pick me up. Not just in a theoretical, how-much-can-you-lift? way, but my body craving the feeling of being picked up and tossed over a shoulder in a sort of caveman way.

It's then I realize that I'm horny for Shawn. Horrifyingly horny about the idea of him picking me up and roughly handling me.

That can't happen.

I turn away abruptly and start getting more ingredients for lunch down from the shelf, some spice jars and condiments. "You should go. You're just going to mess my system up."

"Your system hasn't changed in years, I can tell by the way you have everything lined up."

My hand grasps a bottle of hot sauce briefly, picking it up by the lid. I have half a thought, that whoever used this last must not have screwed it on right, before suddenly it's too light, and I'm just gripping the lid.

I yelp in surprise when the bottle makes its loud impact on the counter, and the last thing I see before squeezing my eyes shut reflexively, is the sauce splattering out of the bottle.

Deceptive, refrigerator-cold drops of it make contact with my face and I freeze.

"Oh my god, are you kidding me," I squeak, and start to go to wipe the sauce from my face, but discover my hands are already wet with it, and I don't know where the closest dish towel is.

"Wow, that got all over you," I hear him from behind me, across the room.

"Eyes, Shawn. It's on my eyes," I tell him, and a second later there's the sound of the sink running. I guess he's rinsing the soap suds off his hands. I can hear him moving around the room. I can't really pay attention to it at the moment, I'm more concerned with if the hot sauce is going to make contact with my eyeballs or not.

My heart is thudding in my chest. I hate getting hot sauce in little cuts on my fingers, I can't imagine how bad it'll burn my eyes. What do I even do if that happens? Would pouring milk in them be the answer? That sounds crazy.

"Did it get in your eyes?" I hear him ask, and this time he's right in front of me, guiding me with light touches to turn away from the counter.

"No, I don't think so. I don't think I can open them," I say in whatever direction, until I feel the counter against my back. I brace my hands against it as he touches just underneath my jaw, coaxing me to raise my chin so he can get a better look.

"Hold still, I've got you," he murmurs, and I feel the cold touch of a wet paper towel on my face. "We're just going to be very careful about this."

I hold my breath and try not to move at all, as his fingers press through the towel and clear the majority of the hot sauce from my face.

With my eyes welded shut like this, the world is reduced to just his hands, fingertips carefully tracing over my face, the sound of his breath and the little warmth that ghosts from it over my skin. My heart is pounding, but decidedly less so from the fear of my eyes stinging.

The heel of his palm presses to my cheekbone, steadying his hand as he touches the wet paper towel to my eyelids, wiping a drip of hot sauce from my eyelashes.

"There," he says at last. "You should be in the clear."

His palm stays nestled against my cheek when I open my eyes.

I wasn't ready for how close he was standing. I used to know this closeness, all the little details in his face.

He doesn't say anything, and neither do I, fearing if we did it would break whatever fragile spell has fallen over us. His hands are warm and big, and I remember every bit about them.

There's almost a gravity present, like standing on the edge of a massive cliff. The edge terrifies you and you don't want to go anywhere near it, but you can't help but be drawn to it, you can't stop peering further and further over the edge, a gentle type of hell.

It's clear Shawn doesn't know how to navigate the lack of physicality between us either. Not touching seems stranger than anything else.

My cheek is pressed hard in his hand, tilting my face up towards his. My eyes flick from his long eyelashes to the hard line of his mouth. I wonder if his lips are just as soft as they were eight years ago. I wonder who he's kissed since we divorced.

He barely blinks, both of us too frightened and suddenly inexperienced in these matters with each other.

The soft, fragile moment slowly fills with horror, as I have absolutely no idea what to do, afraid that it will never end or that it will end awkwardly and terribly.

For a moment, I think he's going to say something I need to hear, like an apology, something heartfelt, some vital key to my closure with how things ended.

"You smell different. It's weird," he says after a moment, an expression like he's personally stumped by this.

"That's not a compliment," I reply flatly.

"I didn't mean it like—"

"I only want to hear two things out of you: compliments that respect my personal boundaries, and 'have a nice day, Elise.' "

He opens his mouth again to protest but sees my expression and thinks better of it.

I swallow and take a step back. "Thank you for getting it out of my eyes."

He blinks, whatever came over us dissipating. "Yeah. Um. Anytime. Let me, uh, get you a paper towel for your shirt."

I turn away and catch my reflection in the tile backsplash over the stove. My apron has taken the brunt of the hot sauce explosion, but my white T-shirt looks like it's been flecked with a red arterial spray.

I take a few more steps back, my heart thudding with adrenaline, slowing down like I'd just come out of a near-death experience.

10

Shawn

I wasn't going to kiss her. *I wasn't.* That would have crossed a line.

Ok, I can't pretend annoying her isn't one of my favorite things to do and that hasn't been my primary motivation, but I can handle being normal around Elise, I think. I can hold still and say very little, and pass for a normal person around my ex-wife, if I really, really need to.

I just don't know that I can juggle that and the knowledge that I've somehow just met my mate.

And, obviously, I won't try to kiss Elise if I have a mate, somewhere. In fact, I'm sure all my complicated lingering feelings about my ex-wife will probably dissolve the minute I actually find said mate again, right?

God, I fucking hope so.

Still, maybe I'm not any more ready for a mate now. Not when I'm still jerking off to the thought of my ex-wife's thighs.

I drag a hand over my face. This is going to be a long week.

This damn house. There's no living here, no avoiding everyone. I don't know why I even came back here. I know for damn certain there's no peace to be found.

I'm working in Dad's old study when my mom steps inside and closes the door behind me. I half-wonder if Elise complained about me to her.

"I'm headed to St. Mary's," Mom says, shrugging into a cardigan. I blink. It's not a Sunday, but I remember my grandparents attended mass even during the weekdays after they retired. I haven't been in nearly a decade.

"Do you . . ." she starts to say, but then shakes her head a little and backs out of the question. "You wouldn't want to come with me."

"No, thanks anyway."

She doesn't leave, though, and I have a familiar sinking sensation in my stomach that I've felt before most lectures.

Mom closes the door and puts her hands on her hips like I'm about to be grounded. "I saw you and Elise talking together earlier."

"We were catching up."

She hums, a note that indicates both that she heard me, but that she's not sure she believes that was all.

I've been a functioning adult for over a decade now, and, somehow, I still feel like a teenager when she does that. All of a sudden, it's like I never actually grew up and moved out and figured life out for myself; I'm just a kid she needs to teach how to behave in the world.

I save and close out of the editing program so I can give her my full attention, taking in a deep, not calming enough breath. I want to have a conversation like rational adults that can respect each other. I'm not going to treat her like a tyrant who wants to micromanage me, and hopefully my mother will pretend she thinks I'm a functioning adult.

"Look, out of respect for Elise and the uncomfortable position we've put her in, I don't want to keep talking about this."

She shakes her head. "It's not about that. I just . . . you know you shouldn't get close to her. Especially not so close to the full moon. Your brothers understand this, I don't know why you have such a hard time with the notion."

I think my mother just implied I'm a slut, but that's somehow not what I have a bone to pick with.

I try not to roll my eyes. "What are you afraid of? That I'll run away with another human? Ruin Logan's wedding with my drama?"

"Coyotes," she answers coolly, holding me in her gaze. "People getting hurt, you included. Hard as that may be for you to believe."

She doesn't want to see me go feral. I know that means she's concerned for my safety, my sanity, my well-being. But it's hard to feel the warmth in that sentiment. I know how easily it becomes a tool of control.

I meet her eye as I shut the laptop. "Except, I've been out in the world, far from my pack. I've lived years without one. I haven't gone feral."

"Would you even know? There weren't any animal attacks here until you showed up again," she says, her voice terribly quiet and full of emotion.

Her words strike a little fear in me, and I try to conceal it.

"You do have a number of other coyotes running around, you know. While it's a lot of fun being the disappointment child, I think maybe you could let someone else have the honors for a bit," I reply, fighting against the urge to snarl and snap.

"Your brothers, Laura, they have all stayed here. They use the brewery's basement during the full moon instead of leaving it to chance. The pack bonds keep them safe."

Her stare is hard. She's so convinced this is the only way to look out for her children.

I sigh, and step back. This is the same conversation we had ten years ago, when she begged me not to move away, and then a couple years later, when she wouldn't hear of me bringing home the girl I'd met and wanted to introduce to everyone. The conversation we had a million more times when I married Elise.

I wish I was surprised that time hasn't altered even a little of her position on this.

I chew on my lip. I'm sure she would be overjoyed to learn that I've found my mate somewhere in this town. But I'm not exactly ready to provide how I know that either, until I've figured out exactly who it is.

Telling her would be giving in. I've held this stubborn position that I know what's best for me for years, and I've paid the price of exile for it. Giving her the satisfaction of being right isn't something I'm ready to do.

The thing is, I couldn't care less about going out and finding my true mate right now. Not when Elise is in the house.

Turning away, her words are aimed at my back. "Having a wolf mate would keep you safe—"

"Mom. Stop it. We're just going in circles on this."

She steps back and lets me leave, but says quietly, "I'll put in a word with St. Michael for you."

My teeth gnash together, but I don't say anything. That was how all our old arguments used to end, before I stopped talking to my family almost completely for a while. She was always lighting candles in my name at her parish and letting me know. Maybe it was her way of saying she still cared, but it felt just as much like a barb.

I don't believe in the church anymore, the teachings, any of it. It was hard to separate the ways it tangled with my wolf, the net I was ensnared in.

I've sat through many masses, but there wasn't ever any specific sermon about what a mate was. Sure, the church made a specific point to emphasize the sacrament of marriage, the importance of having children within that marriage, and raising them in the teachings of the church. I don't know how it took me twenty-five years to realize how culty that sounds.

At home, the conversation connected our wolfish halves with its messages, impressing on us the need for a strong pack.

But I'd been working through the frayed edges of its web for years now. I knew reciting Hail Mary's didn't relieve the excess anxiousness the full moon brought on, but running did. Perhaps what a mate was didn't exist only in the context of God and religion. Maybe it could exist separately.

Like I'm going to just find the meaning of what a mate is to me out in the woods, I scoff to myself.

My feet carry me automatically back toward my old room, a muscle memory about as old as I am. The hallway is dark upstairs; it feels musty and uninhabited as I make my way through it and nearly jump out of my skin when I realize Elise is there, standing in the shadows.

Is no room in this house safe from her? I'm not going to survive this.

"Holy shit," she squeaks, jolting back a step, clutching an armful of plates to her chest. They rattle together, but louder still somehow is her heart rate, picking up dangerously fast.

It makes my pulse quicken as well. It's not that I haven't been able to hear hers before, but I don't think I've ever been as keenly tuned into it. It's always just been in the background.

My every sense feels more precise around her. In the same way I can hear enthusiasm in my brothers' footsteps when they stomp down the stairs, or annoyance in the quiet, steady gait my mother walks with, I know what sort of mood Elise is in just by breathing. She has an intoxicating sort of heat to her, the sort of warmth you feel in the back of your throat after a sip of whisky.

Right now, I can smell the sting of anxiety on her. It reminds me of trying a spoonful of vanilla extract and discovering its taste is purely alcohol. It rebuffs the warmth of its essence.

Clearly the kitchen incident is still on her mind as well. Her cheeks flush as her eyes meet mine, and she quickly looks at the ground again. "You startled me."

"Sorry about that. I didn't think anyone would be up here." I sigh, ready to just leave and forget all this. I feel like I need to keep apologizing. "Um, before, in the kitchen—"

"We don't need to talk about that," she cuts me off quickly. I nod and jam my hands in my pockets. Right.

I glance to the faint moon starting to rise in the evening sky, feeling its presence start to heat my blood, waking the wolf. I swallow and take a step back from her.

"Do you maybe want a light on?" I ask, glancing around for one. My hand finds the antique switch plate. The wall sconces don't turn on when I flip them.

"I tried it earlier. I think these lightbulbs burned out a while ago," she sighs, before her eyes fall back on the wall where she was staring before.

The wall is full of family photos, and unlike downstairs, there are a few that still include me with my brothers. We're all baby-faced and in various states of childish gangly-ness and endless grass-stained knees.

The frames are all heavy with dust, set up to trace the family lineage the further down the hall they go. Photos of Mom and Dad become younger, the photos of my brothers and me playing in the dirt become each of us as babies in her arms, to the one of her and Dad on the steps of a church, leaving their wedding.

I get to the place Elise has been standing, staring. There's a number of pictures of my mom, barely nineteen, standing with her older sister in front of a number of suitcases. The strong resemblance between them remains even with the shaking disposable camera it was taken with.

I can only imagine what is going through Elise's mind. She'd been an only child and her parents had quickly gotten divorced. Looking at our pictures, she probably sees the sort of big happy family she always wanted for herself.

"The nice thing about weddings is they get to be little family reunions, I guess," Elise says, nodding to them with a wistful sigh and a face full of misplaced nostalgia, "What's Deanna's sister like?"

"I don't know."

Her brow pinches as she looks at me. I hate to disillusion her of her fantasy, that a family can be the sum of its happy snapshots. Maybe that happy families can exist.

"That's not Laura's mom?"

"No, Laura's mom is Aunt Jenny, she's from my dad's side of the family. You might see her at the wedding. In the picture is my Aunt Danielle. She died before I was born," I say. "We don't talk about it much."

The crease between her brows deepens. "Oh. I'm sorry."

"It's ok. You couldn't have known."

I can tell she wants the full story but isn't willing to ask.

It's just one of the many things I can't tell her the whole truth behind, even the pieces that I do have. I've gathered some details from other family members, little pieces that fall to the side that were somehow the most important.

Maybe it's the root of everything we were supposed to keep secret. Elise never understood why I couldn't bring her home to my family, and what we were afraid of happening.

"It doesn't sound half so scandalous now, I suppose. Danielle wasn't supposed to have a boyfriend, but she did, and they were caught fooling around. Teenagers in the seventies, I mean, who would have guessed? There was some fear she'd get pregnant, and it would ruin both their futures. Their parents agreed to separate them."

For most wolf packs, going feral is at most an urban legend. And that legend is always about a wolf becoming estranged from their pack, or losing their mate, who in turn loses the will to turn back, often becoming mad with unchecked bloodlust.

It largely depends on who tells the story.

"She was pretty heartbroken. At the time, there were a lot of reports about a wolf being seen in the area, attacking farm animals, pets, you name it. Danielle started hiking all the trails alone. One day she didn't come back, and they filed a missing person's report."

The way my mom tells it, there was another werewolf family her parents had been trying to arrange a match for Danielle with, even though she had insisted she'd found her mate. They hadn't believed her.

"There are some dots there you could probably connect if you wanted to. Mom's never cared to speculate, though."

Mom never had to say it for us to know that she blamed herself for keeping her sister's secret as long as she did. I know she blames me for leaving when I should have known better.

"Sometimes it's just easiest to say that my mom likes to keep her family close." I sigh. "I don't mean to resurrect old arguments, but . . . there are a lot of answers you deserved, that I still don't know how to give you."

I know exactly the words to use, but my jaw welds shut on them. *My mom's every parenting decision is entirely influenced by her sister's death.*

It's too crass, too unfeeling, too rough to do justice for what my mom went through, even if it's the simplest of truths.

Maybe it's easiest to just say no one in my family has ever been to therapy.

I expect to see her eyes harden, the way they always did when this topic came up. Elise had never said how much she resented my family for coming between us in our marriage. She didn't have to, I still knew. It was hurting her, but I couldn't just take her side. Not when I knew turning feral could just as easily happen to one of my brothers. Or to me.

But there's a softness almost like understanding in her face that makes me feel like I should just tell her everything. If only it were that easy.

I press on, gesturing to happier photos, further down the wall. "A little while after that, she got married."

It's not really important to the story that she married the same man her parents had been trying to set her sister up with. That a connection to a respectable werewolf family was more important than her feelings on the matter.

For a few more moments, we stand there, staring at the photos. She's smiling in her town hall photo with her arm around my dad, but I've always thought she looked uneasy, the undercurrent of desperation one might not know to look for. So terrified that what happened to her sister would happen to her that she did whatever her parents wanted.

I sigh and shift my weight from one foot to another. I don't know how I can make Elise understand the fears that were in play then, the same ones that have come back to haunt us now.

"Do you need a hand with that?" I gesture at the stack of plates probably growing heavy in Elise's arms, raising a brow, maybe too abrupt a change in conversation. I don't know how long she's been standing here, staring at my family photos, but we probably shouldn't linger here too much longer.

She starts to shake her head, and then reconsiders and hands them over, wincing at each fragile noise they make as they shift against each other. "I thought I'd get these out of storage now and give them all a rinse, so they'll be ready for the reception. Deanna said there were also some tablecloths up here. I was going to put them in the wash."

"I can show you where we keep those." I nod, taking the stack of plates and internally roll my eyes at myself. Really, I should be making a point of helping literally anyone else with anything else. But I can't help the fact I just gravitate toward her.

I lead her down the hallway to the linen closet, opening the doors to show her the way it's organized.

"There's so much wedding prep left to do." Elise sighs as she follows behind me. "I kinda feel bad. Logan could be having a grand wedding, extensively planned out. But everything feels so rushed right now. If we had more time, I could do more."

"They wouldn't push it back. I think his future in-laws are worried about him getting cold feet."

"If he's getting cold feet, that's all the more reason to delay it. I'd hate for him to get married and then have to go through"—she dares a brief glance at me—"well, what we did."

I feel like I'm supposed to agree with her, say something about how messy and painful divorces are, that we would know, how I hope my little brother never has to experience that.

But it feels disingenuous, and I can't bring myself to say any of that. Not when I don't regret any of it.

I hum back a non-answer. She's painfully close to the way everything connects, but maybe too close to see how. That line of conversation dies as she continues down the hall, taking it in.

"I haven't fully explored upstairs. I mean, I haven't really been at the house much here except when Aiden and Laura want to have a movie marathon because Laura's TV is really small—oh."

She falls silent, and when I turn around, she's not looking at the linen closet, but across from it.

The door still has a handful of stickers unevenly applied, spelling out my name on my old room.

She doesn't pause or ask or anything, just puts her hand on the doorknob and steps inside, the hinges creaking as the door swings open.

I set the armful of plates down on a shelf in the linen closet and follow her.

Elise stands in the center of the room, slowly turning around, taking everything in. The faded blue walls, the little action figures lined up on the shelves, old clothes still folded in a laundry basket, never put away.

It hasn't changed at all.

Nothing's been touched, since I've been staying in a guest room downstairs. In a way it reminds me of how my dad's office was left after he passed, the door simply closed, and everything left alone. It feels like a memorial to a much younger version of myself, someone who never left home and didn't question his parents out loud.

I don't even realize how lost I am in staring at all of it, pieces of myself I left behind without even thinking. The jar full of sharpie markers, a stack of VHS tapes, some still left out of their faded cardboard cases, a sheet of temporary tattoos half picked clean, a stack of CD cases, a number of them open and spread across the top of the dresser, because none of the disks were in the right case, and half of the plastic hinges were broken.

"This was your old bed?" Elise asks, and her voice pulls me from ten, twenty years ago. I blink and feel like I've been three separate people in my life, the person I was with my family, who I was when I was just with her, and the person I've been while alone.

I look up at her, the way she turns and sits down on the edge of it. "Yeah, Batman sheets and everything."

"My god. I never knew what a dork you were," she teases, wrinkling her nose with a smile in a way that breaks my heart all over again. I didn't think we would ever have a moment like this, and now I don't know what to do with it.

I nearly sit on the edge of the bed beside Elise, but manage to stop just in front of her. "Well, I couldn't let you know just how out of my league you were."

She rolls her eyes at my self-deprecating smile, but this moment has a hold on me that tightens with every breath I take.

"You have got to stop flirting with me," she scoffs, but she's smiling so wide, I doubt she believes it.

Elise is staring at me with her big brown eyes. I'm both terrified of what's going on behind them, what she's thinking, and desperate to know. She left me, I don't want her to know about the bits of her I've been holding onto. I can't tell if I'm trying to find a hint of hope in her eyes about what that means.

God, I don't even know what it means.

Maybe it's the way the afternoon sun streams in, cutting the same faded path on the carpet and furniture, bringing out a warm red in her hair. Maybe it's the way Elise and my home are worlds that were never meant to collide. But here they are and if I don't leave this room, this moment, maybe they can exist together perfectly, fitting together seamlessly without disturbing a thing.

Maybe I could tell her I don't regret a thing about getting married to her.

I ache to. The words almost tumble out of me at the same time I feel the urge to just bury my face in her shoulder and take a deep breath. There's something about the way she smells. It makes the pounding in my head stop, the clawing in my chest cease. All I need for the rest of my life is to just breathe it in.

But I would always want more.

And maybe that's why we have to go our separate ways. I wouldn't be able to just leave her alone, to let her live her own life, when I daydream about putting my chin on her shoulder and my hands in her back pockets.

"I'm going to take those plates downstairs," I say instead of anything else, and with that sliver of reality, somehow talk myself into leaving the room.

She doesn't follow me out to the linen closet again, and I'm glad for that much. I need to actually work on staying away from her, not just keep telling myself I'm going to.

11

Elise

Whenever I pass the bakery section of our local grocery store, I stop at the pastry display case for a little while, usually for inspiration. Sometimes I think about what I've already got in my cart and how I could combine it with something as simple as croissants, or if I could swap a different spice into a cinnamon roll.

But this time, I've been standing in front of the pastry display case staring at a fresh tray of Danishes, watching the little decorative lines of icing slowly drip off of them.

You can't call him. You blocked his number forever ago.

I can't even rationalize to myself that I'm thinking about how the pastries should have been given more time to cool so that the icing wouldn't be melting off, or that there's something wrong in the liquid to powdered sugar ratio for the icing to have that consistency.

A movement on the other side of the case pulls me from my thoughts, and looking up, I see the baker in his white smock.

He glances between me and the Danishes, and then raises his eyebrows. "Can I help you with anything?"

"Oh, no, thanks though." I shake my head quickly.

I stare for a beat too long, trying to convince myself to be attracted to the baker. Someone who I haven't been legally bound to before.

He gives me a friendly smile, but it doesn't spark that same heart-thudding, breath-stalling sensation that Shawn does. *Fuck.*

I shuffle away, moving my cart towards the checkout. Now that the menu for the reception has been finalized, I can start getting some of the ingredients before the prepping stage. I've spent most of the day successfully avoiding Shawn, and not wondering about him in the slightest. Re-contextualizing some things about our relationship, maybe.

"Oh, hey."

I still, the checkout conveyor belt snagging a box of flaky salt out of my hands. I know it before I even look up.

I brace myself, and—dear god, he's wearing gray sweatpants, and an old maroon college sweatshirt with the sleeves pushed up to his elbows.

It's not just the way the fabric drapes over his legs and everything in between, it's the way it *moves*. The way the waistband ties frame the imprint of his dick. It makes my mouth go dry. I don't need to be doing this. I remember what it looked like, don't I? Or was my memory on that a little faded as well?

Rationally, I know I don't want his attention, or to be in the same town as him even. I moved across the state to get away from him and avoid this kind of moment.

"Hey, yourself," I answer, as nonchalantly as I can manage, even though I'm definitely on the chalant side of the spectrum. It's fine. I can exist within the same ten feet of Shawn and not be completely weird about it.

"Is that more of the wedding prep?"

"Oh, um, yeah. Some. The Danishes are for me, though."

He reaches over for one of the plastic checkout dividers and drops his stuff on the belt. Literally all he has is toothpaste and a toothbrush. Yeah, he would forget to pack those.

Shawn glances at my cart and frowns. "What Danishes?"

"Oh, um," I say, and in that moment, realize I was so hypnotized by the icing that I forgot to get any. My cheeks flush full red, I'm sure. I can't even think up a good excuse that makes sense to tell him, I just wave the thought off.

"Do you want me to go grab you some Danishes?"

"No, never mind what I said."

His tone borders on *too* pleasant. "It's not a problem, they're just over there."

"No, I, uh, I forgot I decided against them."

"It sounds like you still want them, subconsciously, maybe."

"Oh my god, stop."

I move strategically to the other end of the checkout, where the cashier is piling up my things after she scans them, the cart now between me and Shawn. He leans over the edge of my cart and puts the last couple things I had in there up on the belt and I try to focus on bagging everything up as the cashier passes it to me. It's so hard.

Don't stare. Seriously, don't, I think, even as my vision snags on the way the fabric hangs precariously off one hip. Going over here was a mistake; all it did was make it easier to look directly at him. I swallow.

The moment everything I got is all bagged up and paid for, I leave. I'm not fleeing, I swear. But I do have a pint of ice cream and its staying frozen is suddenly a huge priority.

I pause right before the exit, glancing back at him one last time, and get stuck on what I see. The cashier girl is scribbling something down, and as she hands it to him I realize she wrote her number on the back of his receipt.

Holy shit.

I look away immediately. I have a number of feelings in that instant, none of them kind. That's completely inappropriate, did he ask for it? But also, I should warn her about what he's like, and maybe . . .

I swallow my feelings down. It's none of my business.

I take a deep breath, and the grocery's automatic doors close again. Shawn sees me standing at the exit and jogs over. Oh god, he's going to think I waited for him. I mean, I kinda did. Not on purpose.

Catching up with a few strides, he asks, "Need help loading your car?"

Weakly, I swallow and nod. "Sure."

Outside, he gets to my car first and opens up the trunk. I watch him start loading up bags, and all I can do is stare. It gnaws from the back of my brain until it's at the forefront of my mind.

It's none of my business. But it's going to haunt me.

The question comes out without preamble or any semblance of an excuse. "Hey, did you, uh, date anyone since we . . . ?"

I watch Shawn's expression, the way he freezes ever so imperceptibly, when he suspects a question is a trap.

"Not because I'm, uh, jealous, or anything like that," I say, and wince to hear myself say it. I find my arms crossed over my chest and maybe that's a little too aggressive for this conversation. "I just. I was curious if anyone else had to go through what I did, with your family."

He relaxes a little, the tension easing from his shoulders. He shakes his head. "Oh. No, no one else had to go through that. I wasn't on speaking terms with my family."

I nod. That is the answer I asked for, and yet, it's not the one I wanted to know.

A beat goes by, and I prompt, "Because there wasn't anyone . . . ?"

His stupid, gorgeous eyes lift to hold mine, blinking those long dark eyelashes at me. "Do you think I haven't slept with anyone in eight years?"

The back of my neck becomes hot.

"No! That would be ridiculous," I say and force out a laugh. I feel like I am undoing years of therapy with every word. My cheeks are burning red. "I . . . no. No. I wouldn't think that."

I'm regretting every step I've taken into this quicksand of a conversation, but I can't seem to stop.

"But you've . . . dated, probably, since, uh. In the in-between of then and now, and—" I try to twist it over and over into something not accusatory, but all I manage is to make it not really a question. "Because that would be normal. And healthy."

He nods, and I feel so incredibly transparent in that moment. My only hope is that Shawn's reliably dense enough that he might just take me at my word and not read into my stammering.

He looks me up and down, considering. "What about you, did you date at all?"

I'm not prepared for him to turn the question back on me. I mean, when it comes up in therapy, I usually say it was good to have relationships where I didn't feel like I was going crazy trying to get a straight answer out of a guy.

"I . . . yeah, I guess I did some dating after we divorced." I shrug as neutrally as I can manage. "Obviously none of them went the distance, but I feel like I had some good relationships."

"Oh. That's good. I'm glad. Happy for you," he says, turning away at that moment, and I only just catch the hint of red clouding his cheek as he returns my cart to the corral a couple spots over. "I'm happy for you that you found that."

"Thanks?" What a diplomatic answer. And he said it twice.

We lapse into silence, the only sounds are the highway and the rattle of the empty cart on pavement, unable to look at each other. It stretches several moments, and I wonder if I should take this as a sign to leave.

He looks at the sky, and there's something artful about the shape of his neck against the evening.

"I, uh . . . I tried, y'know. To date," he starts to say, "but . . . I don't know. I think I needed a lot more time away from my family before I could really be my own person. Deconstructing, and all that. Sometimes it would start to go somewhere, then I would remember you, and that would always sort of end the relationship."

"I . . . what?"

I blink. There's some terrible, possessive need to know specifics. Some small island of rationality in my brain knows it'll hurt more to hear them.

Shawn's eye holds on the distance for a moment, then catches mine. He seems to remember himself, or at least realize what he said, a hint of panic in his brow.

"Not that I was always thinking of you when I hooked up with someone else, that would be . . . weird and obsessive," he says quickly, maybe a little too loudly.

Something in my heart softens. I cram my hands in my back pockets, trying to look casual, nothing so obvious as making heart eyes at him "Yeah, you've never been weird or obsessive."

He cracks a bashful smile at that, actually laughs a little. He takes a step forward that borders on invading my personal space, reaching an arm up to grab my trunk door.

I've read the phrase "wolfish grin" before, I've spent too much time on my e-reader not to have. But I don't know that I knew what that looked like before.

Somewhere between the flash of his teeth to the curve of his mouth, I forget where I am. I wonder how many times I'm going to get close enough to kiss him and watch the chance slip away.

"You keep that under your hat, alright?" he almost murmurs, and for a moment, feeling like we're sharing a secret, I remember what it meant to be on the same side as him, to be a team, instead of feeling alone and against everything and everyone else.

He takes his other hand and mimes tugging on the hat I'm not wearing, and my god, he's such a dork, he even hums a little sound effect along with it. Somewhere in the edges of my vision, he closes my car trunk.

He walks away at that, and I watch the way his shirt shifts with every step, the breadth of his shoulders, the way those goddamn gray sweatpants fit him. I am stupid horny for that dork. I can feel my clit pulsing alive like it was about to get some special attention.

I watch him reach into his pocket and toss a little balled up piece of paper into the trash, and that's the sight that makes me get into my car.

Even after I go home, I feel like I have too much energy after that encounter. Just being around him is enough to get me hot and bothered. I can't tell if it's like an anxious sweat or he's hot and maybe I'm ovulating a little early this month.

Because I've seen Shawn's arms before, I swear, without contemplating dropping my panties. Is that just a side effect he had on me that I forgot about?

There's nothing all that different about him now to justify it, either. I mean, maybe he seems a little more mature.

I can't sleep, that's for sure. I pull on a pair of boots and leave the cottage. It starts as just a quick walk to calm my nerves, my body, and maybe tire myself out. I'd give anything to sleep and stop thinking about all this.

I thought I was over him. I guess not, because it hurts too much just to exist in the same space as him, painfully close and still not enough.

I had spent a lot of time mad that Shawn hadn't stood up to his family for me in the way I needed him to, hurt that he hadn't done enough. But I hadn't realized how hard it must have been to have done as much as he had.

I probably would have kissed him in that hallway if the conversation hadn't turned so morose.

I don't know what to make of that little revelation. I mean, I guess family tragedy is always hard to explain. It does seem to me like thirty years is too long to let it control you, but then again, a lot of his family issues never made any sense to me.

Seeing Shawn here with his family contextualizes him in a way I'm not quite sure how to put to words. Something's clicked, and I feel like I understand more than I did when we were married. It's in the little things, the way they interact, the things they do and don't say, cutting around the shape of something I can't quite make out yet.

It's such a small thing. It doesn't make him seem so different now that it's worth trying to reconnect with him at all. Not that I would even want to.

I don't want to feel sorry for him. Not when I've spent years teaching myself to have better self-worth after what our marriage did to me.

It's not really the closure I wanted, but the knee-jerk anger I used to carry about Shawn and how he handled our relationship in the face of his family's disapproval sits oddly cooled in my chest. Part of me still struggles with hurt that he never told me any of those things about his family, but it's not fueled by senseless anger now.

I stop at the sound of a distant howl. Coyotes, I remind myself.

Do coyotes even howl? It's long and low, oddly melodic. And complex. And . . . is that fucking Bohemian Rhapsody?"

No. No way. But I hum a little along to it. *Figaro, Figaro.* Yeah, that's it.

I stand outside a good couple minutes wondering if I'm maybe losing it. It could happen, I've had some pretty weird shocks this week. Another few minutes and I'm questioning if I actually heard what I think I did.

What is going on with me lately? I don't think I'm old enough for even early menopause. Is this what PCOS is? Do I need to Google that again? Is Google actually going to helpfully answer the unstudied medical mysteries that are having a uterus?

Then again, none of that would explain how specks of dirt and leaves ended up in my bed, or where my pajama bottoms went.

Why can't good things just stay good? Why'd he have to show up here and ruin a perfectly fine job for me? Why couldn't things just be easy? Why can't I go back to having my little family? Maybe not a real family, maybe just an overly friendly employer and their delusional catering partner.

No, that was stupid to want.

Hot, frustrated tears well up around my eyes as I linger over it. I just wanted a distraction from all the drama happening at the main house, and now I'd made things worse.

And now here I was, getting lost in the woods because I couldn't stand another minute in the place he'd rejected me.

Why'd he have to ruin our relationship in the first place?

It's dark and I make the decisions of which way to go haphazardly, thinking I recognize the slope of the hill and this cluster of trees until I stop nearly recognizing any of it.

No, I know this path, maybe. I think I can see the house through the trees, or maybe that's someone else's house. But I'm sure there's a bench just around the bend, and it's still part of the grounds. Why couldn't I have just opened a window and done jumping jacks in my bedroom?

It's only when I hear the snap of a branch behind me that I remember the animal attacks.

The woods are dark, the trees almost blending in with the night. But I can see something there, something moving in the tree line. It's only barely perceptible.

I should not have wandered this far.

There's no running this time. I begin to turn and immediately slip on some wet leaves the moment I take a step, just as it snarls and crashes through the bushes.

I stumble into a wide tree, the bark biting into my palms as I try to use it to steady myself, my body ringing with the impact. I'm able to catch myself from hitting my head, but as soon as I look up, there it is, crouching over me, filling up my whole field of vision.

The monster's dark-brown eyes hold me, pinning me to the tree. It's the same beast I met before, I'm sure of it. I know those eyes.

I nearly forgot that strange dream I'd had a few nights ago, with everything else that had been happening. I didn't think it had been real.

There's intelligence in its expression, an understanding I couldn't ascribe to just any creature.

The same as before, it greets me by sniffing me. The creature's snout passes over my shoulder, my stomach, to my hip. It hovers at the crux of my legs a moment, its breath hot against the thin fabric of my pajama shorts.

I hold still, leaning back into the tree bark, though my hammering heart makes me feel like my whole body is trembling.

Last time, it just wanted to smell me, not eat me alive, I think wildly.

A half-baked thought enters my mind and I go with it, moving my knees further apart. I slide down the tree, landing in the leaves with a small thud. My knees spread wide, revealing the growing wet patch on my PJs.

There's no mistaking it for sweat; I can feel my clit pulsing awake with all the adrenaline in my body. My body is empty and needy. I haven't gotten so easily and intensely turned on since I was in college, when every experience was brand new to me.

Look, my self-preservation has never been strong. My heart is pounding in my chest and my clit, and my nipples are hard points that have nothing to do with the temperature. I delve a finger inside, and the pleasure is so much greater than it normally is. A small gasp escapes me.

The creature dips its head, drawing back up with its tongue hot against my thigh, trying to taste me through my pants. The feeling is a tease, and all I can think is that my body needs more.

The beast crouches over me, head bowed between my thighs. I hear a low growl come from it, before it licks me once through my shorts.

At the slight brush of its snout against me, I'm already bucking my hips into that touch. My body feels strange, still aching for touch, for closeness. The way my heart thuds in my chest and my pulse quickens in urgency only fuels it. In this moment, I'll take what I can.

I cry out as I feel its mouth open and its warm breath graze my thighs, followed by teeth. They drag gently across my skin, sweeping from one thigh to another, snagging on my shorts.

I hold my breath, choking on fear as elastic snaps and the beast's teeth shred through my pajama bottoms.

With a snarl, it flicks its tongue against me, and my body goes rigid from pleasure, before melting back into the ground. My knees fall apart wider, and I feel the tongue again.

As needy as my body feels for it, I'm surprised by how good the beast licking at my entrance feels, dragging its hot tongue roughly through my folds, the sensations chasing that rush of terror and excitement.

It licks me thoroughly, lashing ferociously against my clit, then snarling as its tongue delves deep within my cunt, single-mindedly seeking my taste.

I was so sure last time that this was a dream. And now that it's happening again, it feels so real. The heat and pleasure coursing through me are so vivid.

The beast's body hangs low over mine, and—

I know this smell. I used to live here. I used to sleep here, in the bed that smelled like this. I would breathe it in, roll over and stretch and wrap myself in it, and sink back into pure bliss. I used to bury my face in his pillow, steal his side of the sheets when he got up to shower and I was still sleeping in. Then he would sit on the bed next to me while he got dressed, waking me up slowly with languid scratches up my legs, kisses pressed to my forehead. Under his laundry detergent, his shampoo, his deodorant, there was something unmistakably Shawn.

Wolves don't wear deodorant, I think hazily.

It has to be a dream. A stress-dream. I feel weirdly feverish. What's the alternative? I'm hooking up with a monster I encountered in the woods?

My hips buck as its tongue catches my clit again, and I arch off the ground with a gasp.

"Yes, oh my god, yes," I pant without thinking. Its ears twitch, but it obeys with newfound fervor.

My body reacts, my moans growing louder and becoming cries. A new, different sensation enters the chat, as I lose some distant sense of control and squirt, releasing bursts of liquid as my begging for more becomes practically incoherent. The wolfish creature devouring my cunt is only too happy to keep licking me harder, faster, until the sensations peak again.

It feels like an orgasm, it feels bigger than one. All I know is that when I come back to myself, my body is strained and tired, my eyelids are so heavy I'm not fully able to open them for a few minutes.

But I'm back in my bed.

12

Shawn

Staying away from Elise was proving to be a lot harder than I'd anticipated. I keep having the thought that I could grab some Danishes and bring her one, more to make her laugh than anything else. Then I remember specifically I'm avoiding doing things like that.

It's just too easy to gravitate towards her.

After the grocery store-run in, I'm starting to feel that nowhere is safe. I'm trying to stay out of the house as much as I can to avoid my family, staying away from the brewery to avoid Elise.

I keep coming back to that conversation in the parking lot of the Market Basket. Why would she ask me if I've dated after her? She doesn't care. Or at least, I thought she didn't.

But then she used the word "jealous." She seemed a little flustered, honestly. Maybe that just wasn't the word she wanted. Maybe she just brought it up at all so she could let me know she'd moved on, dated other men, slept with them. I try not to grit my teeth thinking of it, but my blood heats at the memory of her saying it.

I knew it was wrong to feel jealous and possessive. It wasn't my place to have that sort of feeling about her. But no matter how many times I'd rationalized over it, it remained. I wanted to pull her into my lap and snap at anyone who looked in her direction.

But I shouldn't. We've outgrown each other, or maybe at least the desperate way we used to need each other.

I'm sitting on the front porch, watching the sun sink lower when I hear raps on the window from inside. I turn around and there's Aiden, bent over to see under the half-curtain, his face nearly pressed to the pane.

"You wanna go down to the Thirsty Turtle?" he shouts, his breath fogging up the glass.

There's really only one bar in town. I've been there enough to know they have one kind of beer, whatever they get from Aconite Ales, and if they're feeling fancy, both red and white wine.

I stare at him for a good long moment, wondering why he didn't just open the window when he starts to repeat himself, louder through the glass.

I wave him off.

"Logan deserves a bachelor party, doesn't he?" Aiden tries again, and I can see the rigid frame of our middlest brother pacing in the background.

"You're really going with that?"

"I don't want a bachelor party," Logan calls, in case he thinks it looks like this was at all approved by him.

"Come onnnn," Aiden groans, then squishes his face more against the window. "When's the last time all of us got any real quality time together?"

He's got me there. I haven't been back here in so long, and maybe they've visited me separately every now and then, but it's been years. Even these last couple days I've been, more or less, avoiding everyone just to keep from getting in more trouble.

The last time we were all in the same place, we were so much younger.

It aches in my chest how much is gone, the way back home with both of them.

I bend down to the bottom windowpane and breathe on the glass. I swipe a couple letters into the foggy pane before it fades.

"He says it's on!"

"It's backward, dumbass," Logan mutters.

"Yeah, and he's dyslexic. I'm getting the keys."

Before I can call off Aiden's plans, he's stomping through the house away from me. Logan gives me a shrug and follows after him. Moments later, they both appear, Aiden leading the way.

"Dude, I gave you like ten whole minutes to get ready," Aiden blatantly lies as he's climbing into his Jeep. Logan, despite his earlier protests, follows him. Probably knows it's best to just give in.

I stare at the two of them.

Either stay out of the house as much as I can, possibly meet my mate in town, or stay in the house to avoid figuring out who it is and having to bring her home, and be cooped up with Elise.

I really shouldn't have come here.

I sigh and after a few moments, hop down from the porch and climb into the Jeep as well. Aiden whoops and revs the engine and takes off with a lurch that sends the St. Christopher's medal hanging from his rearview mirror swinging.

The one and only local bar is the kind of establishment that has every wall covered in taxidermied hunting trophy birds, and, about four months too early for the season, they all have little, felted Santa hats. It's macabre and charming, and a million things I forgot how much I missed. I had never really gotten a chance to say goodbye to this town. I take a deep breath, inhaling the musty old scent of the bar, the way it smells like the memory of home.

"Oh, hey, there's Elise," Aiden says, snapping my attention to him. My head whips around to where he's staring, and sure enough, there she is. It's the back of her head, the messy bun her hair is piled up in, but I'd know the tension in her shoulders anywhere.

"And Laura," Logan points out and waves to catch her attention.

Shouldn't have come here either.

Our cousin hears the sound of our voices through the crowd and stiffens from across the room. Unsubtly, she turns around and catches my eye, and waves us over with the fakest cheery expression I've ever seen.

When Laura's eyes flick to Elise across the booth, her expression drops. Clearly, she's been informed of some part of the recent drama. This whole town is too small lately.

There's no backing out of this moment though, because Elise turns in her seat to spot us coming through the door. Something shutters in her face as her eyes meet mine.

I wonder briefly, mostly in a morbid worst case scenario way, if my mate might be in this bar. There's a cacophony of smells in here, all layered and twisting over each other. It can't be Elise. She is human, and that wouldn't work. Because . . . that wasn't the way it was supposed to work, anyway.

There weren't really other wolf packs in the area, so who would it even be? I'm pretty sure the only wolves around Mystic Falls were my family. I would have smelled another wolf trying to cut in on our territory. Logan had to go all the way to Boston to find another wolf pack. Boston-adjacent, one of those little towns outside the city that still considered themselves Boston-native, like that wasn't half of fucking Massachusetts, but it's like a two- or three-hour drive, depending on traffic.

But Elise's scent rises above the rest, a part of my every breath. I never got the smell of her out of my sheets, all those years ago. I had to get rid of them.

I try to run through my head who I would have met in town. I didn't really stop to talk to anyone or go into any of the shops. I went into the diner before home, but there weren't really a lot of people in there, and I only talked to my cousin.

Maybe meeting face to face is too much to hope for, but having caught her scent without realizing is some special kind of torture. I would just assume some of the guests for Logan's wedding came early, that it would be other wolves from the other family's pack, but there's no way I wouldn't be able to smell them around.

What a time to have met my mate, when my ex-wife just came back into my life.

It sits uneasily in my stomach, the knowledge. I can't really tell anyone here because I don't even know who it is. And I don't want to have to answer how I know, because I'm not about to bring up the knotting thing.

My dad never really talked to us about that in particular, when he was with us. I've mostly heard about how knotting works from my older cousins when they were trying to gross us out with exaggerated stories of how it worked. Not that they were old enough to know either.

I wouldn't have been ready to meet whoever she is anyway, if it had happened to me before I met Elise. Maybe with another shifter it would have been different, and I wouldn't have had to hide all the things I did from Elise, but I'd be stupid in all the same ways. Sometimes, all I can do is look back and sigh and cringe at how I handled everything. With a wolf shifter, I'd be able to be my whole self with her. And I was never going to have that with Elise.

Aiden pointedly corrals Logan into the side of the wooden booth that Laura is on. The things were never really meant to sit more than two adults, so Logan's scrawny ass is in the middle, trying to fold himself smaller, with Laura shoved against the wall. In a way it was the same as when they were all kids, trying to fit more than there were seats for into a row, while I claimed the front seat as the oldest.

I look to the only seat available now, next to my ex-wife. Christ. Now it feels significantly less like the privilege it used to be.

"I'll go get a chair from the bar . . ." I start to say, but glancing behind me, I see all the chairs in the place are taken.

Elise rolls her eyes and scoots over. My knees knock instantly with Aiden's sliding in. I sit gingerly next to her, trying to keep at least a couple inches of space between us, but it is tight.

Logan waves three fingers to someone across the bar, Laura nudges him and he changes it to four. It takes only a couple of minutes for a waitress to bring around four beers. I guess Logan at least is a regular.

Aiden is staring at us intently. Barely a moment passes before he asks, "So, uh, where have you two met before?"

"Oh, we're just directly asking?" Logan scoffs at Aiden before either of us could come up with an answer. "I thought you said we were going to be subtle."

"I was being sneaky about it until you ruined it, man," Aiden exclaims, rolling his eyes.

"That was your idea of sneaky," Laura deadpans. "Was it not obvious to you both that they dated?"

Logan mumbles from his hunched, folded form.

"Yes, which is why I asked where they met," Aiden sighs. "Clearly, I want all the gory details."

Elise glances at me, and I can practically read the thoughts crossing her face. She wants out of this situation as much as I do. If we don't tell them the dates and locations, maybe they won't have enough to put it together. Maybe it's ok.

"We uh. Met at a traffic crossing," she says, glancing at me again. I nod.

"What? That's boring," Aiden interrupts.

"She stepped off the curb too early, there was a car, she wasn't paying attention," I start to say. It was a perfectly innocent meeting, really.

"He grabbed my arm and pulled me back, and we started talking after that," she shrugs, saying it like it wasn't that special. Forgettable, even.

She looks to me, and for a moment, that memory passes between us. I remember every second of it. The way she was utterly windswept by the cold front moving in, and she was wearing some berry lip gloss, the surprise on her face when she'd realized how close she'd been to a much different fate, how fast it all happened, to how that one moment just stopped. I blink and see the new Elise, her hair frizzy and a lot more freckles than she used to have, her expression almost soft.

Laura squints at nothing for a moment. "Wait, you've told me this one before."

"What? No. I wouldn't have."

Wouldn't? Ok, ouch. There's a heart stopping moment when I realize if Elise has been close with the family, would she have unknowingly told them about me? Do they know she's divorced?

"Is he same the guy you made out with like right after he saved your life?" Laura starts to ask, and from the intense red filling Elise's cheeks, she doesn't even need to confirm it. "Oh my god, I didn't realize that was *also* your ex-h—I mean, the same guy. Shawn."

I try not to glare at Laura at that near-tripped-over syllable. She fucking knows.

"It wasn't that dramatic," Elise hisses, but her protest is lost in the table's reaction.

Aiden slaps the booth in victory, Logan elbows him to keep him quiet as Laura's eyes widen comically.

I don't have more than a second to appreciate the way it has apparently been recounted, because I don't remember it being quite that dire, when Laura locks eyes with me.

"Didn't you say that guy had a—NIPPLE PIERCING. Oh my god. Shawn, you have to show us," Laura gasps, eyes wide with my impending doom.

"Ew, no, I don't want to see my brother's nipples while I'm drinking." Aiden immediately grimaces.

"Logan has a tramp stamp," I counter, and for once his mask of indifference slips and he looks mildly panicked.

"It's not a tramp stamp, it's tasteful and off-center," Logan mutters. The attention slides off him quickly, but I know Aiden is going to tease him about it later, and with family it really is about the long con.

"Oh my god. Can I tell them that Shawn's the guy who said the mystical tit-jobs line?" Laura squeals, undeterred, looking like she's been given everything she ever wanted for Christmas. I wish I'd known to tell Elise not to share a goddamn thing with her, but how could I have known they'd be friends?

Elise just looks as mortified as before, shrinking back in the corner.

"Sordid enough for you?" Logan ribs Aiden, looking the most amused he has in a while.

Making the most wildly evil eyes ever, Laura giggles low and loud, "Huhuhuhuhuh."

"Hey, guys, lay off," I start to say, not so much for myself. I don't care if I have to show them where my old piercings have healed over, but I think Elise might crawl under the table in a few minutes.

Aiden catches my drift and looks between the two of us. He says to her in an undertone, "He should be the one embarrassed for that line."

"Let's stop torturing her. Shawn's turn. Tell us something worse than that, I'm sure you've got something," Laura challenges me.

"Shawn does have a lot of bad breakup stories," Logan readily agrees.

Elise looks at me, clearly curious, as much as she's trying to appear disinterested. Maybe she wonders if I ever told my family about us.

"Two. I have two," I grumble quickly. Having their attention just on me isn't better, actually. "From high school."

"Uh-huh." Laura rolls her eyes.

I grimace at myself. That they know of.

"One girl, I really thought he was going to fake his death or something," Laura is quick to explain to Elise, reaching across the table to hold her attention.

I can see in Elise's eyes that she agrees. Instead of amusement, there's a flicker of coldness in her expression, knowing exactly what Laura's talking about.

"You never would make the hard decisions. You always chickened out when it was actually tough," she says, the words cold and cutting, and it doesn't seem like she said it intentionally. Her face has shuttered in a way that, when she blinks, she seems to realize she said her thoughts out loud.

I watch Elise's expression turn into something unreachable.

The table has gone utterly quiet. Aiden swallows. Maybe he thought the gory details would be funny and interesting, and not just all the ways we tore each other apart.

I dragged out our relationship much longer than it should have gone. I should have ended it early, so that it never got to the point of wanting to build a life together, because I knew the whole time my parents wouldn't approve. We couldn't have a human marrying into the family. It weakened the strength of the pack.

Aiden is the first to find the wherewithal to try and change the subject, but I'm too busy watching Elise to listen.

Her face softens a little as she glances to Aiden. He's always had an easy-going charm, and while I've envied that about him, I've never fully felt jealous. But it sits uncomfortably in my chest, a cloying sensation that makes me glare at him unprompted.

Aiden glances at me with a smile on his face that promptly melts off. He makes his sad baby brother face out of habit.

I shake myself and shrug it off.

He's barely a few sentences in about renovations the bar has made when I get up from the table. They fall quiet and I don't hear a thing from them as I leave to get outside.

It's drizzly and gross outside, but I couldn't be in there for another minute.

There are a few hand-rolled cigarettes with a few dried and crushed aconite petals blended with the tea. Usually, I use them to feel a little toasted, since normal substances aren't really enough for our kind. But it's also to keep the wolf at bay. Early on it was harder to control my wolf, and lighting one up was a quick way to calm it down.

It had felt too easy to consider, too reasonable in my mind to dive over the table and grab Aiden by the collar. And for what, because Elise had smiled at him?

That would have been disastrous. Maybe I do need to lock myself in the brewery cellars during the full moon.

The door bangs open a few inhales in, just as I'm starting to feel a little more in control. I don't expect to see Elise coming after me.

She stops a few places away from me, wrinkling her nose. "Is that the hipster-tea-cigarette-shit you always liked?"

I shrug and kind of nod. Not the way I would have described it, but alright.

She looks ready to pick a fight with me, crossing her arms over her chest. "Do you know how bad this stuff is for you?"

"You got statistics on that? I love statistics."

She rolls her eyes, regretting the momentary lapse of judgment that made her offer concern. "Never mind, feel free to kill yourself."

She paces away, reaching for the door to go back inside. She stops just short of it and glares at me. "You don't get to make this harder for me."

"I'm not trying to make this harder for you."

"Then what was any of that?"

"What were you doing, telling our intimate details to my cousin of all people?"

"Obviously, I didn't know that at the time! I didn't know any of that or I wouldn't be here!"

I have to hold back the urge to grin. In some small way, fighting feels more comfortable than anything we've said to each other so far, all the awkward tiptoeing. This is the Elise I remember, ready to die on any hill.

I have always loved this Elise.

"Obviously, you wouldn't be here, you would have left the minute you found out. You would have packed your bags and disappeared without a word."

Her eyes flash with anger. "Don't make it sound like I caved the moment it got difficult. You made it difficult for a long time."

Fury claws up my back, at the nerve she strikes. "I wasn't the one ready to give up on us. Not even after you left!"

"Even after I left? Did you still love me when you were sneaking out of our bed in the middle of the night? When you left me, time after time, thinking I wouldn't know you were gone, or wonder where you were, who you were with? When I confronted you and you still couldn't be bothered to tell me the truth?"

"I wasn't—" I stop short, my jaw tense.

She looks at me, glaring daggers, frowning so viciously, like she can't believe that I had ever loved her.

"Even then," I swear, my voice tight.

Her hand clenches on the bar door handle. Her frown twitches downward like she's trying not to cry. "Maybe to you, it looked like you loved me. But you were just hurting me."

She lets go and stomps away, turning around the corner to the back of the building where the dumpster and stacked crates are.

I hear the way her heart thuds in her chest, the sting of adrenaline in the air, before I hear her scream.

I move before I even think to, catching the way she staggers back, and then I see it.

My hand finds the back of her head and pulls her face towards me, turning her away before she has more than a glimpse of a dead deer that's kind of ripped apart in a way too gruesome to linger over. I've seen this sort of thing plenty in the woods, often smaller animals, often not half-eaten like this. Not decimated. Not done with such a violence that goes beyond simple prey

"I can't look."

Elise has never had the stomach for so much as a teen-rated horror movie.

I put my hand over her eyes without thinking and feel her eyelashes flutter closed against my palm. She curls in towards me, the bridge of her nose pressing hard into my chest.

Even though I can bear to look at the gory mess behind the bar, its existence leaves me unsteady, my stomach turning at what the deer means.

There are only a few werewolves in this territory, and the majority of them are standing right here with me. Any of us could have done this, even me. I'd convinced myself I had such control over my wolf that I'd forgotten what I was truly capable of. And this side of myself was terrifying and dangerous to Elise.

It's every reason I couldn't let her know what I was, why I had to leave her side so many nights, why being with her at all was stupid and dangerous. It had been reckless of me to endanger her by living together.

She could never know. I don't know that I could live with myself if she looked at me and saw that I was a monster. It was bad enough now that she was so close by, when my wolf was hunting, stalking, preying.

I swallow, and it's only a moment before the others are hurrying out. I don't know if they were able to hear our fight over the din inside, but there was no way the three of them didn't hear her scream.

I'll never shake that sound for the rest of my life.

Laura pries Elise out of my arms, helping her cover her eyes on her way to the car.

"What was it that Mom called it? Coyotes?" Aiden offers with a low whistle when he sees the deer, and Logan shoots him a disapproving look.

A few other people start to shuffle out of the bar, also gawking at the overkill, someone immediately throwing up.

"There's certainly something on the loose," Logan says. His stare holds on me, as I glance between Aiden and him. Both their faces are a little too serious.

There's definitely a werewolf turning feral in this town, and it can only be one of us.

13

"Between the two of us," Aiden announces, "we've come up with the Emotional Support Smoothie."

He holds out a cold, plastic takeout cup, wet with condensation on the outside, like he's personally snagged fire from the gods for me and is aware of how cool his gift to me is.

It looks vaguely chocolate flavored and only somewhat frozen. I might have to put it in the freezer for a bit first.

More than anything, it marks just how long I've been sitting on the hood of Aiden's Jeep with Shawn and Laura, not talking. Apparently long enough for the brothers to walk a few blocks and back.

I glance between them. Logan, carrying a few pizza boxes, nods from a few steps behind Aiden, a quiet endorsement of the Emotional Support Smoothie.

I've seen them go through this kind of thinking process a number of times, so I'm familiar with the whole logical path that must have gone down between them: Logan posing that they should cheer me up after what happened at the bar, Aiden quickly chiming in with what always makes him feel better—a protein shake with a little chocolate syrup on the top (something he's come into the kitchen to make a number of times), Logan coaxing the idea into something a little less gym-bro-y.

It's both heartwarming and heart-breaking.

I feel cared for in a way I need more than anything, and it hurts. These are the people that pretended I didn't exist for years, who never bothered to meet me. But clearly Shawn's brothers are caring. I know they are. I've seen it. They've been my family while I rebuilt my life out here.

Shawn frowns at all of it. I guess he's not used to me liking his family more than him.

He's been rubbing my back sporadically between pacing the length of the front porch. I hate that I've been letting him. It's too easy to seek solace in Shawn. I keep trying to remind myself not to.

"Really guys, it's ok. I'm not traumatized, just a little . . ." I struggle for the right word, but nothing fits. Rattled? Nearly hurled at the sight of that much blood?

I sigh and just take the smoothie out of Aiden's hand.

Shawn throws a glare at his brother. "Did you ask for almond milk? You can't give her dairy."

The sensations that pass over me are weird. Heat rises up my neck and cheeks that he's telling his brothers I'm lactose intolerant, but a part of me is oddly warmed that he remembered.

He was always better at looking out for my stomach than I was when we were together. I usually just deal with the miserable consequences.

". . . Where's everyone else's emotional support smoothies?"

The boys and Laura exchange a glance between them.

It's clear they think I'm too much of a wuss to handle seeing gross things. Now that I'm a little less immediately nauseous, I can see that none of them are as bothered as me.

Oh.

"I've seen roadkill before," I say, even though that was a lot worse than any roadkill.

Aiden offers uncertainty, making more eye contact with his brothers than me as he explains, sounding like he's asking a question. "We used to go hunting . . . ?"

"Our dad used to take us," Logan says more decisively. "We're pretty desensitized to it."

Of course. Rich people are fucking weird as hell. They can't have normal hobbies.

I sigh and try not to roll my eyes, mostly to contain any embarrassment at being the only one who's squeamish. "Alright. Well, thank you. I'm gonna let this one firm up in the freezer, it was very thoughtful."

I take a sip anyway, and taste the banana, dates, and blueberries under the dark chocolate. It's heavenly, but I know I'll suffer if I actually try to drink the whole thing.

It does feel a little like handing out treats to a gaggle of puppies that just performed a trick, the way Aiden's smile breaks out across his face. A little condescending, even. But I can do that much to get them to give me some space.

The two brothers break away to bring their pizza boxes inside the Jeep, the sound of Aiden praising his own genius and Logan reminding him it had been both their ideas echoing off the hallway as I'm left with the one brother I just can't seem to shake.

I glance to Laura, my planned ride home. "Are we heading out too?"

"Oh. I was gonna join in on pizza night. Did you want to come too, or would you rather we drop you off at your house?"

I would prefer to go home and sleep the rest of this evening off, but the memory of scratches on the cottage door makes all the hair on the back of my neck stand up now that I've seen the deer. It makes me unsteady all over again. "Um, I'll come over for pizza."

I slide awkwardly off the hood of Aiden's Jeep, and, before I can even take a step toward the end of the parking lot where Laura's car is, she tosses her keys at Shawn.

They hit him square in the chest and he catches them, frowning.

"I'll join the boys in the Jeep," she says simply, "Shawn, you can drive my car back."

"Am I not one of the boys?"

"No, but you're far more sober than I am. You barely touched your drink, and I had two beers before you even got to the Turtle." She shrugs, feigning wobbliness a moment before she sneaks a grin at me.

That checks out, but I also know Laura can drink most people under the table, even if she doesn't look like she has the constitution for it. I'm in the middle of doing the math on how many seats are left in the Jeep, when she hauls herself into the cramped back seat and takes the stack of pizza boxes from Logan.

Oh my god. I cannot believe she just did that.

"Do we believe her, or do we think she's being a little shit?" Shawn asks as we watch the Jeep speed off, and we're truly left alone together, again. I don't know how this keeps happening.

And there he goes, grouping me and him together in a single word that makes my teeth clench.

I should be more pissed off at Laura maybe, but I'm exhausted.

"I don't know how I didn't see it before. Your family doesn't know the meaning of the word subtle, and neither do you."

He sighs and nods and follows me to Laura's car. "Sorry about that. They're . . . well, you know. You've been here. It's weird seeing you all together."

"It is weird. I'm still kind of processing it."

"I don't know that it's ever been normal here. Or them. Or . . ." he glances at me, and then seems to think better of the word *us*, but I feel it hanging there, unsaid.

We were never normal. We tried to be but just couldn't hack it, I guess.

I stare at the car as Shawn rounds to the driver's side. There's something about the way he moves that makes me remember my dream from the other night. Maybe it's the part where I'm continuously finding myself stuck with him, and I can't escape.

I don't usually buy into the dream interpretation stuff, but it's the second time I've had that dream now.

But really, what is it going to tell me that I don't already know? That I'm stressed out about work and my ex-husband being back in my life and now I'm afraid of my attraction to him putting my heart in a dangerous position again, and it's manifesting itself in the image of a wolf chasing me to eat me out?

I feel like it's all pretty clear. And obvious. There's literally nothing else it could be.

Maybe I don't want to look into it, because even if it gives me that kind of clarity, it doesn't give me a solution. At least, a better one than moving out and starting over anywhere but here.

A few minutes go by in silence after we get in her car. Shawn takes forever adjusting every little thing in her car, from the seat to the rearview mirror, the AC vents. I suspect half of it is just to annoy Laura when she has to drive it next. I hold my Emotional Support Smoothie to my forehead, finding some solace in it after all.

This car has never felt so small, but I guess I've never had to compete with Shawn to lean on its center console before.

While my mind is still on that dream, I remember how the beast had smelled. It's weird how those dreams are so intensely sensory. But Shawn is right next to me right now. I lean a little closer and think I can get away with sniffing him.

Nope, he turns right around and gives me a look. "What was that?"

I shrink back to the other side of my seat, practically pressed against the door. "I, um. Uh. Nothing."

It's a deeply guilty and still unsatisfactory answer. Still, Shawn doesn't press it.

"So. Mystical tit-jobs," he says, tilting his head and raising an eyebrow at me. "And you told Laura that, of all people."

I can't help but laugh a little as I cringe. "If you had a story like that, you'd tell it too."

"I don't know that I could admit to falling for a line like that."

"I was twenty! I thought that was about as good as declarations of love got. And you have no room to judge me, you were the one who said it," I bluster, but there's no force or heat behind it.

I watch the smile tug at the corner of his mouth as he keeps his eyes on the road. "I have said every combination of dumb words there is."

"Yeah, you have."

A comfortable quiet falls on us, and I can feel the distance between my shoulder and his, buzzing, burning, itching against my mind and heart. I lean through it, taking the easy way out and just letting myself melt into an old habit.

Just one more time.

The warmth coming off him is worth it, and it feels better than sleeping in on a Saturday. I forgot how he was one of those guys whose body just runs hotter than most. I *think* that's a thing.

I feel the way he holds the breath in his chest, his whole body tensing up for a moment as I settle my shoulder against his. And then how it all seeps away as he lets a slow breath out.

I think he missed this as much as I did.

"I didn't mean what I said outside the bar. I can't actually be mad at you for leaving. Sometimes I wish I could be, but that would be unfair to you. After all the times I . . . never gave you any answers," he hedges on the tail end of his apology.

"That's a weird euphemism for 'snuck out', but whatever." I shrug, but there's no malice in my words. It means a lot that he respects why I had to leave.

"No, not whatever," Shawn grumbles, and scrubs a hand over his face. His grip on the steering wheel tightens. "I lied to you a lot, and I never told you—"

"I know you were out calling home."

"What?"

He struggles a moment to keep his eyes on the road, trying to glance at me.

"I knew you weren't no-contact with them, like you told me. A lot of the time I just had to get up and go to the window. Sometimes you were just outside, talking to your brother or mom or dad on the phone. I felt like I could tell who it was by the tone of your voice sometimes," I say, a secret I never told him before, I realize.

He's fallen quiet, processing what I'm saying.

"I know you thought you were protecting my feelings by just keeping in touch with your family when you thought I was asleep. But it sucked that you felt like you had to hide that from me. All of it sucked."

It wasn't right to ask him to choose me over his family. But how do you love someone who won't choose you? He never had, and that had been the first crack in our relationship. A fault in the foundation, really. He never advocated for me to his family the way I needed him to.

Shawn barely moves even to breathe. I watch his throat as he swallows.

"I know I reacted strongly when you showed up . . . and I'm not apologizing for that," I say slowly, and meet his eyes when he stops at a red light.

He holds my gaze gently and nods a little. I'm surprised he doesn't push back on it.

"But it is nice to get a chance to talk a little again. Even if it's just for some closure. But I'm gonna be real, I think everything makes even less sense now that I've actually met and know your folks."

Bringing up the sum of all our problems, the evidence of the end of us, feels I've drawn a line in the sand. I can see it in the hard line of his mouth as he nods and doesn't push back on it.

The light turns green and the way the car jerks forward feels like it says a lot about his mood.

"Who said families were supposed to make sense?" Shawn sighs. "There's a lot that I still don't really know how to talk about."

I guess his family wouldn't make any more sense than mine did, the way I didn't really end up close with either of my parents. That desperately wanting a stronger connection only made it more difficult to have one.

I watch the sun start to glare against the clouds, slipping down in the sky. We're quiet for a long time, and every few seconds I peek at Shawn chewing the inside of his cheek the way he always did when he was deep in thought.

For a moment, I think he's going to try to tell me something about his family that will offer at least a sliver of clarity.

"I don't know if you still go hiking much, but you shouldn't go into the woods for a bit. Since there's a wild animal out there mauling deer and things," he says, brow furrowed as he chooses his words, not glancing up at all from the road ahead.

I frown a little. What does that have to do with anything we were talking about?

"If anything ever happened to you," he says, but doesn't finish the thought. A muscle tenses in his jaw.

I think about the dreams, the beast I had met in them. There's no reason to, it's just a dream. It's not the same thing as what he's talking about. But I can't help but feel he senses its presence out in the woods as keenly as I do. That all of this tension over the wedding, the issues with his family, and my being here manifest together as something with teeth, a low, constant growl in the background that makes your hair stand on end. It stalks, ready to strike, just when we think we're safe.

Shawn tears his eyes from the road, and when they meet mine, I realize the beast in my dreams has always had his eyes.

"Sure, yeah," I nod and take a sip of the mostly melted smoothie to distract myself with anything else. It's already going down uneasily, and I grimace at it. I hold it out to Shawn. "You can have the rest of this."

His hand grazes mine and the sensation spikes in my middle, an explosion of little wings. Something far worse than lactose intolerance has been churning in my stomach.

Feelings.

Too many to parse through. Every high and every low we ever had, every sweet gesture followed by every problem, every fight and apology and make up.

I should shove away from him, after the number of times I've insisted to Laura that I could never let a guy make me feel so alone in a relationship again.

But here I am, ready to melt into his side if it means he'll put his arms around me and stroke my back and make me feel like I'm the only girl in the world again, even if it won't last.

14

Elise

We get back to the house almost too soon. Suddenly the twenty-minute drive from town to the Hayes House doesn't feel like it's just on the edge of being too long, but terribly short.

He puts the car in park and turns off the engine, but neither of us move to get out.

We're both staring at the house casting a shadow over us, probably both contemplating what more tonight has in store.

"Can't say I had ever pictured bringing you to my family under these specific circumstances," he starts to say, his tone light and playful. "I mean, I know we've both been inside with them already, but it's weird every time."

"Yeah, I never pictured meeting them, period," I say, blatant lie that it is. I had really wanted to meet his family when we had started dating. He'd told me so much about them, and it had all just sounded so perfect. I'd always wanted to be a part of a big family.

Out of habit, I pull out my phone and open up my texts with my mom in case I accidentally swiped away the new message notification away before I saw it, but there's nothing new since last year there.

I let out a slow sigh, deflating a little and leaning forward over my knees. My forehead touches the passenger-side airbag compartment. Maybe I should have just accepted the offer for one of them to drop me off at home. Maybe this is just another in a long line of bad decisions I've been making.

I called her last night too; she still didn't answer. She's always been terrible at getting back to me, I remind myself. I can probably expect a text from her later tonight telling me she's been out of the house all day and left her phone at home, that it's been lost in the couch cushions for days. None of it true, probably.

I'm contemplating the crumbs and paper straw wrappers and crumpled up receipts that are strewn across the floor of Laura's car when I feel Shawn's hand graze against my back. For several moments, he traces gentle patterns back and forth between my shoulder blades.

I can't help but hum a wistful note. It feels good, and it makes the tension in my jaw ease.

I turn my head against my knees enough to look at him. Shawn gives me a little half-smile, and raises an eyebrow, like he's trying to convince me it won't be so bad.

His eyes dip towards my phone screen, a tense line touching his mouth. "I thought you'd gone no-contact with her."

I shrug and put it away. "Not on purpose. That was just a really long experiment to see if she'd ever reach out first."

He doesn't ask if she did, he can probably guess how that went. I'm sure he remembers forwarding me her card, finally congratulating us on getting married a couple weeks after I'd moved out.

He rolls his eyes in a less than subtle way, and I briefly imagine him turning that memory over in his hands as well, when he starts to say, "That's a dangerous game to play—"

"I missed this," I confess, cutting him off, if only to make him stop talking about uncomfortable things.

Shawn looks surprised, pausing his scratching for a second. His face softens then, and he nods. "The back scratches?"

If there was one perfect thing about our relationship, something he did just because it made me happy, it was the scratches. I never had to ask, he always just started doing them. Nothing else ever made me feel so easily wrapped up in someone else's care.

"Well, if we're going to be specific about it, the leg scratches. You could do magic to the back of my thighs," I murmur, like I'm sharing a secret with him. I lean back in the seat and raise my knee for effect, but he takes the motion as an invitation to scratch more of my leg. I close my eyes and let it take me back for a moment.

It's an unexpected memory; one I haven't thought about in ages; one I never really let myself reminisce over. We used to lay in bed on Saturday mornings, doing nothing but chatting and joking, talking about what we wanted to do for breakfast until noon wandered past. He'd be scratching my legs the whole time.

I miss those mornings, what it was like to bask in the whole of his attention for hours.

Shawn coaxes my leg up over the car's center console, and it's all too easy to just let him take my ankle in his hand, to massage the back of my heel.

Despite myself, I giggle. "You cannot be out here grabbing random ladies' ankles."

"Just the ladies I know, gotcha," he replies with a wink, and I cannot contain the laugh that little gesture evokes in me. I wince my way through it because I know, I know, I know, I'm not supposed to laugh with him anymore. I can't resist it, it's just so easy.

Shawn leans across the center console and threads an arm under my knees, pulling them up to my chest. It's all to create access to the back of my thighs, and he begins drawing long trails of pleasure up and down.

I can't even snap at him for encroaching on my personal space; it's exactly the way we used to be, and it feels too good. This asshole and his magic fingers know all of my weaknesses.

"Ugh, yes, just like that," I nearly moan, my head tipping back and closing my eyes just to enjoy it. When I open my eyes again to glance at him, I realize in just that moment how close his face is to mine.

There is such warmth and depth in his dark-brown eyes. I sigh, and it feels like an admission that maybe I am shallow enough that I'll let a pretty face fool me. I had let it convince me it was worth being hurt for. But it wasn't just Shawn's features, it was how he made me feel, how he took care of me. It was the many evenings we fell asleep on the couch in front of the TV, my cheek pressed against his collarbone and his arm around me, drawing lazy circles on my thigh.

He reaches out and tucks a lock of hair behind my ear, and his fingers trace down from my jaw to my chin, where he runs his thumb over my lower lip.

I don't know if the feeling building in my chest is the need for him or for closure, but this is neither.

"Elise, I don't want to leave things like we left them all those years ago when you didn't give me a choice," he admits. Every word he reaches for feels deliberate. "I don't want it to be how we remember everything we had."

I can't breathe or swallow or think. I know the ache he's talking about, how the way we ended eclipsed everything good that we once had. For ages, I couldn't even let myself remember the good things fondly, only the pain of how much I ached to have a taste of that again.

The words come out of me quietly. "How do you want to remember us?"

His hand on my leg tightens as he holds my gaze, and for the briefest of flickers, his eyes dip to my mouth. It feels like permission to shift towards him, to nose my way into his space and graze my lips to his.

I want to. I will. I'll let myself have this.

But his hand catches hold of the side of my face, keeping me in place. He doesn't pull back, but keeps our foreheads pressed together, our noses just a hair apart.

Even though his grip is strong it feels shaky, like he's holding himself back. He takes in a deep breath, letting it out slowly. I let myself sink into that moment with him, the memory of what it meant to be held like this, to feel utterly safe and protected from whatever else the world could bring.

For several moments, all I can hear is my heart in my ears when he breaks the quiet. "Like this."

He presses a kiss to my forehead, and for a second, I feel whole. In a matter of seconds it's over, the moment is gone as soon as it happened. He opens the driver's side door and the cool rush of air from outside brings me back to the present.

I push back into the passenger seat, and as I'm figuring out how to bend my knees the right way to get my legs over the center console, I'm wondering how he was able to get my legs over there so easily. I'm not thinking about that kiss. I swear to god this better not have gotten me wet. I try not to wonder, would Shawn . . . no. I shouldn't even consider it, really.

Maybe it's a good thing we don't desecrate Laura's car. But also maybe she deserves it for enabling this.

That wasn't really a kiss, that was barely anything, and yet, it was like plunging into an intimacy so deep I couldn't see the end of it. It doesn't make sense that it could just vanish into thin air again so quickly.

Shawn gets out of the car and stretches, and maybe I enjoy watching a little too much. God, he always had amazing arms. And he's got this litheness to him, like all his joints are just a little bit detached.

He looks like every guy that was just out of reach, that was just a little too good to spare a glance at me. But he was mine, for a little while.

Or at least I thought he was, before I realized he never really would be.

I stare a little too long, and he's rounded to my side of Laura's car. He opens the door and offers me a hand to help me stand up. The way he leans against the open door makes it seem like such a simple, casual gesture. I blink a couple times and take it. Not that I need it, but maybe there's closure in feeling his hand envelope mine.

And if I hold on a few seconds longer than I should, it's still definitely for closure.

We walk inside the Hayes House, and I can see his brothers in the dining room already, dividing up the pizza. Laura's commandeered half a white-sauce pie, Logan and Aiden have already taken all the pepperoni slices.

I can hear Deanna just inside the dining room, "Laura, will you tell Aunt Jenny she still has yet to send me her RSVP card. She hasn't answered any of my texts."

"We can't just assume she'll be there? Mom's not going to miss her godson's wedding."

"Oh, I suppose," Deanna sighs, and when her attention turns to us it stops us in our tracks.

"I was wondering where you disappeared to," she says, her eyes flicking between Shawn and me. The suspicion in her eyes is a little jarring. She's always been warm towards me, more than business partners needed to be.

But the way she's looking at us makes me feel like we're teenagers caught out after curfew.

Even though she's talking to her son, I feel the need to explain that Laura insisted we take her car, that's all that happened.

It's the first real reminder from her that she never approved of us together, for whatever reason. I'd never had to deal with it in person, but I wonder if even after her knowing me and being so friendly, she still would have disapproved of us?

It's a strange line to draw, mentally.

I don't know that I like what it says that they all just assume I'm clearly an ex-hookup of his. Or what it says about him. It falls in line with my worst perceptions of him and reaffirms all those old hurts.

"I didn't think we were that far behind," I say, putting a few steps of space between me and Shawn, hurrying ahead to the dining room. In my hope to not be alone, I think I've just invited myself into a den of wolves. They're going to keep staring at me and Shawn, watching our every interaction, just like at the bar, but now with Deanna.

Dinner is painfully quiet. We sit around the long dining room table, too much space between each of us.

"I hear you five went to the Thirsty Turtle," Deanna offers after several minutes of the only sound being chewing.

"Logan's bachelor party," Laura explains.

"Oh. That's nice." She nods, clearly more occupied with her mental list. "There's still a lot to do. We should finalize the seating plans. And Aiden, you still need to find something to wear. You can take Shawn with you when you go into town. Logan, I need your opinion on bunting."

Shawn and I may have undeclared history in her eyes, but we're all here as part of the wedding planning party. It's nice that there's more important things happening than my drama with Shawn.

Logan is quiet. He usually is, I guess.

"We're going to have a lot of guests here at the house soon," their mother continues, looking prepared to assign us all additional duties.

"Hopefully the wolf attacks don't scare them off," Shawn mutters, interrupting that train of thought.

His mom looks at him. I can see the tightness in her jaw as she works to figure out how to respond to him.

"I'm sure there aren't any wolves. Probably coyotes. They're much smaller animals, but they can make a real mess. It's usually because people aren't locking their trash properly, it brings them into town," Deanna goes on.

A week ago, I would have taken her word for it. I don't know how to begin to tell her that what I saw was too big and savage to be a coyote's work. The way the deer had been ripped apart in grand, arching slices.

I swallow at nothing, and fidget with my napkin.

"So, Elise went to the bachelor party as well?"

"She is a friend," Logan shrugs.

"Catching up?" Deanna prompts with a glance to Shawn as she takes a sip from her wine.

"A little," he says, and once again I can feel them all itching to ask more, but Deanna's watchful eye seems to be holding her sons from inquiring for details again.

"It's been a few years since we talked," I say, trying to thread the line of lying and telling them enough truth to not have to remember details later to uphold our charade.

"Would you say it's accurate that you ghosted me?" Shawn asks, giving me a little teasing smile. After how quick he was to bring it up earlier, I'm surprised he looks so blasé about it.

Deanna frowns, and glances at Aiden to clarify. I guess he is the youngest in the house. "Ghosted? What does that mean?"

"When you don't call someone after a date, ever. Vanishing on them," he tells her in an undertone, though the whole table can hear it.

Eyes flick between me and Shawn, and I can see them trying to imagine us on an unpleasant date. At least Shawn didn't imply I was a hookup to his mother.

"Some dates are bad enough you'd rather both just forget about it." I roll my eyes. Ball's back in Shawn's court.

"Oh. Well. I am a very bad date," he informs his brothers, to their bemused looks. "Just in general."

"Always late," I add.

"And underdressed." He nods in agreement.

"Forgets his wallet."

"Accidentally stepping on your toes."

It's a little too easy to smile, to fall into this rhythm that used to be second nature to us. I catch myself and realize that this little ping-pong we used to do is not the best idea right now. I stop myself from adding anything else.

"So, uh, who's on the guest list?" Shawn asks, directing his attention to Logan.

This whole dinner has been one awkward moment after another.

Logan fails to answer. He shrugs a little.

"Mostly just family," Deanna answers for him.

"Very traditional," Aiden puts in as he catches my eye, making eyebrows. Maybe he thought that needed clarification, except I don't know that he's explained anything.

Shawn shrugs at Logan. "Can't say I'm one for tradition."

"You've always had to be a contrarian," Deanna says dryly.

Shawn doesn't respond, and dinner falls silent again. The sound of chewing dominates the big, well-decorated room.

"Are you still married?" his mother asks, cutting through the silence. Clearly Aiden's impatience for subtlety comes from her side. I'm just glad I don't choke on my food.

I exchange glances with Shawn. Does his family not know we got divorced years ago? Do they think he's been living with me this whole time, and that he just came up alone?

Shawn doesn't answer but holds up his unadorned hand.

Deanna rolls her eyes, and glances at me. "These boys always think they can lie to their mom. Darling, I saw you take it off earlier."

Pizza crust clatters loudly against a plate, but it's nothing against the way my heart startles at the thought of Shawn keeping his ring.

"Mom," Shawn says, his tone warning, but I'm too stunned by the revelation.

He still wears the ring. Or he has it on him, at least. I left mine at that little apartment years ago.

I'm too stunned to think; it's all I can do to make sure my face doesn't show what I'm feeling when Shawn makes careful eye contact with me. I'm sure I shouldn't hold his stare, that Deanna is watching the two of us, gauging my reaction, but I can't help it. The thought of him holding onto it sits strangely in my chest. Fills my chest with goddamn butterflies, and I can't decide whether they're a parasite or not.

It aches for me to want to relish in the feeling, how much I miss what being loved by him felt like.

But I can't just let myself enjoy the feeling. Not after the way we ended. I can't bring myself to believe that he ever cared so much for me.

Deanna doesn't seem to get what she wants from her provocation, or maybe she does and she's just better at concealing her intentions. "Well. You should make time to call her and let her know how you are. We wouldn't want you to neglect her."

I can see how she must think that would sound normal to an outsider, if a little passive aggressive. But I can't imagine why she would think of herself as the neglected party. She was the one who told Shawn he had to choose between me and his family.

I still honestly can't believe they hated the idea of me so much, that they can't even remember my name, just that I was a grudge worth holding all this time.

"Can you tell we like you better?" Aiden says to me with a smirk.

Deanna gives her son a sharp look. "We're not going to embarrass Elise this evening."

I'm not sure what Aiden is implying, that they would take me over this stranger they've never met; they somehow prefer the me they met versus the one they refused to meet.

They would have never bothered to get to know me.

Here we were with this great relationship, genuine warmth, and they would have chosen to never know me. No, what's worse—we could have had this. We could have had an even closer and warmer version of this, but they chose not to by never meeting me. They never deserved it.

Deanna breaks me out of my thoughts, glancing to me sidelong. "Did you not know?"

So, that's what she wanted to learn. There's a faint sense of relief, at least, that she hasn't figured us out yet.

I don't know how to voice that I didn't even know there was a third brother, let alone that it was him. It's actually strange, now that I think about it, that there was no trace of him here. I haven't seen any pictures of him in the family photos downstairs before, though there are plenty of his brothers playing together as children.

"Mom, don't," Shawn's voice warns before I can answer, redirecting her attention.

I can feel the intensity of their matched glares burning through the air. I wish I knew what was going through his head.

Then he gives a little shrug and pushes back from the table. "I think I'm done. Can I take anyone else's plates up?"

I swallow and look at him. It was getting harder to exist in the same house as these people.

15

Shawn

It turns out I don't actually remember where any of the plates should go. And I'm not sure which of the pretty wood panels in the lower-shelf units conceals the dishwasher, so I opt for handwashing the plates and propping them up to dry on a dish towel.

I used to really hate doing the dishes, but right now it seems like the only thing I can do that doesn't start more shit. I keep thinking things can't get any worse, but that bar keeps being pushed, all too often by my own family.

Of course, my mom is quick to find me after dinner, showing up in the kitchen doorway when I'm halfway through my task.

I gnash my teeth together. I'd like to just ignore her for the rest of tonight, maybe tomorrow too. Instead, I glance at her, working against the muscles in my jaw to find what I can even say to her.

"You had no right to tell Elise about my ring."

"So, you hadn't told her," my mom observes, like she has everything figured out, and I resist the mighty urge to roll my eyes. No, I didn't tell my ex-wife I kept both our wedding bands out of sentimentality. I wonder if she'd have done that if she knew who Elise really was.

I feel my hackles rise in response, when I catch sight of the waxing moon in the window, pale blue in the early evening, inching its way to full. Its influence on our blood is the last thing we need right now.

There's something so repellent about this conversation, something almost physically nauseating. We've had this fight before, with and without my dad present, a hundred times. Ever since I met Elise and was naive enough to tell my mom about the girl I'd been smitten with.

"I just don't think it's smart to spend so much time with her. She's busy prepping for the wedding, and you . . ." she trails off, but I feel like I know the next words by heart. They've been carved into my chest.

"You shouldn't get involved with her, Shawn."

"That's—" I bite down on the words before I can say them. She's not my wife anymore.

My claws puncture the soapy sponge clenched in my first. Anger burns up through my veins, I can feel my transformation threatening to unravel my rationality with feverish, raw, unmitigated fury.

I step back, shutting the water off in the sink and putting the unfinished dishes aside. I take a long, deep breath through my nose.

It's not nearly as calming as I would like it to be.

"I can't deal with this right now," I tell my mom, expecting resistance. "I'm tabling this for tomorrow, ok?"

"Shawn, we need to talk—"

"I am not *fucking* able to have a rational conversation right now," I snarl, unable to contain myself, my every nerve a live wire.

It breaks my heart to see the genuine surprise on her face. For all our fights, there are so few times I've actually yelled at my own mother.

"I need a breather. Tomorrow, ok?"

She glances at the window, and slowly nods. With that, I leave the room, the house, the property.

It's too early in the evening to shift, but I feel the need to go running in the woods and burn off the anxious, angry energy thrumming through my veins. If I'm dead tired, at least I won't start more shit. I hope.

There's a wolf going feral in Mystic Falls, and I'm terrified it might be me.

I don't know for sure what was left of that deer behind the bar was my wolf's doing, but I can't rule myself out. Every night closer to the full moon, I lose a little more of myself to it. I don't always remember why I have to pick little clumps of fur out of my teeth.

There was one time in my memory that our dad killed a coyote just before a full moon. He'd been pretty unpleasant to be around during the day in that period, there had been some issues with the brewery that he'd been stressing over.

As glad as I am that he's gone, some part of me wishes he was here so I could ask him questions about it. The wiser part of me knows I'd never really been able to ask him anything.

This last week, it's been getting harder to control my wolf than it usually is near the full moon. The aconite ale hasn't been doing enough to keep my wolf at bay since I got here. Just going for runs until I was too exhausted to do anything except collapse in my bed wasn't helping the way it usually did either.

Maybe it's because I've been avoiding finding my mate. There's only a couple of things that will drive a wolf feral: losing one's pack, and being kept from one's mate. Well, I've lived without a pack for a while, it can't be that.

I don't know how to begin looking for my mate. I could try to follow a scent, but I'd need to pick it up first. While my knot may be the main evidence I have that she exists in Mystic Falls right now, it's not exactly something I can search dick-first with.

Besides, I wasn't really sure I wanted to look for my mate. When I thought of my parents' union, any bond resembling that didn't feel like something worth wanting.

What would be a mate outside the ideas I was raised with? Hell, what was even a healthy marriage?

I never wanted to be like my father, having the final, unquestionable word on everything. That I couldn't bring any concerns I had to him without expecting it to result in a lecture and feeling like I was in the wrong no matter what. Growing up with it was bad enough, but I couldn't imagine having that in a life-long partner. Even my failed marriage seemed better than that. I couldn't count how many times Elise had pointed out flaws in my thinking, how often I had been relieved that there was someone who I could be wrong out loud to, and not feel shame or guilt about it

No one ever said it explicitly, but a lot of what I learned from church was that if it felt good it was probably a sin. Guilt as a lifestyle had been inescapable until her.

It had always been safe with her to be incorrect or have weird little shortcomings. I smile, remembering a lazy Saturday she had handed me her phone and I'd passed her my laptop. I called her dentist to make her an appointment because phone calls still flustered her, and she went through my email draft to a client to word it a little more professionally.

And then we got up to make dinner together. She hated touching raw chicken, so I always did that part, carefully trimming the lines of fat off the edges. In that little apartment, we had a gas stove that I absolutely hated. Perhaps I had been spoiled by growing up with a sleek glass electric range in my mom's house, that didn't seem quite as dangerous as sparks, gas, and open flames. I'd hand Elise the ingredients as she asked for them and scratch her back while she stirred them around in the pan; at least until she started piling up dirty dishes for me to wash.

I miss the home I used to have with her, the evenings with my hands becoming pruney under endless dish soap and hot water while we planned out our week. Perhaps a mate wasn't grand or romantic or even mystical at all.

No sacraments, no rites or rituals. Just someone who made the mundanity of life feel wondrous.

Of course, it took me a couple minutes before I even realized I started filling in the idea of a mate with just her. I need to stop doing that. I sigh as I take another wandering turn down another street.

There're a few leftover summer fireflies floating out of the grass, especially the taller, wilder areas that bleed into the woods. The meandering jog is just starting to make me feel better. The winding hills are steep and more difficult than I was used to in the Boston suburbs, I'm halfway to town when a sound stops me.

There's no mistaking it. The sniffles are coming from a nearby house, all too familiar.

I stop and sigh when I can see her from the street. Elise.

I don't know what instincts led me here, since I wasn't really paying attention where I headed on the jog, but from the front of the house I can smell Laura's car freshener still faintly hanging in the air. I can assume my cousin dropped Elise off after that train wreck of an evening.

More than that, I can smell her. I feel like I could find it and follow it from across the country.

I scrub a hand across my face. Don't go in there. Don't make things worse than they already are. Especially after the incident at the bar. Especially not now, when the moon is rising.

But it's Elise. I can't ignore her when she's crying.

The door is wide open to the cool autumn air, and I tug open the screen door to stand on the threshold, giving a quick knock.

Elise looks up from where she's sitting at the little dinette, immediately inside the front door. The place has the same charm as her old apartment. I recognize a lot of her things from when we used to live together, plants and quilts and endless goofy oven mitts stacked everywhere.

She spares a glance to me, before her face crumples further and she buries it in her hands.

I pad my way into the room on bare feet, just loud enough that she can hear me. I pull out the chair next to her and sit down, facing her.

"Hey. Hey, shh. Tell me what it is," I murmur, the words as quiet as I can manage. The sound of her crying is maddening, like I need to run out and claw through something to make things right for her. I can't tell how much of that is how I feel and how much of that is the moon.

I scoot closer, and thread my arms around her waist, wherever it is in that big sweater, and rest my chin on her shoulder. She doesn't pull away, but slumps against me.

"I hate it here," she mumbles.

I nod. That's fair. I kinda do too.

She doesn't ask what I'm doing here, or how I found her address.

Her phone is still open on the table to her most recent calls, and there's at least ten calls to her mother; it doesn't look like any of them have been answered. My heart pinches at that, my hand curling into a fistful of her sweater. I have to force myself to release it.

I start drawing shapes across her back over the top of her sweater. She always enjoyed that. "I'm sorry about tonight. I don't know what they said to you but . . ."

She shakes her head. "Not me."

I wait for her to explain, as she wipes at her eyes with her wrists, more tears coming regardless. Eventually her breathing moves from sobs to shudders. She leans into me the slightest bit more.

"I guess it should be obvious. I've been here a few years; you haven't been here. And when you chose me, you chose . . ."

Her lip quivers. She can't bring herself to say it.

"Wrong?" I finish quietly for her, and she nods.

"And they never let you live it down," she blubbers, all red faced and tear streaked. It's oddly endearing.

All I can do is agree. "Not yet, at least."

"Did no one reach out . . .?" she starts to ask.

I don't know that I can deal with the thought of her worrying about me. God, I can't have her crying about feeling alone and thinking about me being alone.

I drop my gaze to the floor. I nod a little. "Aiden did a couple times. Logan, once. It hasn't been that lonely."

"Three times in eight years?"

"Well, when you put it like that," I say, and attempt a smile, but her face starts to crumple a little more. She scrubs at her face with her sleeves, uselessly.

"I'm sorry you had to choose between us. I'm sorry I let you choose me," she cries, sniffling into my shoulder, her tears and whatnot seeping through my T-shirt.

It cracks my chest open, and I'm doing everything I can to hold it closed. There's too much about her that I've buried, and this week has been digging it all up.

I don't have an answer. It shouldn't have been a choice at all. And this whole facade we're putting on is just more evidence that we could have had everything, if only she'd been allowed to know the family's secrets. Or even just exist with the same level of knowledge as she does now. My mother's insistence on keeping only werewolves within the family has always seemed overblown to me, but now more than ever.

Instead, I busy myself finding that spot under her bra line that always itches, that she can never reach right. My palm flattens against her back and my thumb strokes against the spot, and she lets out a little noise of contentment stretched out on a sigh.

Her sniffles start to abate, fewer and further between. It feels all too natural to have her in my arms.

If I do nothing at all, maybe this moment will last forever.

Her bra straps relax around her shoulders, and she realizes then that I unhooked it.

"Shawn," she warns, but the way she says my name, it sounds like she wants more.

"Elise," I breathe, as my hand returns to the spot that her bra has dug lines into her skin, scratching much easier with it out of the way. "Anywhere else?"

She shakes her head, and I can tell she's trying not to sound too satisfied by my answering touch. But she's never really been able to hide how much she likes it.

My fingers slide down her back, and she arches into my hands, her qualms about the bra slipping away with the tension in her muscles. Her head tilts up with a soft little moan.

Here she is, in my arms, the moment I never dreamed I would find again, and again I freeze.

I glance around, before leaning in and pressing my mouth to hers, not closing my eyes until I'm sure my mouth is next to hers—for a sudden and irrational moment, I fear I'll be clumsy and miss.

I've done this before, of course I know how it works. But I'm also sure there's no chance I can do this right. It needs to be perfect for her.

Her mouth is as soft as a sigh, and a tension I didn't know I'd been carrying with me eases as she presses into it, a hum of pleasure caught between us as she snags my lower lip with her teeth.

When she pulls away from the kiss, our gazes linger a little too long. One of us needs to blink or breathe or step away. I don't think I'll be able to, and my heart might break if she does first.

"Stay," she whispers, and that word alone sunders any possible protest I could make. She touches my cheek as she tilts her head to kiss me again, her mouth impossibly sweet.

Her caress is slow but firm, until I close my eyes and settle a little closer to her. The kiss was a careful, gentle sway, soft and sensual, with no pattern but the pull and slight retreat, the back and forth that rolled between our mouths against each other.

"You don't want me here," I remind her, because one of us is going to have to find the strength to walk away from this.

"I want to feel good for a minute, I don't care what it takes," she says, and I believe her.

All I can do is make things worse for you later, I want to tell her. But she takes my lower lip and worries her teeth into it. She threads a hand through my hair, the other hand tracing my jawline as she sucks harder on my lip. My hands pull her body closer to mine, and soon she's out of her chair, straddling my lap.

"I know how to make you feel good," I assure her, because I know I can manage that much. I can feel my cock hardening under her pillowy thigh, straining against my jeans. I trace the curve of her neck with my mouth down to her shoulder, inhaling her scent deeply. "I miss the way you taste. The scent of your underwear after you've been working all day."

Elise whimpers in response, but I know what she likes to hear.

"Just this once," Elise tells me as she kisses me again, because she knows this is a mistake as much as I do.

She invites my tongue into her mouth with a brush over my teeth from hers.

I pull her closer, my touches growing rougher, more desperate to feel what I can while it lasts.

I half-want this to be quick, to get it out of our systems so we can remind ourselves we were always a mistake, that chemistry fades. But in the next thought, I want to draw this out, to really witness every moment. To really take my time if we truly only had one more time.

I palm her breasts, finding a nipple with my thumb and rolling it to a tight peak as she gasps and presses further into my touch. She shifts her hips and grinds against the bulge in my jeans, the friction so good it nearly renders me breathless. I groan, wondering how I can make "just this once" last forever.

I cup her ass as I pull her nice and close, squeezing handfuls of it through her jean shorts. Then I find one of my favorite places to stroke, the little fold of space between the curve of her bottom and the fat of her thighs. It's tantalizingly close to her center, already damp and needy. My claws start to press out of my fingertips just as I'm thinking of how to get her out of her shorts. The fabric of her underwear snags easily in my hands, and I think I might have just torn a slice through part of them by accident. Shit.

Touching her like this is making me overwarm, like a fever is building in my veins. My body is threatening to shift, my muscles burning to stretch into a form that feels more natural now.

I feel like a teenager again, about to come in my pants from barely a touch, all because the girl I'm obsessed with is straddling me. I wonder if she knows how easily she can reduce me to a pathetic puddle of want and need for her.

God, I really am about to come in my pants like some inexperienced whelp, because a new tightness swells against the seam of my jeans. Fuck, my knot.

"We can't do this," I pant, pulling back from her. Before I can even begin to offer maybe I'll just lick her until she can't take it anymore. My blood heats at the thought, and I know I wouldn't be able to control myself and keep from shifting if we tried.

She pulls back, her chest heaving with her breath, confusion slowly crossing her face as she takes in my meaning. I close my eyes because I can't look at her and hold my resolve. I know it's a complete turnaround from what I just said, and that I can't explain why I changed my mind.

"It's not, we're not getting back together. Shawn, I'm not asking anything like that. We wouldn't do that," she says, explaining it like I've misunderstood something.

"No, no we wouldn't. But we can't just do this for old time's sake either."

"You don't want to?"

"It would be a mistake," I lie through my teeth. Nothing about her could ever be a mistake, or the wrong choice. But we can't do this. I can't put her in that kind of danger. With my knot present and my wolf ready to seek my mate, I can't know she would be safe if we went any further.

"You don't want to."

Her voice shakes just the slightest bit this time.

I can hear the question she really wants to ask embedded there. *You don't want me?*

"No, no, I do. Believe me," I plead, and grit my teeth as my knot strains against the edge of finishing against the perfect heat at the crux of her legs. "I just can't do this knowing you might regret it tomorrow."

She nods and slides out of my lap, but there's hurt in her eyes she's trying to hide. I get up, every movement unbalanced. I want nothing more than to pull her in close and kiss her again, and to tell her I'm sorry, among everything I've always wanted to tell her.

But I can't. We don't have that anymore.

So, I leave Elise's cottage, not really knowing where else to go.

It's never been like this before with her. But it can't be Elise, it just plain can't. I would have known. It would have happened when we were dating, or the year we were married for.

If I was going to knot in Elise it would have happened eight years ago.

16

Elise

The fall leaves crunch underfoot as I step outside the brewery and check my phone, taking a quick break from catering duties. Even though I'm catering the Hayes wedding, the brewery's industrial-sized kitchen has the space and equipment I need. Really, it's not all that different from regular weeks catering events here.

Earlier, my hands were too crusted over with dried frosting when my phone vibrated in my back pocket to check my messages. I take a deep breath, considering the row of missed calls to my mom from this last week, and the singular text I got in return.

Sorry, it's been a busy week.

I don't want to call her again.

I think even a few months ago, I would have been relieved to see her trying to respond to me, making as little effort as typing out a sentence, even if it were to break bad news. I can't bring myself to feel guilty that I'd be shamelessly thrilled if my mom remembered to invite me to someone's funeral.

She's never been a person to run to and just hold my hand while I cry out everything that's been weighing on my mind. The prospect of calling her back is as weighty as anything else

I've felt these last few days, getting tangled in my feelings about Shawn and his family.

But right now, her attention isn't what I want. Maybe some deeply buried part of myself wants to feel like I'm not alone in all this, that I could just hand over the bulk of my emotional burdens to someone else, or just have someone whose lap I could cry into for a while.

But it's not my mom, and it never will be. I'm just going to have to handle this on my own.

I switch to scrolling through my email app, taking a few more moments to myself before I head back in. A couple old clients are having events I could cater, one said she would recommend me to a friend that had a more long-term job open.

And after Shawn rejected me last night, I'm grateful for a bit of hope for life after Mystic Falls.

I feel dirty. I shouldn't have come onto Shawn. I don't know what I was thinking, trying to hook up with him. But I knew he could make me feel good. I just didn't think he wouldn't want to.

I mean, I guess I should have been ready for that. I did leave him; why would he want anything to do with me? Just because we're back in the same place doesn't mean we have any kind of want or need for each other again.

I mean, maybe I hadn't been thinking that because Deanna has liked me so much these past few years, and his brothers, that they'd be happy to see us together, that things could easily pick up the way we left things off. It would be like they'd never refused to meet me, heartbreak simply forgotten. But I hadn't been thinking or wanting that. Because that's dangerous hopeful thinking, and I can't allow that.

I don't want to go down this line of thinking more than the million times I've already been through it.

He could've at least decided he didn't want to take me up on my offer before he started touching me. Even his rejection isn't enough to throw cold water on my libido, it seems. I guess that's a win for therapy.

For maybe the hundredth time today, I think about texting Shawn. Not that I even have his number. I don't think I could get it from Aiden or Laura without some pretty judgmental looks, either.

The brewery's back door swings open abruptly, and some stupid part of me hopes it's going to be him, that we can have a private word about what happened.

But it's Deanna. "Oh, Elise. Good morning."

She looks just as surprised to see me out here, standing on the little platform of the loading bay. People really only hang out here on their smoke breaks.

"Sorry, I was just stepping out for a second," I start to say, when she cuts me off with an apology.

"I'm sorry if dinner was a bit awkward last night."

Deanna looks me squarely in the eye as she says that. It doesn't sound deeply heartfelt, but there's sympathy in her voice.

It's honestly caught me so off guard all I can do is stare back at her. This is not at all what I expected, especially after how she acted last night. She takes that moment and puts a gentle hand on my arm. She wears a solemn expression.

"Elise, I value our relationship. You've been wonderful to work with, and pleasant company outside of work." She glances away towards the woods on the hill, where the Hayes House stands, just on the other side of it. She chews her lip a moment. "So, I hope you understand how much I value you, when I say you shouldn't spend too much time with Shawn."

I frown. My heart is pounding in my chest. I have to look away. My hands are automatically tight fists at my side, and I try not to overtly show that I've been dreading this.

"I . . . um, uh," is about all I can manage to say.

Not exactly the kind of confident dressing-down speech I'd rehearsed and tweaked in my head for so many years. It's a lot harder to summon those feelings of indignance at being dismissed when she just said she values me.

I don't know how to respond, except to turn a little away from her.

She takes her hand off my arm, but hovers nearby. "Did he tell you he was married?"

I swallow. This conversation might not be what I was afraid it was, but I'm not sure where it's leading. She seriously thinks we're still married, after all these years? Did he never tell his mom we got divorced?

"I mean," I stammer, not really sure what I mean. What do I even say? Yeah, I'm well aware he was? Or, no, actually to correct you Deanna, boss, I'm pretty damn sure he's as divorced as I am.

"I saw him take his ring off the other day, before he went to talk to you," she sighs, a faded disappointment crossing her features. She glances at me, misunderstanding my shocked expression, and giving my hand a sympathetic pat. "And I'm sorry you had to learn the way you did, last night."

"He, um . . . I know about the falling out you two had. That he didn't come home for years."

"He's filled you in on that much, then?" Deanna sighs, rolling her neck as she digs her hands in her pockets. It's a movement that is so quintessentially Shawn, it's actually jarring to watch. I don't know how I never noticed it before.

"We haven't talked in years because I disapproved of his marriage when it happened. But that doesn't mean I want him to be unfaithful to her. And for that much . . . respectfully of your feelings and hers. Please don't be one of his mistakes."

I think my ex-mother-in-law just asked me not to help my ex-husband cheat on me. Ok, now she can absolutely never know because I'm not going to be able to explain that.

I'm quiet for several moments. It softens something in my chest to hear that she cares in that small, weird way.

Deanna glances at me, eyeing my lack of a reaction. She shakes her head a little, staring off into the cool gray afternoon, and then smiles to herself. "Don't worry, I'll lecture him too."

I nod. Glad we're both getting this talk.

For a moment, I let myself stand outside and just enjoy that moment, the easiness between us that existed, before Shawn showed up and upended everything.

I used to believe that Shawn's mother could only be cold and unfeeling, and it was hard to see why he still wanted to be in contact with his family.

But I know Deanna, and I can see it all together now. She's not like that.

I also know there are no more pictures of Shawn around the house, and that makes my heart break for him.

I've barely said a word this whole conversation, and the words that are waiting, heavy in my chest, are all that I have. I can't ask her. I have to. I need to know, even if it doesn't seem like it should be my business.

"Why didn't you approve of her?"

Deanna's gaze grows distant, and I wish I could see what she does. "I'm not sure it even matters any more. I wanted to keep him close to home, and all I did was push him away, and lose years we could have had. I thought we might patch things up after his father passed away . . . but he wouldn't even attend the funeral. And now that he's home again, I'm falling into old habits. All I do is pick fights."

It's not the answer I'd hoped for, though, honestly, I'm not sure what I wanted her to say.

She pauses a moment, running a hand through that perfectly coifed bun she always wears, raking a path of destruction through the neatness. "Maybe if I hadn't reacted the way I did, I could have eventually convinced him to move closer to home. Perhaps there'd be grandchildren. I'd retire and become a nanny. But she was a Baptist, and that was supposedly worth sacrificing a whole future for."

Non-practicing Presbyterian, but whatever.

She gives a short laugh, not cold or sharp, but warm and wry, like she can't believe herself. It pricks something terribly painful in my heart to imagine that.

"That is the problem with babies. You think you're going to teach them anything, but, truthfully, I think they make up their minds on who they are before they learn to talk. And when they're adults, all you can do is hope they'll make the right decisions. I wish I'd known that when I first had them."

"Oldest siblings are always the practice child," I joke ruefully, and it pinches something awful in my chest. That was one of the first things Shawn and I connected over.

Deanna grimaces, but I can see it's to fight a smile. "Before Logan and Aiden were born, I took Shawn to the beach. He was maybe two years old. I had so many fond memories of going there with my sister. We started building a sandcastle too close to the tide, so the water would fill the moat. But a wave pushed us over and I wanted to keep his head above the water. I didn't even see the way I held on too hard until we went back to the car; I left all these bleeding nail marks in his arm."

She pauses for a long moment, letting herself grimace and cringe at the memory. "Not the first or the last time I felt like a bad mother. You hold on that tight, you leave claw marks."

I can hear it in her voice, how the pain of one tragedy is so much you can't but create more.

Then she gives herself a little shake, stepping away from her memories. "I'm sorry, I've kept you out here far longer than you probably intended. You don't need to keep listening to me ramble—"

"—I couldn't get my mom to call me back," I blurt out, confessing to her. "And I think I'm finally ready to stop trying. But Shawn came back home to see his brother get married. I think that means you've still got a chance to repair things."

She holds me in her gaze, and I think I see her eyes become glassy with emotion. Then the door next to us pushes open again, breaking whatever moment we were having as another brewery employee brushes past us.

"Um, I was just stepping outside for a moment, anyway. Fresh air," I tell her, taking a quick step away. Deanna nods, as I grab the door while it's swinging shut to head back inside.

I glance at Deanna, but she gives her head a little shake, indicating she means to stay outside a little longer.

"Fresh air and better signal. For some reason, inside the brewery it's downright awful," she sighs, taking her phone out of her pocket. She leans against the platform railing with it before her, some brightly colored app on the screen. Even the boss needs her match-three games.

"Don't tell the boys," Deanna says in a conspiratorial undertone, quirking an eyebrow. "I used to give them so much grief over their video games."

I can't help but smile back and imagine what that was like.

17

Shawn

The next day passes exceptionally quietly. I know, because Aiden texts me.

When did you start grinding your teeth?

I look up across the room and attempt to relax my jaw. Aiden's always had the keenest sense of hearing out of all of us, but this is ridiculous.

"There's no way you can hear that," I say out loud, and he doesn't look up from the coffee table. He's spread a bunch of printed-out pages that he's cutting into name cards for seating. Clearly Mom's been putting everyone to work.

I'm restless enough that I've been considering volunteering to help out, but that would mean talking to my mom, and that's been off the table since pizza night. Elise actually put a note on the kitchen door not to bother her while she was working on food prep, and Logan's been Logan.

"Every time you walk around downstairs," Aiden says, waving the scissors around for effect. "Being in the same room with you is a bit much."

I've been trying my best not to think about Elise, or last night. I'm failing miserably. I'd been so tempted to go back and kiss her breathless and make her whine with pleasure, that

I ended up going for a run until I was too tired to think, just following the paths that were as familiar to me as breathing.

With everything going on, I've barely paid any attention to the scene I'm supposed to be editing; I just keep playing it through and hoping one of these times I'll remember what I was supposed to be doing. I hit the spacebar a little too hard to pause the program.

I pull the headphones off and get up from the window seat, moving to leave the room.

"Let me know when you get to the folding stage on those place cards," I call over my shoulder, to a non-committal grunt from Aiden. Fine, I guess I don't have to help him if he's gonna be like that.

"Elise doesn't need you to keep bothering her, y'know."

First of all, rude. I'm not that predictable. I stop in the doorway. "Who said I was going to bother her? I could be going anywhere."

Trying to look casual, I lean against the doorjamb, crossing my arms over my chest. ". . . I mean, did she say something? Did she tell you I was bothering her?"

Aiden rolls his eyes, but he doesn't look like he wants to chide me about it. "You've got it bad."

I sigh and scrub a hand over my face. He's right. Bothering her is the only thing I want to do.

"You know, if you hadn't told me it yourself, I'd think you two knew each other a little more than just a couple of bad dates," Aiden says, snagging part of my attention.

I shrug, looking out across the empty hallway. Mom's probably asleep in bed already, the sun is setting, I don't see Elise's car in the driveway.

Maybe it's safe to practice a tiny bit of honesty. It doesn't come naturally at this point. Admitting the truth feels more like lying than lying ever did.

"Yeah, alright, I might've fibbed a little. It was a little longer. I didn't want to get her in trouble with the mothership."

"So, she is that human you weren't supposed to marry," Aiden says, and my full attention snaps to him.

This little shit. Did Laura tell him? There's no way he just figured it out on his own. I would have put money on Logan doing the math for when I left and whenever Elise showed up, putting pieces together.

For my least observant brother, I wouldn't have thought he'd be the first to figure it out.

Instead of answering, I push off the wall and close the heavy wooden door to the den, its base sliding across the carpet. It's about as close to soundproof as this house gets.

Aiden looks absolutely delighted with himself. He punches the air, before offering a low whistle and wincing. "Yikes. That's messy."

"Yeah. Well, I wasn't about to tell Mom she was right. 'Wolves can only mate with wolves' and all that," I say. Even years since I'd last heard it, I still say it with the same inflection our mom did when the drama initially went down. She'd become a broken record about it, and that became the only thing she would say on the matter.

"Well, it could have been worse. What if Elise had been a Protestant," he chuckles, and takes a swig of his beer, "—and Dad was still alive."

"Well, yeah, I guess it *can* always be worse. Our parents could always have had even more insane, outdated rules." I throw a flippant sign-of-the-cross and roll my eyes.

Aiden grimaces. "Don't do that, you'll give me flashbacks. Remember when he burned my Pokémon cards for being devil worship? I cried so hard I threw up, man."

A short, dry laugh escapes me. I remember that. I also remember Logan and I pooling our allowances to buy him a couple packs of cards, making him swear he would never take them out at home again.

We stare out across the lawn, my thoughts turning toward Elise. She used to do that kind of thing. Small gestures that went a long way. Whenever she poured herself a glass of water, she made one for me too. The instant ramen cups she hated but always kept a stash of them around because she knew I preferred them over the good stuff.

". . . I cried pretty hard after she left. She didn't say anything, she just left. And I know I made it hard on her. She was right to leave, but it still hurt," I say, looking at the window, gauzy curtains filtering the last light of evening through them. "I think I stayed in bed for days."

I glance at Aiden, whose face is contemplative. "Did you throw up, though?"

"After trying to drown my sorrows, probably. I don't remember."

"Well, if I loved my Pokémon cards more than you loved her, maybe it wasn't meant to be, ya dingus."

"I think you've blocked out the part where you stuffed your face with a dozen saltines covered in cream cheese first."

"Oh. Yeah. Did you know Elise has a bougie recipe for that? It's so good. She's made it for my birthday like three times now. Seriously, you're not allowed to do anything that's going to jeopardize that."

"That's all it takes, huh? A lifetime of brotherly love for some Boursin on crackers?" I chide him and move back to the couch he's on. I nudge him over with my foot, and he sticks a pillow between us, as if that'll shield him. He mutters something about it not just being Boursin.

This particular couch isn't all that long, so I end up folding my legs up on the couch between us instead of stretching out.

I can't bear to think of our relationship as a complete mistake, but there's plenty I regret. Back then I was young and just stupid and hubristic enough to think I could make it work with a human, that she would never have to know.

Of course, it didn't work. Of course, it all went the way my parents said it would, and I'd been too proud to admit that, to return home at all.

And here I was, still too proud to tell her.

I'd hoped I wouldn't have to show her the worst parts of myself; that I could bury it. Perhaps that was the problem at the root of it, that you can't really be known and loved if you hide half of yourself away.

I've turned these thoughts over hundreds, maybe thousands, of times in my head. I don't think I've ever said them out loud before, because they sound just as selfish as the first time I thought them.

"I just wish . . . I don't know. Maybe that she would have tried to stay. Choosing her over you guys was the hardest thing I ever did. And the minute it got difficult for her, she was gone."

"I think it's ok to feel like that, even if it's not fair to put that burden on her," Aiden says, surprising me. I watch him as he takes another printout of place cards, the scissors carefully gliding through the page.

"We all want someone to choose us, at the end of the day. But I think because our family put you in a difficult position, you didn't really choose her either. You could have told her what was really going on and given her a chance to choose all of you. But you hid behind our rules, because you didn't think she'd stay if she knew what you were."

I stare several moments at my brother, increasingly concerned that one of us is having an aneurysm or something. "What the fuck, dude."

"Oh, did you miss the part where she's one of my friends, and this is what she yells at the TV on movie nights? It's been real obvious to me, the whole time."

"Yeah, I guess I did miss that part. I don't think I was physically here for it."

The heavy back door creaks open, and Logan stands on the precipice, threading his arms through a jacket. He nods to the both of us, "I'm heading down to the catacombs, you want a ride?"

I blink. We haven't called the brewery's basement that in ages. I would be surprised if the graves of Aiden's many deceased goldfish are even there anymore, our mom always did hate that he kept burying them in the basement's dirt floor.

"It's not even the full moon yet," I complain with a glance to the window, its ghostly shape creeping up in the sky. "And we're not kids anymore, we have some control now."

"You think you do."

Ladies and gents, my brother. He knows how to kill a vibe wherever he goes.

Logan doesn't look like the responsible type, with his long hair, piercings, and tattoos, a visual rebellion no matter what detail you stop on. But his default demeanor has clearly changed. He just always seems like he's waiting for me to be done with my bullshit.

He's right, but I don't want him to know he's right. I don't know how I'm going to make it through the next few days. I've been doing a pretty terrible job of leaving Elise alone. We're almost to the wedding, and almost to the full moon. But with all the wolf sightings and rumored animal attacks, if one of us is starting to turn feral . . .

I can't imagine it's either of them, they both seem so normal. Well, as normal as any of us have ever been. If it were me, wouldn't I be able to tell that something's wrong? At least, besides everything else that has been messed up lately.

Logan scoops up a six pack of cans with the Aconite Ales branding that I hadn't noticed on the floor before. "C'mon, I'm leaving. We've been experimenting with a honeysuckle and aconite blend. It's got a more traditional ale flavor profile, less of the aconite's bitterness."

"Look, he thinks he's going to lure us into the basement with a new flavor of ale," I scoff to Aiden. If there's one purpose I have in life, it is to annoy Logan.

"For the love of God, Montresor!" Our little brother grins, and mimes pounding against a brick wall. It makes me crack a smile. Some jokes never die.

"Don't tempt me." Logan rolls his eyes, looking like he's trying to play along. "Come on. With all the coyote sightings, I'd hate for one of you to get pepper sprayed by some hikers."

His words are light, but I can tell he's worried. The eviscerated deer is still on my mind, and clearly his as well. But I don't think locking ourselves in the basement is the answer.

"If one of us is going feral, the last thing I'd want is to be stuck in the brewery basement with him."

"We're all here together, we can't go feral," Aiden says, as if that puts the whole matter to rest. "I mean, you're with us now, and we're about to join with the Carrington pack. That's more wolves in the family than we've ever had."

"Yeah, there's a real sense of community with a bunch of strangers." I can't help but tack on a little snark to Aiden's optimism. He's an extrovert, so of course joining with a bigger pack sounds like a party to him.

"Then why are there still coyote sightings?"

His expression falls a little, and he rubs the back of his neck uncertainly. "Maybe there really are coyotes."

Logan doesn't look impressed, of course. "So, are you coming?"

"Nah, dude, he's gotta go annoy his girlfriend," Aiden blabs, and I try to kick him through the pillow. He gives me his puppy eyes, and I glare at him, hopefully communicating that if he tells Logan I was married to Elise, I will make him regret it.

Logan gives me a side eye as he settles against the doorjamb. "You two have been getting pretty friendly. Are you sure that's smart?"

He's never been a snitch, but he does have our mother's *Are You Sure That's Smart?* glare down pat.

"Since when does Shawn do smart things?" Aiden snorts, his grin immediately falling when I shoot a glare at him.

I'm not sharing a couch with a traitor, so I get up and toss the other throw pillow at Aiden, directing my words to Logan. "I don't need this from you and Mom, ok?"

Logan crosses his arms at me like he's in any kind of authority. An older-brotherly annoyance rises in me. I'm not about to take direction from the kid whose face I used to wipe Cheeto dust off of, even if he is right.

He continues to lean in the wide-open doorway, making it impossible for me to leave until he's gotten his way.

Instead of doing anything so obviously guilty as crossing my arms over my chest, I take one of the cans of ale out from the plastic loops that hold the pack together.

"I don't mean it the way Mom probably means it, you and humans and all that," Logan says quietly, leaning towards me, even though there's no way Aiden can't also hear it. "She is right though."

That makes it sound like I have a weird, specific human fetish that I had to break all our rules for. Not really how I would frame it.

Still, Mom had never put it in the colorful terms that Dad did. She had always just reminded me, *"Humans don't know how we do things."*

Gentle words with a difficult meaning.

I bristle and resist the urge to roll my eyes. "Dude, if you have something to say that Mom hasn't yet, you should get to your point."

"Ok," he shrugs, and says simply, "Elise is my friend, and I don't want you to hurt her. Again."

I pull open the tab and the harsh sound stings the air.

There's no way Elise told him enough of what happened to merit him saying "again" like that. There's a slight chance Laura told him whatever version Elise was willing to share with her. It's possible he's just imagining that because clearly it ended badly before, it was my fault.

Logan eases into the room and hands one of the other cans to Aiden, opening one for himself. He sits down on the coffee table, and if I wasn't currently the problem child, I would have tattled on his ass so fucking hard right now.

"Back at the bar, she said you lied to her," Logan chides, leveling a cool look at me. His tone drops into a low disapproval that manages to mock both me and Aiden, *"Dude."*

The level of judgment in that one word. I guess they all must have heard us fighting the other day outside the bar after all.

"That's what I got from the other day," Aiden adds. Yeah, these little family togetherness moments are just so important.

"Just say you eavesdropped and move on," I reply dismissively.

"Well, did you?"

I look at both my brothers in disbelief. They're ganging up on me, to defend my ex-wife to my face. It was bad enough when it was Aiden hounding me, but if Logan is joining in, I don't know how I'm going to get out of this conversation.

"Of course I did."

Aiden's brows scrunch together in abject confusion, before devolving into that kicked puppy look. He had the gall to be disappointed in me. He lives in a world where lying to people you love doesn't need to happen, because he follows the family rules.

"You would have done the same," I almost snap at him in defense.

"Neither of us would've gotten into that situation," Logan snipes unhelpfully, but at least he picks up my meaning, and has the presence of mind to close the living room door again.

Aiden, unfortunately, hasn't been paying attention, ever, I guess. "What situation?"

"She caught me coming back from my . . . midnight runs a couple of times. She's a light sleeper, and, in the moment, I didn't really have a good explanation," I mutter. "It sucked, and it was clear I was lying to her, but that was the only option. I wasn't going to spill family secrets."

I would have thought this was obvious. At least these idiots could have picked a worse time and place to confront me about this. By now Elise has already gone home for the night.

It's likely the least of the many reasons wolves keep bloodlines within long established packs, but it's not exactly easy to keep one's lunar transformations a secret when living with someone. My brothers probably never had to consider just how difficult it is because they've only ever lived at home.

I'd thought Elise understood something about me. She commiserated with me about fucked up family dynamics, how hard going no-contact was, what it meant to give up on the idea that our parents would love us the way we needed them to, when the pattern of their damage was imprinted upon us.

But it had been clear she was looking to replace her family with someone else's, and I knew that would never happen with mine. Of course I lied to her.

"Oh," Aiden says, looking guilty, and then mumbles, "Sorry. I didn't think it was that. I just thought—"

"That I'd actually cheated on her? Of course," I grumble, perturbed that my brothers would think so little of me. "You guys have anything else you want to say to me? Logan, clearly you've had a chip on your shoulder since I got here. Come on, out with it. Get it off your chest."

Logan says nothing, just rolls his eyes. He looks like he's regretting offering any kind of olive branch.

"I can only speak for MYSELF," Aiden says, shooting a glare at Logan, ". . . but it sucked when you picked some stranger over us. It hurt, man."

Logan glances at me for half a second, his eyes lifting and falling imperceptible as a single breath.

There was a point when Logan and I were best friends. We were closer in age to each other than with Aiden, who'd been the baby stumbling to follow us around. We'd only grown apart as we'd gotten older.

I chew the inside of my cheek. Not the way I thought that would go, but I don't feel right apologizing for choosing Elise. I've never had it in me to regret choosing her, and this past week has only made that clearer to me.

But I am sorry for the pain that it caused.

"Yeah," I nod slowly, "—and it hurt when you guys sided with Mom and Dad."

Maybe they hadn't realized that's what they'd done. They were as young and immersed in our family's bullshit as I had been, and they had never left home the way I did. But that was still effectively the choice they had made.

For a moment, there's only quiet. Too much of it, filling the rifts between us.

Instead of responding, Logan downs the rest of his ale and swiftly cracks open another. I'd grab one too if it didn't mean moving closer to him.

"I think it's super lame that I'm the only one in our messed-up family that even tried therapy." Aiden sighs, but I know he's not going to make a dent with Logan.

"I don't need therapy, I'm fine."

"I'm also fine."

"Good to know we're all perfectly fine."

And no one is going feral, either. Yeah, that checks out for this family. Just pretend nothing is a problem, it'll go away sooner or later. I imagine that's what happened when I left.

I wonder if Logan sees it too, watching his expression. His jaw is tight, but I watch the half-smile that flickers across his mouth. He doesn't look at me but raises his eyebrows. "Do you guys wanna go light a soccer ball on fire?"

I follow his eyes to one of the pictures on the wall, where the both of us are no more than thirteen, our eyebrows singed off, grinning like maniacs.

The nostalgia of that question is touching, honestly.

"Yeah, alright. We're probably too old to be grounded." I scoff but still feel all mushy inside about it. I didn't realize how much I missed this kind of bonehead shit. "Aiden, you in?"

He grins wide and takes an ale from the pack. "Burning all the leg hair off our shins is gonna be such a great look for the wedding. We should all wear shorts to show it off."

Logan smiles back, it doesn't quite reach his eyes. He looks tired.

18

Elise

It's one of those dark, rainy mornings where the night holds on with both its hands, covering all the windows with dreary clouds. I couldn't go back to sleep, so I texted Deanna that I was coming over early to get some work done. It's been on my list to gather a bunch of the herbs Deanna's been growing for a personal touch to the food, so I'll have time to wash and chop everything slightly in advance. There's still so much wedding prep left to do.

I turn on some of the greenhouse lights, grab some garden shears and a basket to carry it all back in.

It doesn't escape my notice that it's yet another morning like the ones in all my dreams where I wander into the woods and get cornered by a wolf.

But I'm awake this time. I'm sure.

I haven't been able to sleep. Not since I overheard the brothers talking in the living room yesterday. I'd been just outside, packing my equipment up in my car, when I heard their voices. I hadn't meant to listen, until those words—

She said you lied to her.

Of course I did.

I had hidden in the doorway, unable to stop myself. I couldn't just go into the living room where they were and interrupt them, but I had to know. And now I wish I hadn't.

I watched Shawn from the reflection in the glass cabinet, just the hunch of his shoulders as he leaned against the sofa.

It cracked something in my chest, to hear him say that.

I don't know if I believe it, or if I just want to. That's the treachery of him. It was always too easy to love him, to want to forgive him. And I can't believe myself, how ready I was to want that. It's like I learned nothing.

His brothers didn't press him for more explanation than he gave, which is utterly baffling to me. They don't want to know what he was lying about? They just kind of shrugged and accepted it as a normal thing.

My heart has been nonstop thudding in my chest for hours, the edge of unease that just won't peak.

I don't know where my head's at. Shawn insists he lied to me for a good reason. I'm having the weirdest stress dreams about this wolf I keep hearing doesn't exist.

This is only happening because I stupidly let myself care about him again. It shouldn't matter that he admits he lied, that he still thinks it was the right thing to do.

I don't know that I even care what he lied about.

I don't know what to make of any of it. I don't know why stress dreams about the animal attacks would lead me to that. Or maybe it's because I went to bed horny after getting rejected by my ex-husband. Truly a plethora of options, really.

After cutting dozens of chive blossoms, a bunch of lemon grass, and pulling some heirloom carrots and radishes, I walk across the lawn to the kitchen's back door. I stop halfway through pushing it, when something catches my eye.

There are fresh scratches in the paint, cutting down through the wood.

Not many, like a frantic, frenzied clawing of an animal trying to get in, but a careful, deliberate slice next to the latch, suggesting that it could have opened it, but chose not to.

I let the door fall closed and stare out the kitchen windows again for several long minutes.

It's dark enough outside that I can nearly believe that dreams are real. To fully believe there's a creature out there, regardless of what Deanna says, and it's stalking me. Is it the creature that ripped apart that deer, the source of the animal attacks? Or am I just buying into my own weird stress dreams?

I don't know what makes me think a kitchen knife will defend me against such an enormous and ferocious beast, but I grab one before going over to another window that faces the woods. It's still too dark to really make anything out, just shapes blurred by the rain.

But I see it. The wolf.

My head feels heavy, my hands too tight around the knife as I watch the creature I've seen in my dreams emerge from the woods. Heat creeps up my neck, my breath stalls on my chest, my hands grow clammy.

In the same heartbeat that I'm afraid to encounter it again, curiosity—morbid and aroused—holds me in place. I can't believe I'm seeing it again so close to the house. Something about how I had only seen it in the woods before made it feel less than real, made it easy to convince myself it was a dream.

The barest shreds of dusk peak though the woods, capturing and turning the unmistakable silhouette of it, and filling it in with detail as it saunters towards me.

It slows its tired pace, coming to a stop maybe a hundred yards from the house.

I put my hand up against the kitchen window to hide the light's reflection and make it easier to see into the weak morning light.

The wolfish creature hunches down in the grass, each moment looking not quite the same as it had the second before.

My nose nearly touches the glass.

The beast rolls its shoulders, and stretches its arms overhead, suddenly far too human, far too familiar. My heart stops.

Shawn.

My heart is thudding in my chest. I can't think. I don't know how to process what I just saw. It couldn't have been Shawn all along. I know what I saw. I know the wolf was right there. But how can Shawn be both himself and that beast?

I stagger away from the window. I catch myself against the kitchen island, holding on for support as my knees feel less than sturdy.

I don't know what to think. Reality and those dream-like encounters in the woods are crashing together.

I look up at a flicker of movement in the corner of my eye, and Shawn steps through the kitchen doorway, appearing tired, carrying an air about him that is far too serious, a little scary even.

His dark eyebrows draw together when he sees me. "What are you doing here?"

I gasp, startling back a step. I don't know what to think. I just saw him—he was out there. He wasn't human, he was something else, some kind of creature, something out of my nightmares.

The ringing sound of metal against concrete pierces the air, the cold sharp edge catching my heel as it rebounds.

I don't have time to think or react—somehow, I'm up on one of the tables before the knife hits the ground again, Shawn's hands digging into my thighs as he sets me down.

"Shit, Elise," he mutters. The storm door slams behind him, rain flecked across the screen so heavily it blurs together the autumn-colored mountains behind him. "What happened to kitchen safety?"

I don't understand how he can joke like that right now.

"You startled me," I say, and despite being the one bleeding, I feel like there's bigger, more important things to worry about.

He raises his eyebrows at me and takes my ankle in his hand, lifting it up enough to press the edge of his T-shirt against my cut, where the knife glanced off my foot. A little spot of red wells up through the white fibers.

I don't know that I even felt it happen with how preoccupied my mind is. My hands are clutching his arms, when did that happen?

It's just Shawn, *my* Shawn. The way he's always been . . . but he's not.

Shawn is a . . . werewolf? I just saw that with my own eyes. I'm trying to process what this means. Are the things I think I know about werewolves true, or is he something else entirely?

He doesn't seem quite himself, the man I know in the daytime. Or maybe, I've just never really seen him, knowing all that he is.

He breathes heavily, the flush of red up his cheeks. There's rainwater dripping off his face, his hair and clothes are soaked, the scent of the woods on him.

My eyes rake over the way his T-shirt stretches across his shoulders, down to where he's pulled the edge up, revealing the thick trail of hair disappearing into his unbuttoned jeans.

"What are you doing up so early?" he asks again, his eyes searching mine carefully.

He wants to know if I saw him.

There's a flicker of tension in his hands against me, like he wants to dig his fingers in to grip me hard, but he's doing his best to hold himself perfectly still.

My heart thuds in my chest. If he didn't tell me all those years ago, if he never told me, he wouldn't want me to know now. I haven't had time to think what knowing this means to me, or what it might mean to him.

I don't know if I can tell him what I saw.

"I couldn't sleep," I tell him, swallowing hard against my uncertainty. "Stress dreams."

His grip tightens protectively against me. "Is my family getting to you?"

I give a half-hearted shrug. I was just starting to deal with all that, but this is all getting to be too much.

He nods a little, letting his gaze drop from my eyes as he starts drawing slow, comforting lines up and down the whole length of my legs, and it should not be making my blood heat the way it is.

A noise escapes me, a breath of relief that rides a little too close to sensuality. He always knew the places to touch me, even just to comfort.

The world is condensed to just our breath clouding in the space between us, that seems to grow smaller the more aware I become of it.

Shawn is the creature that's been chasing me in my dreams. My body reacts with sudden, prickling awareness, as the meaning of that dawns on me. He's the one that eviscerated that deer behind the bar, the one scratching up my doors, following me. Maybe that should inspire an all-consuming fear, and maybe it does, but it doesn't feel entirely like fear.

It feels like my body coming alive with that same need and willingness to surrender, to let the creature he is ravage my body any way it wants, not as some roll over and let me survive instinct, but because I want it.

A fraction of moan escapes me as I realize that, arching into his touch. I can feel my clit pulsing to attention as he stands between my parted legs. This is not the time.

"You can't keep teasing me like this," he pants, and presses a kiss to the side of my neck, just below my ear. He stays there, heat radiating off him, his body hanging inches from mine.

"I've been the tease? You left me hanging." I gasp, thinking about the other night in my cottage.

"I had to. I've been trying to stay away, but it's almost impossible."

I stare over his shoulder, wondering what he means by that. Is that connected to what I just saw? Is he able to control himself when he becomes a beast?

But there isn't time to linger over every question I have, to try to figure out the answers. Shawn is here, now, touching me. A beast, the beast I've been dreaming about running into in the woods, maybe.

I'm wet when his fingers move lower, skimming up my thighs and then finding my folds. Pulling my underwear aside, he drags his fingers through, parting me with embarrassing ease with how slick I am.

He pauses only to taste the wetness off his fingers.

A jolt of arousal makes my hips jerk. I hate that he remembers just how to turn me on, but at the same time, there's something about being known and remembered so well that it lays me bare and doesn't even give me the chance to hide my feelings, that makes me want to melt in his grip and give into it all.

"God, Elise. You don't know what you do to me," he sighs, something gravelly in his voice. "I think I've had dreams about the way you smell."

My heart is thudding in my chest. It's equal parts terrifying and arousing to imagine the depth of that statement. Maybe because I've also been having that dream about him.

He's never *eaten*-eaten me before, right? Yet, I'm still starting to worry that he will, that the power he moves with is the same as the wolf's. He could tear through me easily, and perhaps chooses simply to touch, but I want to know what the extent of that power feels like.

"I want your fingers in me," I gasp, feeling my body respond.

"I can't," he groans, the gentle graze of something sharp but well-handled against my skin. I'm too distracted by his mouth on my neck to see if it's nails or claws.

"Then your tongue," I say, and he stills. "Don't you miss the way I taste?"

The words are too bold to have come from me, and for a second, I regret saying it out loud. But the beast from the woods has done nothing but try to lick my cunt, and if that was him, I guess it makes enough sense for me.

He doesn't answer, but his eyes remain on me.

For several agonizing seconds, I think he's going to reject my offer just like the other night, but then I watch the last of the resolve in his eyes snap.

He hooks his hands under my knees, pulls my hips to the edge of the counter. I squeak in surprise, because I don't think I've ever felt him throw me around quite like that before.

He starts slow and reverent, the heat of his breath ghosting against my needy sex. He takes in a deep inhale, followed by a groan. I thought I was wearing shorts at least, but after the way he ripped through my underwear the other night there's a good chance this is now a terrible denim skirt.

I wriggle against his iron grip on my ankles that keeps my legs spread apart, when he parts me with his tongue.

"Shawn," I gasp, my hips bucking into his mouth when he delves his tongue deep into my core. The heat of it makes me forget what I was going to say, except, "Oh, god, keep doing that."

Every stroke of his tongue that makes me keen with pleasure grows closer, a heat and tension building deep in my core. Heat spreads through my body, and I feel tingles up to my shoulder blades.

After a few tantalizingly slow laves against my cunt, he finds my clit and focuses on it, and my body traitorously threatens to orgasm before I've enjoyed enough of this.

It's too much, it's too intense.

I bite my lip to hold back a cry, grabbing fistfuls of his hair as I rut against his face for every greedy taste he takes from me, riding out my climax.

"Tell me you missed this," he growls with a dark note of jealousy before dragging his tongue hard against me, every additional stroke against my over-sensitive nerves makes me moan. "Tell me you thought about this when others tried to please you."

I should maybe kick him for just assuming I couldn't find good sex with anyone after him, and I think to say as much to him when his tongue delves deep within me again, unsated. I whine in response, lifting my hips to shy away from the intensity of the pleasure.

"You don't have to compete with guys I broke up with"— I pant, my body just a mess of aftershock twitches—"but I did. I thought of you every time."

His hands dig hard into my hips, spurred by a possessive surge, something sharper and thicker than his nails creasing into my skin. I get a glimpse of the fur starting to cover his arm for just a second, before he unleashes another vicious focus on my clit, and my head tips back involuntarily with a gasp.

Suddenly, his tongue feels a little different than I'm used to, a different texture, rougher, hotter, more ravenous against my sex. Each drag through my folds that reaches my clit makes me whimper for more. My hands are twisted in his hair like I'm hanging on for dear life. He's always known how to make me feel good, but I had no idea how much he was holding back.

It doesn't cease, even when I struggle against his hold on me, even when I can't keep fully quiet. If there's been a deficiency of orgasms from my last partners, he's more than making up for lost time.

My thighs clamp together around his head, my hips bucking again as he licks me through another orgasm, not stopping for as much as a breath.

I think I forgot he was like this. Maybe convinced myself I'd made it up that he had to put me through a couple orgasms before he'd even get a condom out.

"Slow down," I pant, tapping at his shoulder, the top of his head, whatever I can reach. His grip on my hips remains, but he at least parts his mouth from my cunt.

He drags his teeth against the fat of my thighs in a way that is familiar, but also, I completely forgot he always did that, and it makes a lot of sense now. I think. There's a lot of little things I just brushed off that are starting to make a weird sort of sense, reinforcing what I can't believe I saw.

Shawn is a werewolf. The werewolf I've been having dreams about. The wolf I've been ready to ride in what I'm not entirely sure were dreams now. It didn't seem possible that it could have been real.

I lean up on my elbows as Shawn plucks one of the clean dish towels up from the stack and dries his face with it. He starts to offer it to me, when he stills, and then I hear someone coming down the stairs.

I scramble to push off the counter, tugging down my less functional shorts to cover myself. The kitchen light flicks on before I finish checking myself over.

Logan stands in the doorway. His eyes fall on us immediately, looking rather unimpressed even as Shawn leans against the counter to hide his erection. It's probably fairly obvious we weren't just chatting at five a.m.

"Christ, man. Now I owe Aiden money."

Logan saves most of his judgment for his brother, barely glancing at me. I turn and head out the kitchen side door before my embarrassment can catch up with me.

A different sensation does instead. Something splits, and it feels like I'm standing on the edge of my dreams and my usual reality. Logan showing up reminded me of everything I'd been willing to put aside earlier.

Shawn may be the beast my body has been craving, but he's still my ex-husband.

19

Shawn

"Did Dad ever talk to you guys about knotting?"

I ask the question under my breath, the words barely audible.

The small clothing boutique isn't devoid of other people, but the two with supernatural hearing glance at me with near identical expressions of horror and incredulousness. Logan is halfway through buttoning up probably the fifth suit jacket he's tried on, frowning impressively more than usual. The shop is nicely kept and there's a lot of what I think are vintage prom dresses all in plastic protective bags.

It's not a question I ever thought I'd ask, but I'm starting to feel a little desperate for brain cells. Not that I think I'll find them among my brothers, but I would die before I asked my mom or Laura.

My brothers aren't a better option by much, though.

"Whoa, dude, we're not talking about that," Aiden dismisses it immediately, his words a hiss as he glances around to make sure no one else in the store heard me.

"We didn't need to bring you along," Logan mutters, turning back towards the mirror.

I was in the middle of catching up on work, crouched between the couch and the coffee table my laptop is set up on, when I got dragged into more wedding prep. Some people had come by to decorate the house, and our mom had rounded us up into Aiden's Jeep and told us not to come back until we all had something appropriate to wear to Logan's big day.

"Sorry, let me just Google werewolf puberty." I scoff and roll my eyes to push away my own embarrassment.

"Hate it, hate it, hate this conversation," Aiden mutters, scooping one of the pretty throw pillows off the waiting room couch. He plops back on the seat, covering his head with the pillow.

"Fine, never mind."

Logan shrugs out of the suit jacket and pulls another off the rack. He jerks his head to move his hair out of his face as he starts buttoning this one, and glances at me from the mirror. He prompts tonelessly, "And you brought this up because . . .?"

If it were anyone but Logan who had found Elise and me in the kitchen before, I'd have thought they were behaving a little chilly towards me. But with Logan it's always been a little hard to tell.

He's well aware I need to keep my hands off Elise. She wants me to. I want me to. Or, she did, but it seems like she's changed her mind, and now it might just be down to my ability to say no to her, and if that's all that's holding me back, I don't know how I'm going to manage to keep it together for another few days.

Considering the fact that my knot's been showing up every time I touch her, I'm more than a little confused.

Theoretically, I should be obsessed with finding my mate. I mean, all the stories you hear about it from distant cousins during reunions, that's how it goes. Maybe it has about as much merit as their urban legends about going feral. Still, it doesn't make sense that all I can think about is her.

As an experience, as a sensation, these thoughts felt out of place with the rest of the spirituality my parents had impressed upon me. Like a mismatched patch hastily sewn into a larger tapestry. Is it just because we used to have a connection? Not a wolf-y, supernaturally charged connection, sure. But we used to be solid.

I can't be so much of a fuckup that I can't get the mystical fated mate thing right, can I?

It's all a bit much to explain in the middle of a second-hand clothing boutique, however.

"I mean, not that werewolf families are all that pro-sex education to begin with," I grumble, failing to actually come up with a coherent excuse. Things I could have thought about beforehand, maybe. "All I know is some really uncomfortable points Dad made about the knot, and that whole thing about the church and not spilling any semen, all-life-is-precious kind of thing."

"Hey, what now?"

I turn back and glance at my brothers, a little perturbed by the mix of concern and confusion on their faces. "Did Dad not give you the anti-masturbation talk?"

"Wow, you really were the trial and-error child," Logan says, and while I have always felt a particular kinship with packages that get absurdly dented going through the mail, his remark feels an awful lot like finding a "FRAGILE" sticker that's been punctured by the corner of something else.

"Whatever. I mean. I hate feeling shitty about wanting to know things. I don't know about you, I've never been with another wolf."

They both glance away at that, a different sort of energy hanging in the air. I hadn't put a lot of thought into it before, but there aren't exactly other packs in our area, and for the number of times I'd seen both of them sneak out of the house, I doubt they've fully kept faithful to the pack rules.

"It only happens when you find your mate," Aiden supplies, not really muffled by the pillow, reaffirming everything I already know and offering nothing I don't.

Probably in an attempt to change the subject, Logan points out, "Would there be animal attacks happening if finding your mate was an easy thing?"

"We're not talking about that either," Aiden grumbles through the pillow, and on that I agree with him. It's not exactly great conversation to wonder which of us might be running mindlessly bloodthirsty through the woods. He puts the pillow aside and sits up. "Those things don't have anything to do with each other."

"Sure they don't. Mom just married the first wolf she found for no reason after her sister went feral."

"What? No. You don't think Mom and Dad were in love?"

I blink in surprise.

I guess Aiden, being the youngest, doesn't remember the rocky start they had, before they settled into a more amicable pattern. I'd never really thought of them that way. I don't know how he can know our family history and not think they started as anything but duty and convenience.

I glance at Logan's reflection as he faces the mirror, fidgeting with the non-pockets of the jacket. His expression shadows over, his mouth grim. "I don't think it's something worth holding out for."

Yikes, dude.

There's a long silence over all of us, Aiden glancing at me and making eyebrows like should we be trying to unpack that with Logan or just pretend he doesn't have the most depressing mindset to be going into the rest of his life with?

I hadn't really put a lot of thought into why Logan was following through with our mother's wishes, why he'd never wanted more for himself. I'd just assumed after it went so badly for me, my brothers decided that was enough proof for them, that they needed to keep to the tradition of marrying into other wolf packs. I hadn't considered that Logan didn't believe romance was worth trying for because of our parents.

I can see why he'd be a little pissy about my flaunting my not-relationship with Elise around the house.

The shop's door dings the bell hanging on its corner, and the feelings that twist in my stomach conflict wildly. It's Elise and Laura stepping into the shop, glancing around at the second-hand boutique.

"Wow," Laura says flatly, wrinkling her nose, before her eyes even find us. "Did we all just have the same idea?"

"Was it 'I'm not buying a whole brand-new suit for this weekend'?" Aiden offers.

"Or 'Shit, I don't have anything to wear, and this is the only place nearby I can probably find something'?" Elise sighs, crossing her arms and looking unimpressed with the three of us, even though she's clearly in the same situation.

Her eyes fall on me, and something in her posture tightens, almost defensively. It's almost startling to see her acting like a cat with all its fur standing on end, even as she fights to hide it.

"You're going to be there? I mean, I know you're going to be there in the house at the reception, but I didn't know if you were going to be there at the wedding." I stumble through the surprise and my sudden inability to coherently form a thought.

There's something a little too rigid about her stance. This whole crazy situation she's had a perfect poker face, but now something just feels off. Did one of them say something to make her uncomfortable? Or had the early morning moment between us crossed a line?

She gives a little shrug, trying to be casual. "Just something a little nice. I just didn't want to be working in my jeans like I usually do when everyone else is dressed up, like professionally underdressed."

"You never look underdressed," I offer in what I hope is a neutral voice and not at all trying too hard.

Aiden and Logan are inevitably rolling their eyes and repeating what I said mockingly under their breath, like I'm not bound to hear it. Aiden makes some grotesque kissing noises like he's twelve until I throw a glare at them and wave a gesture for them to cut that shit out.

It doesn't really help.

The moment Laura and Elise disappear off to the side of the store where the dresses are, I mouth at my brothers, "I will kill you."

Aiden and Logan raise their eyebrows at each other, before apparently deciding they don't care.

"Fucking try it. I'd love a distraction," Logan sighs, picking at a loose thread on the sleeve of the jacket.

"Yeah, you won't, coward," Aiden echoes, and I am this close.

Instead of responding, I glance in the mirror Logan's been standing in front of all afternoon, watching Laura disappear into the racks of clothing when Elise heads for the dressing room, a couple options already picked out.

I swallow. I should stay right here and finish up. But I also want to apologize for the other day. I can't stand the thought of her being upset about something. It claws up my insides to think I might have done something that hurt her.

"I'll be right back," I tell them, not that I think they're paying attention.

"Don't do it," Logan replies without looking over his shoulder. He doesn't have to say anything to me about my behavior with Elise, for me to know he thinks it's a bad idea, but he probably enjoys gloating some, and who am I to take that away from him? When I keep walking away, he mutters to himself, "What happened to exercising a little self-control?"

"I didn't agree to that," I reply under my breath.

There's plenty of self-control happening here, demonstrated by the fact that I'm only going over there to talk to her, and not to whisk her away somewhere just private enough for round two. And now that I've thought about it, there's a lot more self-control needed.

Whatever. If anything, when I'm around Elise I feel better than normal. The itch in my bones disappears, and I finally feel like I can think. And at that point, I come back to the conclusion that if I feel fine this close to the full moon, it can't be me that's going feral. It can't. I don't know who my mate is, but we've never been separated like my Aunt Danielle and her mate were, so that wouldn't be actively driving me off the edge.

I wade through the overstuffed racks of clothing over to the other side of the store by the dressing rooms, where Elise is, digging my hands in my pockets. After this morning we should probably talk a little, considering how we definitely crossed a line we said we wouldn't at the start of all this. I dunno, maybe there isn't all that much of a line between a little light fingering and sticking your tongue inside your ex-wife, but I feel like there is.

Elise steps back when she sees me, and it kills me that she looks afraid.

"Hey," I offer softly, a gentle, verbal olive branch. After this morning I'd have thought she'd have warmed up to me a little more, but there's something in the way she's looking at me that wasn't entirely there before. Did I just not notice because we weren't exactly making a lot of eye contact?

She glances around for Laura, for the others. She's clutching the clothing hangers of the dresses she picked out like they're for protection.

I try to catch myself before I frown in reaction. For the record, no one's ever liked me less for eating them out before, including Elise. If I remember correctly, that's usually the kind of thing that inspires more touchy-cuddly feelings in her.

What the hell did I do?

"I'm, uh . . . sorry about this morning," I start off, hopefully quietly enough that my brothers won't hear, or at least not loud enough to catch their attention.

Elise just shrugs and pretends to return her attention to sorting through a rack of dresses, but she doesn't even glance at some of the ones she adds to the pile draped over her arm, keeping a wary eye on me. "What's there to be sorry about?"

The words "I'm sorry I ate you out specifically after I said I wasn't going to do that" just aren't going to happen while my brothers are here, but I'm sure she has to know that's what we're talking about. And all the other moments I haven't been doing a great job at staying away from her.

"Uh, well. Y'know. I'm just trying not to make this whole ordeal harder for you, crossing lines we set pretty firmly at the start of this and all that," I remind her, just in case she'd forgotten that whole fight we'd had about it just a few days ago.

She glances at me warily and starts walking away to the dressing rooms. "You didn't make it harder for me, it's fine."

The way she darts behind the safety of the thin plywood door and quickly locks it says otherwise.

I follow her and ask over the top of the stall door, "Really?"

She waves an empty plastic hanger at me, and I back off a few feet. I can see her kick off her pants in the few inches of space under the privacy screen, and the top of her head over it.

Right. Stay away, sit still, no touching. The spirit is willing, but the flesh is weak. I jam my hands in my pockets and wait for her answer.

"I've made my peace with everything that happened between us. Found the closure I was looking for. I'm good now, Shawn."

I frown. "When?"

"I don't know . . . I overheard you talking to your brothers the other day. About the way you lied to me. It made me upset at first, but the longer I think about it, that was never really the issue."

Sometimes I forget humans can eavesdrop too. "It wasn't?"

"No."

She doesn't elaborate, of course, just shimmies out of one dress and into a different one. I catch myself biting one of my knuckles, staring hard at the sliver of her I can see between the door hinges and the wall. After this morning, the need to touch her is overpowering. My cock twitches at the barest glimpse of her shins under the door like some kind of repressed Victorian.

"Hang on. If me lying to you wasn't the reason we got divorced, what was? No, for real. Why'd we split up then?"

"Shawn, we can't keep doing this. There's nothing left between us to repair, I don't know why you keep digging. We're not . . . we're not going to get back together, or anything. Obviously."

She sighs and leans against one of the dressing room walls.

"Obviously, pssh, yeah," I repeat, because yeah, we're totally on the same page. I hadn't been hoping that she'd just fall into my arms after a couple of orgasms, wanting to see if we could make it work one more time, or anything else along those lines. Not at all.

"I'm leaving after this whole wedding is over," she says pointedly, a little bit exasperated, like she doesn't believe I'm agreeing with her.

"I'm leaving too," I add, and honestly, it does now sound like we could just happen to leave in the same direction, if she wanted to. Apparently, I don't actually know the reason she doesn't.

Whatever idiot thing I'm about to say next dies on my tongue when she opens the door and I get to see what she's tried on.

That is not just fancy work event clothing. I've seen the early stages of Elise's attempts at professional catering clothing, the black dress pants and button-down shirts. But this is something else entirely.

It's a little black cocktail dress that hugs her middle a little too well, and my mouth goes dry at the way the fabric clings to her hips, her legs, highlighting every curve and movement.

It's cheesy, but I like her in satin. I recognize it instantly, a memory blooming from the shiver of fabric as she turns. She had another skirt like that when we lived together. Every time she wore it, I found myself worshiping with my head between her thighs.

She hovers in the doorway apprehensively, before turning around and pulling her hair aside.

My jaw physically aches at the sight of her bare neck and shoulder. It's more than just the want to kiss, to carve into that spot that always makes her breath hitch with the blunt edge of my teeth.

Momentarily I forget where I am, until she asks, "Can you get this zipper for me?"

I blink, and finally notice the open back of the dress, the way the zipper is caught in a tangle of thread halfway up.

I stand next to her and help, cutting through the threads with a claw that pushes out of my skin all too easily. I try not to move at all when my knuckles graze her back, making her shiver.

"I'm just now realizing what a sin it is that we never went to any nice places together," I murmur, my other hand finding hers and immediately tugging her into a little twirl before me.

She glances at me, still wearing one of the suit jackets from the other side of the store over a worn T-shirt.

"You don't clean up so bad yourself"—she laughs, finally looking less tense—"but when you elope in Atlantic City, the dress code is flipflops and tie-die shirts."

"I'm serious. Clear your calendar, we're crashing galas and black-tie events for the next . . ." I trail off and clear my throat, stop spinning her around.

I'm struck by the thought of what could have been. That in a more perfect set of circumstances, we could have stayed together, driven up here for the wedding together, my hand on her knee the entire trip, been welcomed at the house together. We could have had entirely different lives and found ourselves back here, if only I'd made it work. I could have brought her home, tried harder to make my mother listen. We could have done things right.

Elise comes to a standstill, facing me.

I stare at her, willing myself to not fall in love with her again. Even as I think it, I know it's too late. Ten years too late.

"Did it ever upset you that we never had a big fancy to-do . . .?"

Elise's eyes widen just the tiniest bit, and I hear her heartbeat quicken, I feel it as if it's my own. I watch for a too-long moment as she fidgets a handful of the fabric of her skirt.

"No, never. I was happy with . . . what we had," she finishes a little lamely.

Her answer doesn't sit well with me, but I can't tell if I don't believe her because it doesn't sound like she believes it herself, or because I don't want to believe it.

"I wish we'd done things differently."

"It is what it is, Shawn."

"No, I should have tried harder to make it work. I knew my mom would love you if she just got to know you. I knew it. And look at you, you fit in better here than I ever did."

"Shawn, no. I'm happy we divorced. It was the right decision."

"What?"

Elise turns away from me, stopping in front of the mirror, moving as if she's testing out the dress, but her eyes are unfocused as she speaks, not really watching her reflection.

"We were too young. I didn't know how to calm myself down when we started fighting. All I wanted to do was hurt you the way I was hurting. I needed time to grow, to learn how to be better. I don't think I could have learned that if we had stayed together."

She stays quiet a long moment, letting the truth of that statement sting and reverberate throughout the air.

My gaze falls from her to my shoes. Eventually she moves back to the dressing room, and I hear her start to unzip the dress. I take that as my cue to leave her alone, but she starts talking again. It's quiet, almost a mumble. I'm not entirely sure she's speaking to me, but I halt and listen.

"Sometimes people get divorced. Sometimes it's a clean break, and they can just move forward with their lives and forget about that little blip. They can go on to find new partners, make new families. I think that's really the best-case scenario for everyone involved."

I find myself standing right outside the dressing room door, my palms pressed against it. If only it was just a flimsy plywood door that stood between us, and not miles of an emotional gorge I carved myself.

"How is that the best-case scenario?"

The tips of her shoes in the gap between the door and the tile appear, nearly toe to toe with mine. I feel her head knock slightly against the door, and can feel her presence so close to mine, depending on the door to hold us apart.

I know too well what Elise crying looks like. Sometimes it slips into my dreams, the way her face crumples a little, her lower lip wobbling as tears start to creep out over her eyelashes.

I can hear it all in her voice as she speaks.

"Because the other option is that it isn't a clean break. Sometimes there's a little girl who was supposed to have a family, and she gets left behind for the new families. And, god, I can only imagine what it's like to have someone choose you over everything else, to think you're worth it."

I don't ask her what idiot would ever think she wasn't worth it, I already know.

20

I have been simmering on this thought nonstop.

Shawn lied to me. Shawn *fucking* lied to me. We lived together for two years, and I never put two and two together. I feel so stupid.

It's been a quiet day; guests will start arriving tomorrow. People have been in and out, decorating the place. I've been staying in the kitchen at the Hayes House pretty much entirely, trying to keep my hands busy.

If I keep working, maybe I won't have time to think about anything. I won't have to confront what I saw—the wolf, the transformation, Shawn standing out in the morning mist.

Maybe I could convince myself that it was a trick of the light, the way the dawn was scattered through all the trees, but the feeling of his claws on my skin, careful and precise, made me sure of what I had seen.

It cast all the dreams I've been having in a new light. A startlingly clear light. The full moon coming out from behind a heavy cloud and lighting up the night kind of clear.

The last of the preparations for the wedding are coming together, and everything that was just recipes and massive grocery shopping trips are suddenly food prep and an endless number of dishes to be washed and dirtied again.

For maybe the tenth time today, Aiden pops his head in the kitchen and raises his eyebrows at the batter I'm stirring and asks, "Can I have a taste? What if I use a clean spoon this time?"

"Logan, can you deal with your brother?" I huff, sidestepping one brother to call out to the other. Logan's made himself pretty damn scarce lately, and I've taken to just demanding his time out loud in any direction. Eventually he shows up.

"She said we could taste test the first batch," Aiden says before I can ask Logan to cart this annoyance out of here.

"I did not," I snap, and catch myself. I'm getting way too prickly, and they don't deserve it from me. We're all stressed.

I pause and take a breath, pinching above the bridge of my nose like it'll do anything to relieve the pressure mounting behind my eyes. Logan and Aiden watch, waiting for my next direction.

"You can each have one only, but only if you clean those trays first. I need them to start baking the next batch."

That will get them out of my hair for a moment.

Despite the whirl of people coming and going, working in the kitchen feels both overwhelmed by company and desperately alone. I need someone to talk to about what I saw the other morning, but I can't.

The Hayes brothers bicker over who washes and who dries the trays as I add the final few cups of flour to the batter and start to stir again.

And like all the other moments I'm not currently multiplying measurements, suddenly I have all the time to think.

For the last day or so, I have been struggling to keep my cool. Whatever appearance of calm I manage externally is out of sheer catatonic shock. How can it both be that there are really werewolves, and that the one that's been showing up everywhere is my ex-husband?

Even when I talked to him in the boutique, it didn't seem real enough. He was just Shawn. He looked the same as he always did. It didn't seem real that he could be something else, perhaps even something truly dangerous.

I wanted to make sure I knew, that my brain hadn't just malfunctioned that morning. Lack of sleep making me see things, maybe, I thought. Nope. I downloaded one of those sleep monitoring apps and propped it up against the window, recording the edge of the woods in the early hours of morning, and I'd seen it again.

If Shawn's always been this kind of creature, was he telling the truth to his brothers?

Shit, his brothers. I hadn't even thought about how they were a part of this. Are they all wolves?

All the hairs on the back of my neck stand up, and I stop stirring the batter. Slowly, I lift my eyes to the two brothers chatting in front of me.

Aiden is rambling, ". . . I could never move to a bigger town, man. It's getting crowded enough with all the wedding guests coming here, I could barely find any parking this morning. And then Mom snapped at me for leaving out that newspaper talking about the wolf sightings—"

Logan rolls his eyes and sighs and flicks him with the damp dishtowel.

"I mean, coyote sightings," Aiden corrects himself awkwardly. They both pause and glance at me, a moment more telling than anything else they've said.

Oh. My. God. They're all werewolves.

If I hadn't seen it with my own eyes, would I have even connected the dots? Or would their terrible attempts at keeping this a secret continue to fly over my head?

I drop my gaze quickly, and they go back to cleaning the last few trays. It's really just a quick rinse with soap.

Shawn, ever a master of timing, picks that moment to duck into the kitchen, making a beeline for the coffee maker, where a half-full pot of coffee has long gone cold.

My teeth grind together as I glance at the three of them. These fucking assholes. They've just let me stay in the dark about this.

And all the dreams I've been having about meeting a wolf in the woods and letting it lick me to completion . . . my cheeks flare. If they're all wolves, and we're in supernatural territory, was there more meaning to my dreams? Maybe they weren't just my subconscious stressing out about the wedding prep and Shawn showing up and expressing it through the coyote sightings?

And Aiden has teased me for believing in déjà vu and intuition. I'm going to smack him for making me think such things were silly and just too supernatural to exist in reality.

Flustered and trying to keep my sudden anger in check, I let out a breath that is a little too exasperated to be a sigh.

All of their eyes immediately snap to me, and their attention feels heavy on my skin. I take a deep breath through my nose. I glance at Shawn. I've been living here for years without werewolf wet dreams. Those didn't start happening until *he* showed up.

He's the only one I'm really mad at right now, and I want to see him squirm.

I meet each of their concerned gazes briefly, and shrug. "I don't know why everyone keeps talking about the coyote sightings. They're so . . . common."

"They are?" Aiden asks, a little too much concern cracking his voice.

"Yeah, I don't think I've ever lived anywhere that there weren't a lot of wolf sightings and animal attacks," I say out loud, trying to sound as casual as possible. I glance between everyone else in the kitchen. "Lately there's been a lot of scratch marks on my doors from wild animals. They just come right up to your house, it's so weird."

Shawn looks like all the blood drained out of his face as he concentrates on pretending to sip his mug of coffee, and, honestly, if I've taken a couple years off his life with that comment, I'm fine with that.

"That . . . that's so scary," Aiden fumbles to say when he fails to hide his horror.

"I just thought it was normal," I insist, and then look pointedly at Shawn. "Don't you remember? I would say it was pretty frequent in . . . college? I think we met when I was in college."

"I didn't really pay attention to the news back then," he says weakly into his coffee.

Logan is glaring daggers at Shawn with more emotion than I've ever seen out of him. I'd just hoped to imply there were plenty of other werewolves out there, but it seems they got something else out of my comment. I wonder if they've noticed a wolf has clearly been stalking me these last few weeks.

With the ferocity in Logan's expression, I think it's safe to assume they're all wolves. And if this is a family of werewolves . . . suddenly it makes a lot of sense why Shawn and I couldn't be together.

Maybe we were a mistake from the beginning.

Shawn slinks out of the kitchen, a maybe-not-so-metaphorical tail between his legs. Aiden and Logan continue to try to communicate behind my back as I turn my attention back to the stove. I can see them mouthing and gesturing at each other in the reflection on the polished tile backsplash.

I don't care if I've just kicked the hornet's nest. Or a better metaphor involving a wolf den, whatever.

Unsurprisingly, I make it through the rest of the day with as little contact with any of them as I can, with no effort on my part. Aiden all but runs in the opposite direction whenever I step out into the hallway. Logan is somehow less reachable than usual.

And Shawn finally made good on his promise to leave me alone; of course, it's when I actually want to talk to him and finally get some answers.

After a long day of rechecking that I have everything ready for the wedding tomorrow evening, I find myself staring out the back door of my little cottage, turning the same tangled web of thoughts over as I dunk a peppermint tea bag in a mug of hot water.

I want to sit down, just the two of us curled up in one another like we used to on Saturday mornings and talk through every little thought and worry I've got buzzing around in my head. I miss the way he would help me unspool my line of thinking and find all the frayed edges and help me wind it all back into a tidy little bundle.

I need to confront him about this, but I'm not sure how. He could just deny it, and I'm sure he would. If he wouldn't tell me when our whole marriage was at stake, why would he just give in and tell me now?

The thought makes a hard, painful lump rise in my throat. I didn't know that whole time. He managed to keep it so under wraps I never even suspected. Maybe our whole relationship was really a sham.

I stand at the doorway for so long, the mug grows cool in my hands.

There were many nights toward the end of college, the evenings I worked in my apartment, sitting at my desk by the window for hours to get my papers written, Shawn would come home to find me sitting in the dark. I'd hear his keys jangling in the door, the floor creaking underneath as he crossed to me, and found the light switch. Every single time, I'd never realized it had gotten so dark, until that moment he came home.

It's not quite a full moon, but it lights up the night spectacularly. It doesn't even really feel dark out. It looks so much like the not-yet-morning hours I've given up on jogging during.

A thought, barely more than an impulse, leads me to roll the back sliding door open and step outside.

Of all the times I've walked into the woods in my dreams, I haven't had a purpose in mind. And sure, it's only eight p.m., but who says it has to be three a.m. to run into your werewolf ex-husband in the woods?

21

Elise

I have been power-walking the hills of Mystic Falls for the better part of an hour now, and I have yet to flag down a particular werewolf. Jogging went away pretty fast, because I don't have that kind of stamina, unfortunately. I'm a fucking chef, not a marathon runner.

It's times like these that I miss Boston's public transportation system, something that never happened until I moved out here. Fucking mountains. Ugh, this is why Shawn was always complaining about there being nowhere good to hike when we were together, because he was used to roaming around actual fucking mountains.

Low-key, a lot more little things like that are starting to make sense.

I peak over a hill and check my watch. Eight forty-five. Maybe it would be quicker to just call him, if I hadn't blocked his number and deleted his contact info off my phone forever ago. I was really starting to regret that, even if it had been justified at the time.

Evening creeps up around the edges of the horizon. It's one of those summer nights that bleeds into the day, staying up past its curfew.

I look around and recognize most of Mystic Falls. Large rocks jutted randomly out of the landscape amongst low, wandering fieldstone walls that one could easily step over. There's the occasional building that dots along the winding mountain road, most structures sagging from their years: paint chipped and wood rotted. Even the lasting fieldstone structures had a handmade, cobbled quality to them. I find the shape of the brewery just a service road away from the main highway, the tall, brick-walled factory on one side, renovated glass walls of the offices and outdoor tables on the other side standing sharply out from the landscape, the only recent construction in sight.

And then, further up the road, the familiar slant of shoulders, the faded back of a band T-shirt I remember wearing to bed a number of times.

"Shawn!" I call out, perhaps not as loudly as I should to get his attention. Even from a distance away, he turns around, and I see his expression shift to alarmed the moment he catches sight of me.

He glances between me and the brewery, and after a moment, decides to cut through one of the fields to meet me. The mist hangs low over the ground, and I finally get close enough to him as he steps over one of those meandering fieldstone walls to me.

"What are you doing out here?" he asks, glancing at the sky, the ghostly, almost invisible moon creeping higher overhead.

"Looking for you."

"Yeah, but . . ." he glances back at the sky one more time, like he's worried it'll swoop down on him. He eyes me carefully, a muscle tensing in his jaw.

The last ten or so feet between us feel like they might as well be a hundred more, when he finally sighs and shakes his head. He glances over his shoulder one more time, and then sits down against the wall.

"You already know."

Instantly, my throat feels tight. It's not the way I wanted to broach the subject, for him to just throw the truth at my feet, as if it weren't even worth it to say it out loud.

No, I'm resolved to squash any guilt I have about not telling him I saw him shift from one form to another. He's had years to tell me himself. It didn't feel like betrayal, but a void between us, a cruel gap that lived between our hearts, a murmur between chambers. It was the first broken seam, the chip where all our issues wedged themselves and pried us apart.

"You knew in the boutique, then too." He digs his hands deep in his pocket, his mouth set in a hard line. "And you were just going to wander around for how long? Elise, if you know, then . . . God, what if I hurt you?"

"I don't think you would have."

He groans and leans back, bringing his hands up to scrub over his face. He looks pleadingly at the clear, fading blue sky. "You don't understand. I'm not myself when I . . . I don't have the ability to rationalize and control myself as well as when I'm human."

I bristle, unable to keep it out of my tone when I say, "Well, if I don't understand, clearly there's a reason for it. You didn't tell me anything!"

He doesn't even meet my eyes. "I always meant to tell you, really."

"When? When were you going to tell me? Eight years ago?"

"I wanted to tell you . . . I've needed to tell you. But the truth was harder to express than I thought," he says, and I do understand that, and sympathize.

It was definitely not on my bingo card for reasons our relationship crumbled; I don't know that I would have believed him if he'd just told me, how I would have reacted if he'd tried to show me.

"I was afraid you would leave me if you knew. Even though it was inevitable that not knowing would eventually drive you away," Shawn says. "And I couldn't bring myself to let go of you. I always knew you were too good for me. And when we were falling apart, I kept convincing myself if I could just keep us together, we'd make it through and be happy. But it was unfair to you, and . . . I'm sorry. I wish I'd ended things before it got to that place."

I can see the way he must have thought he could keep me and his family both happy.

"Fuck, Elise. I would have told you if I'd known how," he says, voice hoarse with emotion. He shakes his head and swallows. "I still don't know, honestly. Maybe it doesn't matter, we'll say goodbye after the wedding anyway."

He takes in a deep breath, glancing up at the sky again like he's keeping an eye on the clock, not yet hurried enough to leave, though. I don't know whether to trust that. He's always been a leave-the-house-ten-minutes-late kind of person.

He scratches at his chin, keeping an eye on the sky rather than look at me. "The closer we get to the full moon, the harder it is to control ourselves. This is my family's curse. And for all I know, I'm going as feral as my aunt did. I've already hurt everyone by coming back. You shouldn't come outside in the evening anymore."

"You never hurt me when we were in the woods—" I start to say, but catch myself. I had sort of assumed the dreams were something more than dreams. Like they were clearly about him, even if I hadn't recognized him in them at first.

His expression narrows. "What? What are you talking about?"

"Nothing, sorry. Just a dream I had."

Shawn pushes off the wall, his curiosity moving him. "What dreams?"

"Meeting you out here, finding you in the woods. All those times I've seen you in the woods, and we . . . I-I mean you," I start to make gestures and immediately abandon them.

He backs away a step, like I'm the dangerous one, or the weirdo who's willing to fuck any wolf I just met in the woods. Like he's not literally the wolf.

"You've been meeting me in the woods?" I hedge and grimace, mostly to just stop digging my own grave. "Or it's a dream. I'm pretty sure it was just a dream."

He looks utterly bewildered. He sort of shakes it off, and I don't blame him for not wanting to try to make sense of the dreams either. "Look, I just want you to know I'm sorry for everything. This is why I couldn't tell you where I was. What I was. Why we . . ."

He trails off, but I know the words he won't say. Why we can't be together.

Maybe it was always destined to end. This was why his family wouldn't hear of him bringing me home. Maybe he always saw telling me as what was always going to be what broke us.

I swallow and push forward, crossing the distance between us to stand. I get closer, and realize, the transformation is already creeping in along his edges.

Already, his teeth look a little sharper. Traces of fur and whisker started slowly peeking through along his jawline, his brow, his arms. I can see the way his fingernails have lengthened and become thick, dark; the way the process bruises his knuckles.

Despite it all, I reach out and carefully touch his face. He closes his eyes and lets out a breath, looking like he's trying his best not to lean into my touch.

I rake my fingers into his hair, cupping his face. "So, what do we do with the whole wolf thing?"

A glassy glint of vulnerability in his eyes, Shawn asks cautiously, "Do you think . . . is this something you could put up with?"

"Shawn . . ." I swallow. Looking in his deep-brown eyes, I see it. The fear that this was something he would have been correct to keep from me. It wasn't a secret he had kept to hurt me, even if that had been the outcome.

"Maybe we could figure this out. Give it a try," I offer just as hesitantly, ultimately hedging on what was in my heart.

"Yeah?" He nods, looking painfully hopeful and still uncertain.

My hands already threaded in his hair, I tilt his face towards mine and lean in, pressing a kiss to his mouth.

My forehead touches Shawn's, and I sigh deeply, the sound almost blending into the chorus of the few September crickets left. My throat feels tight, like at the end of a good long cry.

I brush my tongue over his lower lip, and then against the edge of his teeth. Shawn leans into the kiss and within a few breaths, it becomes deeper, full of teeth dragging against skin, nipping at one another.

A low growl thrums through his chest to mine and makes the hair on the back of my neck stand up. The prick of fear under my skin, the urge to glance at the sky pulls me away, out from the kiss.

Then he moves me bodily, a display of unexpected strength. I let out a little squeak of surprise as he gathers me up in his arms, his grip digging into my ass while he pulls me to him, the fat of my stomach against his bony hips.

And something else. The longer I stay with my body pressed to Shawn's, kissing him, the more apparent it becomes, digging hard into my stomach. I shift just enough to make space to trace the outline of his hardened cock through his jeans.

"You're cute," I tell him, if only to see the way the color rises to his cheeks as he glances away from me. He's even cuter when he's bashful.

"If you only knew what you do to me." He sighs, and I lean my head against his collarbone, listening to his muffled heartbeat.

Tomorrow's the wedding. There isn't a whole lot of time to do everything I want with him. I want to bring him back to my cottage and curl up on my couch with him for the evening, even though rationally I know that's impossible.

He must have a similar thought, because he kisses the top of my head with an air of finality.

"We should get you to the brewery sooner than later, maybe you can call someone to pick you up from there. Someone not related to me, hopefully." He grimaces, making a vague gesture to the rest of himself, "You don't want to see me this close to the full moon. This is bad enough already."

My heart pinches at that. I don't want to leave this moment with him feeling like this is still something to hide from me.

In a moment this vulnerable, I want him to feel cherished and worthy of love, but I don't have it in me to just tell him I love him all of a sudden. Maybe I never stopped, but I can't just bare my heart like that. I'd been burned by loving him before.

But I could show him, and maybe that would be enough.

An idea strikes me as my hand slides down his stomach, stopping at the top of his jeans.

The breath stutters in his throat, and I can hear his teeth click together. He pulls out his phone to check the time. I glimpse the 9:03 on his screen before he puts it away.

"I have . . . maybe another hour before I really need to go. I can usually hold it off that long, at least."

"So . . . what you're saying is we have at least fifty-five minutes to get over there, and maybe five minutes to spare?"

He chews the inside of his cheek, a hand covering his mouth as he considers me. "Maybe more like three."

With one hand, I unbuckle his belt, pop the button, tug down the zipper of his jeans. He glances over his shoulder, but doesn't stop me from getting his dick out in what might technically count as public. I suppose someone could take ten minutes to walk over the hill from the brewery and see us, or drive past us at seventy-five miles per hour.

I finally slide an open palm down the hard length of his cock, finding the opening in his boxers to pull it out, my hand wrapping around the base. I watch Shawn's eyes flutter closed and his mouth bite down on the pleasure of that first touch.

My breath catches a little as I let myself glance at his cock and realize it's not quite how I remember it. It's thicker, flushed a deeper, needier red, his cockhead taking on a slightly pointed tip, more distinct veining down the shaft. I hadn't fully considered how complete the transformation under the moon was.

Realizing his cock is even a little wolf-y right now, makes my clit pulse alive. Maybe all those weird dreams should have prepared me a bit better for how intensely this would turn me on.

I give him a light, experimental stroke, and tilt my head and look up into his eyes.

His nostrils actually flare.

In my hand, I feel his cock twitch, and I can't help but smile. I move back a step, slipping to my knees.

Bringing the tapered tip of his cock to my lips, feeling its heat against them, I lick in small teasing flicks, listening to every reaction in his breath. Taking the head into my mouth a little bit more each time, I stroke what doesn't comfortably fit, my hands wrapped around the base.

"Go easy on me," he says, the sort of self-deprecating joke I'm used to from him, and there's something I can't quite make out. There's a dark, low, smoldering heat in his voice I'm not familiar with.

He must know I would take that as a challenge, so I dip down to take the head of his cock in my mouth for a good, hard suck. He makes a strangled noise, his hand tightening on my shoulder.

I lave my tongue over the head and up and down the length of him, but I don't think I could even attempt to deepthroat him for the life of me. Nope, a girl has gotta have boundaries.

I gather up all the saliva in my mouth and draw one last, wet, messy stripe up the underside of his dick. Then I pull back, kneeling on the ground. I tug my shirt up to my collarbone and pull my heavy breasts out of my worn sports bra.

A moment of self-consciousness passes over me. The ways my body is different now, the weight I've put on, the stretch marks, the way my breasts don't have the buoyant bounciness of a twenty-year-old, and are just probably a few too many inches lower than he remembers.

My heart stammers for a second, and I wonder if I should reconsider this, glancing up at him.

Stunned is a very good look on Shawn.

"You haven't changed a bit," he says with no shortage of awe, his hands cupping my breasts, his thumbs finding and toying with my peaked nipples, his attention rapt over them.

"Well, maybe just a bit." I try not to smile.

I lean forward, my hands skimming over my breasts, sitting up a little straighter to bring them up to the same height as his hips.

I cup my hands on either side, pressing them together, enveloping his cock entirely. The slick path of spit on his cock connects to my sternum, making it a little bit easier to get some movement started.

His head tips back as he sucks in a sharp breath, enjoying the stroking up and down his shaft. I watch the way his chest rises and falls in time with my grip coming up over the tip, squeezing the softer head.

We start with a few slow, experimental thrusts, adding more saliva to his cock to make the friction between my breasts a little easier.

Before long, he's rocking his hips into my chest while I clutch my tits around his cock.

I've done so much avoiding him lately, even when I kissed him the other night. How many times did I even look directly at him this week, until I was kneeling between his knees, stroking his cock?

Time has cut into his face, there are creases around his eyes that didn't used to be there. The years have definitely blurred my memory of him. Or maybe back then I'd been too busy curling in on my insecurities to really, truly look at him the way I am now.

When his cock pushes up between my breasts, there's just enough bend in my neck to drag my tongue over the head of his cock, or to give the occasional teasing suck between every few strokes.

I don't know what Shawn thought was mystical about my tit-jobs, I thought they were fairly standard.

His shoulders heave with a labored breath and he grinds out, "Fuck, I'm not going to last long."

Before I can make a teasing comment in return, I feel something else start to disrupt the rhythm of my tit-job. A swell towards the base of his cock, growing more prominent with every pass between my breasts.

I slow my heaving bosom, taking his cock in my hands again, laying my eyes on this new addition. There's a bulging knot split by a seam of veining, swollen near the base of his shaft. I could feel a more intense heat coming off the skin as a bead of precum welled at the tip, his balls tightening below.

I trace my fingers over the formidable curve of it, marveling for just a moment. Is this supposed to go inside?

"That's my knot." Shawn sighs, the muscles in his neck tense as his chest rises and falls with heavy breaths.

"Knot?"

"It's . . . kind of a wolf thing. I mean it is a wolf thing," he mutters. He glances away from me, dragging a hand over his face, but I can still see the rush of red peeking between his fingers. "It's for mating."

"You never knotted with me before."

"Maybe we weren't ready for that," he pants and swallows. "Wolves mate for life. Or you're supposed to."

There's something about that statement that makes me bristle. Maybe it's the guilt I feel at leaving without a goodbye, or maybe it's that I'm still gun-shy at the thought of commitment.

Whatever it is, I drop my eyes to the ground at his words, not really able to handle the weight of that statement. Part of me wants him to explain what he means by that, but I can't stop and interrogate him about it, so I just focus on finishing this.

"Elise—" Shawn starts to say, interrupted by his own climax. He comes with a groan, hot spurts of his release painting my clavicle, my neck. It cools almost the second it touches my skin, but there is something extremely gratifying about his climax dripping onto me. It's interrupted by a stinging pain in my shoulder creeping into my awareness, as he grips me too hard.

His cock twitches the last of his release against my tits. A low, guttural rumble in his chest becomes a snarl, the corners of his mouth dragging down. My eyes widen, seeing him shift further into his wolfish form. It's startling to witness, hearing the creak and snap of bone.

I can't help but recoil.

"Ow!" I hiss, pulling back out of Shawn's grip, but that only makes it worse. I realize as he lets go of my arm, the tips of his claws pull out. They had dug in, perhaps even emerged further as he'd gripped me through his climax.

I fall back on my ass, scooting away from him in the dirt. I clutch a hand over where the pain in my shoulder is, and my palm comes away wet.

"Shit, Elise, I'm sorry," he starts to say, but the words are tainted by the wolfish gnarr now in his voice. He starts to reach a clawed, jagged hand to me.

"It's ok. It was an accident—"

I glance at my hand, the way my palm is fully red with my blood. I can see when the metallic scent hits him, the way he shudders and shifts a little more into the monster he was afraid I would see.

He looks horrified with himself, but it's hard to decipher the human expression from the wolfish features surfacing. He backs away, stuffing his cock in his jeans haphazardly and clearing the fieldstone wall behind him in a swift movement. "You need to get home, lock the doors."

"Shawn, I know you didn't mean to," I plead, almost yell, after him. He's halfway across the field again when he stops and barely turns to me.

"Elise, please. I couldn't live with myself if worse happened."

The fading sun catches and reflects a bit of scarred skin on his arms, a few thin scratches where his coat doesn't come in.

I can see them then, the marks his mother left in his arm, scars nearly as old as he is, before he turns and runs away.

This whole fucking family, man.

22

Shawn

I'm fucking losing it.

I can barely think. Even turning my head a few degrees feels like the world is spinning, tilting on a new axis as my bones try to shift, to complete the wreckage of myself. Holding it back is like holding my breath for too long. The pain and discomfort, pressure and itching in my bones is dizzying.

I can feel it in my jaw as palpably as I can feel hunger or exhaustion. The need to close my teeth around her soft, yielding flesh overwhelms me. Some terrible part of my mind is telling me that I could shift and catch up to her in seconds. Just thinking about her makes me salivate, and I hate to imagine why.

I don't want to chase Elise. I can't. I won't.

I rarely draw out the shift for so long, but I have to. I need to hold it off as long as I can, to get myself into the brewery cellars so that Elise will be safe.

I'm finally coming to grips that everything I've ever done with Elise was a mistake. It was a mistake to involve her, to put her safety so immediately in the path of danger. Every moment I have ever loved her has been selfish. All it's done is hurt her.

I rinse her blood off at the outside spigot at the brewery, a tap meant for watering the shrubs that line the perimeter. It's not enough to get rid of the smell completely, but it helps calm me down some. I feel less like a monster I can't get away from.

I've never voluntarily locked myself in the brewery's cellar, at least not since becoming an adult. It wasn't really our choice when we were younger.

I'm starting to feel like it might be the only good idea I've had in weeks.

I should have never let her near me. I should have said no when she'd started kissing me, should have pushed her away. I knew it was a bad idea, but I let my desire to hold her, to breathe her in and spend every second I could with her outweigh her safety.

Her knowing what I am didn't solve problems the way I thought it would. Every problem we ever had comes back to what I am, the nature of my monstrosity. Perhaps things were better when I'd been able to keep it from her, and the worst I'd ever done was break her heart.

But her blood on my hands . . . I tore up her arm without even realizing. All I wanted was to hold her, and I couldn't manage that much.

Despite being nine p.m., the brewery hasn't yet locked up for the weekend, and I spot why as soon as I enter the brick building.

My mother raises an eyebrow at my partial shift. She hasn't even started to shift yet, a testament to the control she's mastered in her age. I know she has her flask of aconite tincture in her purse, and I'm sure she'll have a quieter night than I'm in for.

"Shawn, what are you—" she starts to say, surprised to see me here. Her brows narrow and pinch together as she spots the blood on my shirt, and she doesn't bother to finish her question. "Are you alright?"

I shake my head a little. I don't know what's wrong with me, why this full moon is so much harder to bear than any other has been. I'd been a fool to think I knew what control was, that I had enough, when the shift could be this bad.

I take another step inside, shutting the door beside me.

She frowns. "You smell like Elise."

I'm not about to tell my mother I just left Elise alone in a field with my cum drying on her neck and gouges in her arm. Running away from her is simultaneously the most dickish and smartest thing I've done.

My mother sighs, glancing away from me. "That's disappointing. Even after she knew you were married."

The last time she started this conversation on a similar note, I'd been ready to snarl at the slightest provocation. Tonight, I'm just defeated. I don't have it in me to respond with any ire.

"I've been divorced for years, Mom. She knows that."

Deanna looks at me, her glare suddenly much sharper than before.

I can't help but scoff, rolling my eyes. I can't do anything right in her view. First, I marry the wrong sort of girl, then I commit the terrible act of divorce when it doesn't work out.

“But your ring—”

“Yeah, I have hers too. I carry my regrets around on me.”

It’s been tucked into my wallet long enough that it’s imprinted into the leather.

I can’t even meet her eyes. I glance around the lobby of the brewery entrance, the way the furniture has changed since I was last here, and fall into a seat along the wall, no will for any of it anymore. The need to shift fully still sickens me, like my wolf is trying to lunge its way out of my throat.

I really am going feral. I wonder if my Aunt Danielle felt like this. Too bad I can’t ask her. Then again, I probably wouldn’t exist if she were alive.

I double over, hunched against my knees almost instantly. I swallow, clasping my hands together behind my head, taking in a few shallow breaths.

“She left me. All my bullshit was hurting her, and what we had wasn’t worth the pain I caused her. I wish I’d been able to see that when I needed to. You were right, in the end.”

Even as I admit it, I’m still not ready to hear *I told you so.*

I expect my mom to bring up the sanctity of the pack, but the lectures I could repeat in my sleep never come.

For many moments, there’s utter silence, and I can only hear the creak of my bones pushing against each other. My mother’s heels click against the tile floor as she crosses to the bench. It creaks as she sits down beside me.

“Oh, my baby. I’m sorry.”

Her long nails comb through my hair. Her elbow rests against my back as she continues the motion, and I find myself leaning into her side.

I close my eyes, too raw to find healing in it. If I'm going feral, being with my pack should keep me safe, even if it doesn't feel like it.

"Don't say that. You think I make stupid choices."

"Shawn. I just want you to be happy. I want the best for you. For all my children to stay safe and never let the world put you through the things I've seen." She sighs, as I find the wherewithal to sit up a little more and turn enough to look at her. The crinkles around her eyes deepen as they become a little glassy. "But ever since you came back, I see a ghost every time I look at you."

"Danielle." I exhale. It hasn't escaped me that I look more like my aunt than anyone else in my family.

My mother shakes her head. "My little boy."

I search her warm, brown eyes, and she withdraws her gaze, clasping her hands in her lap. "Sometimes I wonder if I wanted too much for you. I put too much pressure on you and pushed you away."

This might be the first calm, easy conversation we've had since I've gotten here. It's a home I haven't stepped in for years.

I swallow, taking that in. I haven't felt like I had my mom in so long. My throat tightens as the emotion swells in my chest.

Her expression is soft, as she says, "I doubt you will believe me, but I'm proud of you in a lot of ways. You made it out in the world alone, something that terrified me."

Those words don't quite sink in, the way I thought they should. "You can be proud of me when I haven't made the same choices as Logan?"

"You're different people. I am proud of him for taking on the family business and making connections in a way I wasn't prepared to teach him, after your father passed."

"He's just doing what he thinks Dad would have wanted him to do."

A smile twitches at the corners of her mouth. "He's downstairs. I imagine he can hear us."

"Lovely. I'll go talk shit to his face, then," I grumble, forcing myself to stand. The night is getting darker, and I ought to remember why I came here in the first place.

Her hands tighten together in her lap as she looks at me, her brow pinching in concern. "You look unwell. Did something happen?"

I think for a moment of telling her everything. I think about all the times I wanted her to be there for me, to hold me and tell me everything was going to be alright. All the times I was too afraid of her disappointment to admit my flaws to her.

I give my head a little shake. "No."

The stone steps down into the brewery's basement feel too familiar as I descend, finding the dim lights already on.

We'd only ever used the basement for the nights of the full moon, when our curse was at its worst. The rooms are spaced far between, each with a heavy sliding door with a lock that requires opposable thumbs to open.

It had been a necessity in high school, when my wolf was especially hard to control. When I'd gone to college in another state, it had become necessary to figure out something else—running, aconite-laced drinks.

Eventually I got the hang of it, if only tenuously. I could be sure my wolf would run the hills of empty woods, maybe stalk a deer. It would stay instinctually away from people, I'd found. When I came back, I couldn't stomach the thought of spending the night down here anymore. It was the first of many fights with my family.

There's something about the cellars that reminds me too much of church. Maybe it's the stone walls and floors, reminiscent of a cathedral. Not for its splendor, but for its coldness, its discomfort. It's kind of hard to keep furniture in the cellar rooms, seeing as it gets wrecked and splintered every full moon.

Downstairs in the brewery's basement, there is a plain-looking door that only my family carries the keys to—the scene of many a sleepless night.

The whole basement looks old, but there's something about this dusty, vacant oratory that makes everything feel a little worse. I wonder if it was ever brought up to code. Maybe there's radon down here.

Maybe it's the gouges scratched into the walls.

The far wall is divided into four stalls, each separated by thick stone partitions. There are gapped sections of the masonry with iron bars crisscrossing through it, allowing us to glimpse one another. High up on the back wall, there's the thinnest sliver of sky through frosted glass, confessionals to the moon.

It looks awful and medieval, but whatever. It's necessary. I need to be sure I won't be able to go after Elise.

God, just thinking about her hurts.

I don't know what to think. What my mom said about Danielle being kept from her mate didn't make sense. My circumstances aren't the same, how could I be kept from a mate I've never met?

But what if I let myself entertain the thought that even if I never knotted in Elise before, that she could still be my mate? If I just ignore every reason it didn't work out before?

The thought brings a sort of restlessness that lights up my nerves with energy it's hard to place in my human body. I need to move, to express it, but it's got this tail-wagging giddiness to it that shaking my hands out doesn't quite reach.

My next thought makes all of it dissipate instantly. She left. She chose to leave. And even if I do buy into the idea that our souls are somehow cosmically intertwined, how cruel would that be to her? How can I tell her this is what I think, what I feel, without feeling like I am cornering her into being with me? That I am just manipulating a narrative to get what I want out of it?

And even if she feels the same, accepts all of it wholeheartedly, how can I be sure it won't just end the same way it did the first time?

It doesn't matter, then.

I go in and sit down with my back to the wall; I can see Logan is already locked in for the night.

"This is the sorriest stag night I've ever seen," I tell him, but even as I say it, I think how much I would have wanted him there for me the night before I got married, instead of a bottle of beer.

Even a full-moon night like this, laying on the ground with nothing to do but wait for it to be over. I have so many memories of sitting as close to each other's doorways as we could, reaching under the gap to move the little plastic pieces around an old Battleship board, chatting aimlessly about everything and nothing for hours.

I'm about to ask him if he remembers playing Battleship with me, when he interrupts the silence.

"You know, I always thought the prodigal son story was bullshit."

So, he's still pissed at me.

Once upon a time, this asshole was my favorite brother. It kinda sucks that it's just defaulted to Aiden.

"Yeah, you would. I figured it was just someone making up bullshit to make a point," I evade. "Should have had a better point."

The quiet is grating.

Logan is eerily calm for a full moon. Or maybe it's really just me that can't handle it tonight, for some reason.

The itching pressure in my bones is going to last until I shift fully, but it's so overwhelming this time I don't want to just lean into it the way I normally would. It feels like giving in.

I find myself staring at one of the only decorations in the cellar, an antique painting of Saint Patrick. I mean, I know it's St. Paddy, but it does just look like a guy in a black cloak and bare feet carrying a baby deer away from its mother.

Our dad hung that there after Logan and I had gotten into some trouble. I don't even remember what it was, just that Dad hung it there with the intent to make us think deeply on our Lycan condition. Given what it stands for, I'm honestly a little surprised no one bothered to take it down.

"Why are we supposed to venerate the guy who's supposed to have cursed us?"

"Why are we taught to respect our parents?" Logan counters a little too quickly.

"Jeez. Ok, edgelord," I sigh.

A few beats go by in the nothing, the quiet. I have to get up and pace rather than sit down in the corner.

It's a fever, it will pass. I close my eyes and try to just endure it.

After several minutes, Logan interrupts the silence. "I've never really had it in me to believe."

It's not much of a confession. I think I've always known that about him.

I glance sidelong at him. Logan's always moved fluidly through life, sidestepping what annoys him. A refusal to be second in command, to answer to a power higher than himself. The way to be more powerful than god is to be a nonbeliever.

I can see the way the wedding is frustrating him. It's not something he can just dip out of. There's a tension in his jaw that has been there since he was a kid. *He must have some serious TMJ,* I muse to myself, and roll my jaw in sympathy.

"You know what it's like to be married, right?" Logan asks, as if his thoughts can't help but wander in the same places as mine. The normally defiant edge in his voice is gone for something almost casual. "For however long it lasted."

I sigh and put my back to the wall opposite the confessional window. "Two years, for the record."

He raises his eyebrows. "Impressive."

"Shut up."

"You're not going to tell me about it?"

"Getting divorced?"

"No, when you got married. Famously, I was not there."

"Oh, you know. We went down to the courthouse in a couple of tie-dye T-shirts. There's some terrible photobooth strips that are almost too dark to see anything, we got those from walking around the boardwalk after."

That night was a new moon, I remember because I'd specifically planned that out. I vaguely remember some half-baked intent to keep her up all night and then waking up at noon, not sure when holding her close became sleep.

The memory makes me smile, and then wince as my claws push a little further out.

Through the latticed opening, Logan looks thoughtful. Then he asks, "How'd you do it, knowing you were making a mistake?"

Yeesh, rude.

"I didn't think it was a mistake. It was the best day of my life. I'd do it again in a heartbeat."

He doesn't reply.

Maybe he just wants reassurance he's making the right decision. It must feel like a big leap, and he's too much of a cynic to believe in himself.

He always has been. I remember him being too frightened to bike without the training wheels. Also picking him up after he fell off my bike, putting Band-Aids on his knees while he sniffled and promised not to tell Mom.

"She had a lot of money to pay in taxes," I tell him, weaving this little story for him. It makes me miss being a big brother. Just a little.

"It was uh . . . self-employment tax stuff. Anyway, she couldn't cover it all, and I was already in love with her. It started out as a joke. Filing as a married couple would save her the difference in what she owed, and a marriage license was like, less than thirty bucks. We were already married by the time I told Mom about her."

Maybe it's going over fond memories, or that it feels like coming home for the first time in ages, even though I've been here all week.

He doesn't add anything else for a long moment. I think he's done talking to me at all when he says, "I hope the pain was worth it."

"What do you mean?"

"Getting divorced."

"You know, you're so much fun to talk to. I don't know why we didn't catch up earlier."

He rolls his eyes in response, like I'm the asshole for not accepting his condolences when they were presented with such careful and empathetic tact.

Whatever. I'm just going to keep ignoring his attitude. There's not much else I can do while sitting penitent.

I put my head between my knees, my claws raking through my scalp. The shift feels oddly suffocating this time, like I can't breathe in deeply enough.

"And then when Elise—ah, fuck."

I look up, and there's no mistaking it from his expression. He heard me say her name. Fucking tripping at the finish line. Great job, man.

Logan's dark eyes hold mine, his brow furrows. I can hear his teeth grind together.

23

It's the morning of the wedding, and I keep looking for Shawn every time I get a few spare seconds. When I got to the Hayes House, Deanna answered the door, and said they would be back soon.

It's kind of getting on my nerves that Shawn is actually doing a good job of avoiding me, or at least better than the rest of his family. I've barely seen him.

And, like, I guess he wouldn't want to see me after he just kind of abruptly left last night. But I need to talk to him.

I've been over the order of things I have to put in the oven a dozen times. I have everything I need prepped, but I feel like I need to just stare at the trays and agonize. It's too quiet.

A couple days ago, I had planned to tell Deanna I was going to move after all this was over and figure out an end date for our contract. The plan was to go back to packing up my things after all the dishes were done. The money that would have been a down payment on my cottage would be a cushion while I rented and looked for new contacts. One of my cooking school friends actually replied to my message and knew a restaurant that needed a new sous chef. It wouldn't be working for myself, but it would be a good opportunity.

No more Shawn, no more Hayes family, no more werewolves.

No more anyone.

The thought isn't reassuring the way it was supposed to be. I don't have a family here; these people are not my friends. They're the same people who would have rejected me before.

Laura's always good company, I think as I wander upstairs, but it sinks my heart a little, knowing that I won't be able to hang out with her after I leave. Maybe we could keep in touch, but texting every now and then just won't be the same as hanging out on her terrible couch with a pint of melted ice cream.

In one of the guest rooms, I catch sight of Ava—Laura's friend—and what I'm assuming is the back of Laura's head. Ava has a couple flowers pinched by the stems in one hand, and a couple of hairpins in the other. She's decorated Laura's braided updo with a variety of little buds.

Leftovers from the flower arch, I realize as I get closer.

Ava has been here today about as long as I have. Laura stopped in earlier to introduce her florist friend to me, before showing her the backyard. Every time I glanced out the window, the clearing before the woods was a little more fairytale-like. Ava waved at me through the kitchen door every time she passed by with another box of flowers, and I kept wondering where she was going to find more places to stick them.

"Someone actually got attacked and chased by a wolf a couple nights ago," Ava says when I walk in the door, the smell of flowers greeting me. Her eyes are wide and genuinely worried. "It's so scary what's happening."

"Oh! Those hikers, right? I heard they just saw something they thought was a wolf," Laura says, waving me in. Apparently, Deanna's rule that they weren't to encourage the rumors didn't apply to her.

"My high school best friend," Ava continues in a hushed voice. "I had just lent her my coat the day before it happened. She sent me a picture of what was left of it when she got away."

"Oh, shit," Laura murmurs, looking genuinely bothered for a moment, before she throws me a half-hearted smile. I ache to comfort her, but that would mean telling her that I know everything when I'm not supposed to. Maybe it would be too much of a shock during an already difficult moment.

At that, Ava puts down the handful of little flower stems, and takes out her phone, swiping through to find the message and show us. "Terrifying. I can't imagine what I'd do if that happened to me."

The photo on her screen was bone chilling.

I could barely tell that it was a coat, just a shredded pile of fabric and zipper. Half of it looked like it had been torn off, maybe left on the trail with the wolf. It couldn't have been Shawn that chased the hiker, could it?

I swallowed, reluctant to even think about it, with the emotions that mixed uncomfortably in my stomach: fear for the hiker's safety, worry about just how much control Shawn had as a beast, and I cringed at myself to admit that I felt the tiniest bit jealous. It was completely irrational. If he didn't have control over himself as a wolf, I couldn't exactly get mad that he was sniffing other girls, right? And there wasn't even proof that it was him, for all I knew it could be any of the others.

"Oh, have either of you seen Logan?" Deanna sighs, sweeping into the room with her usual exasperation with the people around her.

She catches sight of Ava's phone screen, and her mouth immediately becomes a hard line.

Laura, for once, looks guilty. "Sorry, Aunt Dea."

"Girls, let's not bring today down with . . . just put it away," she says, and it's hard to miss the way her skin blanches.

I have to wonder, then, about her. Shawn said this was his family's curse. If it includes everyone, even his mother, how long has it been going? And if his mom is also a werewolf, then that story about his aunt . . . what really happened with her? He said something about a wolf being seen in the area before she disappeared.

She had been the wolf. And she'd been so alone.

I swallow, thinking about the way Shawn had struggled against the beastly transformation last night.

Deanna sighs and says to Laura, "Do me a favor, if you see him, will you get him to do something with his hair? He's always been difficult about that."

"What, like a bun? French twist? High ponytail?"

"I can fishtail braid," Ava offers brightly.

Deanna waves a hand, checking her phone briefly. She says over her shoulder as she leaves us, "As long as it looks presentable."

"Ooh, what if we do a bun, but we stick some flowers in it," Ava whispers to Laura, eyes lighting up with her idea. Her hand dips into the box of flower bits preemptively.

Laura snorts. "Good luck with that."

"Ok, maybe no flowers. But there's ribbon, and who would say no to that?"

I think she may be the only person in this house having a fun time with the preparations. I envy her for a moment.

She might also be the only other human in the house right now, until my waitstaff get here for the reception. My plan is to prep them while the guests arrive and are being seated, and then at least catch the end of the ceremony from the back row.

"Well, until then . . . Elise, I've got plenty of rosebuds," she offers, wiggling her eyebrows. I can see her planning how she's going to pin them around my bun already.

I smile and give my head a little shake. "I'm going to be in the kitchen all day, I can't. I don't want anything falling into the food while I'm working."

"Oh, yeah, I guess," she admits, and the thought does seem to deflate her enthusiasm for a moment.

"But I will say yes to the ribbon."

That seems to satisfy her. Ava jogs across the room and ducks into the little ensuite bathroom where Laura's fold-out makeup case has been spread out across the vanity, looking for the roll of ribbon.

I glimpse some movement out in the hall, and my heartbeat picks up for a moment hoping it's Shawn. It's not. Still, I call out, "Logan!"

I swear I can see the thought of just ignoring me tense up in his shoulders. He stops and turns around reluctantly.

"What do you want?" he says, instead of a greeting, and it's oddly cold from him.

"Your mom said you'd be coming back with Shawn?" I start to ask, but the words become quieter as he glares at me. It's the same sort of pinched look he normally reserves for Shawn.

"What could you possibly need from him right now?"

Ok, the attitude isn't cute. I'm about to tattle to his mom in a second if he keeps this up.

"Never mind. Just get in here." I roll my eyes and wave him into the room, and he begrudgingly follows in. "Laura, he's all yours."

He looks tired, more than usual, dark circles under eyes, his long hair loose and untamed. He's barely made an effort to get dressed for the event, just wearing formal black pants and a mostly buttoned white shirt. You'd have thought he was a waiter instead of the groom.

"And what do you want?" The question is directed at Laura with his usual tired exasperation, and she is clearly used to it enough to not take offense.

"There's some time before the lady of the hour gets here, so I was told to do your hair. Since clearly you weren't going to," she says, with just a hint of a fiendish smile.

"Hm. Yeah, no. See ya," he says, as monosyllabic in his word choice as he usually is.

"Get back here," Laura grumbles, lunging quickly enough that she can put a hand across the doorway before he can walk back out, but he ducks under her arm fluidly. Laura only succeeds in catching him because she takes a dive and catches her arms around his neck.

I know now that they're both werewolves, but watching the way they move and interact, I'm surprised that I never suspected anything before. It's not unsubtle.

Eventually Laura tugs him back into the room and he sits in the chair, leaning back slowly, like he's expecting torture. "Put the scissors away."

"Relax, I'm just going to braid it."

"What's that for," Logan asks through gritted teeth, when she plucks up the pre-heated hair iron from the nearby table.

"A straightener. You've got those weird ponytail crimps in here," she says, as she starts to drag it through his hair. "I keep telling you not to do that when it's wet. Like, have you ever used a blow dryer? A diffuser?"

"Every day, obviously," he sighs, slumping defeatedly in the chair.

Something about the cadence and efficiency they bicker with makes me wonder if they've been having this conversation ever since they were kids.

"Ava, can you bring me some ribbon too? And grab my concealer. Jeez, what's wrong with your face, dude?"

I hear the sound of Ava rummaging around through Laura's makeup case, while Logan grumbles something back to Laura, but he falls silent as soon as she slips out of the guest bathroom.

"Which concealer?" she asks, her brow furrowing. She glances over her shoulder where Laura points. "You have like three different kinds, and they all look ancient."

"Oh, never mind. I'll grab it." Laura tosses the straightener aside on the vanity, and heads toward the bathroom. "Logan, stay there. I'm not letting you go out there with bags under your eyes."

Several moments pass, a small quiet falling over the messy guest room. I wonder if Laura can't find the specific concealer she's looking for either. I watch Ava drift back to the box full of flowers, glancing between Logan and anything else in the room. Every so often I glance back out the window with half-hearted hope that I'll spot Shawn. He's gotta get here sooner or later.

"Are you in the wedding party?" she asks, and goes for one of the smaller boxes, full of little pre-made miniature bouquets of purple and white flowers, tied with a lace bow. They all have pins on their backs. I realize as she selects one, that Laura has one pinned on her dress as well.

I'm surprised that Logan full-on glares at her, withering her friendliness on the spot. I'm almost ready to chide him for that, the way all the cheeriness she brought with her vanishes. I know he's having a hard time with the whole wedding thing, but he still needs to be nice to people.

"Yeah," Logan mutters after a long moment, his mouth a hard line, his stare set dead ahead, unseeing. He has such a talent for making a single syllable sound barbed.

"I'm supposed to pin these on everyone who is," she tells him, offering a friendly, if shy, smile. I almost feel the need to warn her that he's been about as cuddly as a porcupine all of last week. She holds out the little bouquet for him to see.

He doesn't answer, eyeing the flowers like he expects them to bite him. He doesn't nod, but he tilts his head to the side a little, allowing her to step closer.

An awkward few seconds filter through, and Ava decides to just go ahead and do her job. She takes half a step toward him and slips a hand delicately under the collar of his shirt, tugging a pinch of fabric taught to guide the pin through.

I watch a muscle tense in his jaw, his nostrils flare with his breath.

I don't see it happen, but maybe she accidentally pricks him with the sharp end because he grabs her wrist suddenly, snatching it away from him, pin and all. They lock eyes for a moment, and time seems to stop. It's hard not to stare, though the two of them are so agitated by whatever just passed between them that they don't notice my rudeness.

Ava's the first of us to break away from it.

"I guess you can re-do it later if you want, um," she mumbles, glancing from his hand on her wrist to him.

He lets go of her and stands, brushes out of the room in a couple long strides.

Ava glances at me and mouths, *what the fuck*, and I give her a sympathetic shrug and equally wide-eyed expression. She looks a little upset but tries to shrug it off, pinning it to her sleeve instead.

"Whatever, I worked hard on these, and I don't want him to have one anyway," she mutters, waving her hand a little to admire her work. "Fuck that guy."

"Yeah, I don't know what's eating him." I nod, when I hear Shawn's voice downstairs that moment and honestly take that as my cue to leave. I say apologetically to her, "I'm going to be right back."

I step out into the hall, but it's empty.

Ok, now I'm getting a bit pissed off at Shawn, I can feel it heating up my skin. I know he's upset, but he can't just avoid me forever, can he? Like, that's got to be the only reason I'm feeling warm under the collar every time I look at him.

When I get to the top of the stairs, I can see the front door wide open and a few guests in their formal clothes stepping through, being greeted by Deanna. Some of them receive warmer greetings than others. I watch as one woman, tall and skinny with gray hair and fun looking earrings stops short of embracing Deanna and gives her a semi-pleasant smile.

"This is Elise," Deanna introduces me as I'm halfway down the stairs, and I put on my customer service smile to conceal my disappointment at getting swept up into something else. She raises her eyebrows at me. "Darling, I have some fires to put out, would you show Laura's mom to the patio?"

I'm not going to be right back, and I'm not going to find Shawn, it seems.

"Jenny Brandford," the woman tells me when I reach the bottom of the stairs, offering a hand and a much bigger smile to me.

"Oh, Laura's one of my favorite people," I tell her, shaking her hand briefly. "Laura's upstairs, if you're looking for her—"

"She'll find me if she wants. I live in town, and I see her maybe twice a year as it is," Jenny laughs, dropping that tidbit and moving on without a second thought. "How long have you been with the family, dear?"

Jeez, does anyone have a good relationship with their mom?

"Four years," I answer without really thinking. It was the sort of question I got a lot earlier in my career when I was a private chef. "This is my first wedding, though."

Jenny pauses, closes her eyes, takes a deep breath, then raises her brows. "You sure smell like one of the family."

I . . . don't know how to feel about that.

She links her arm through mine, and I lead her towards the back doors.

"You're in for a treat. It's delightfully pagan, the excessive drinking, seeing the couple disappear into the woods, the chase, the mating bite . . . god, it reminds me of my youth," she tells me, with drama in her voice that is plenty reminiscent of the way Laura tells stories.

She pauses to lift the edge of her sleeve, revealing a smattering of scarring near her elbow.

It takes me a moment to realize what I'm seeing is a pattern of teeth.

"Oh, wow," is all I can think to say. What am I supposed to do here, hike up my skirt to show her my knee and say, *I got this one falling out of a tree at seven?* Or do I ooh and ahh over her bite mark like it's got fourteen-karats?

The patio doors close behind us as she boasts, "I had a true mate, rare as it is. Unlike my brother and Deanna. I always knew they were wrong for each other, but it was hard to explain. I think it might have been easier if he'd known what it was like."

"How did you know?" I ask before I can stop myself, and she gives me a smile that feels, honestly, a little patronizing, as if there was no way I could know what she was talking about either.

Still, the urge to impart her wisdom wins out.

"I felt my mate's presence linger with me, that we were linked together even beyond this Earth. I dreamed his wolf was stalking me, marking his territory," she says wistfully, and I feel there's a real beauty to what she's talking about.

A little girl with a fluffy tulle dress bounces to Aunt Jenny's side and grabs her hand, scrunching her nose. "Uncle Rob peed on you in your dreams?"

Aunt Jenny lets loose a rather canine-sounding growl and the little girl runs off before I can get her name. It's ferocious enough that it makes the hair on my arms stand straight up, and it's all I can do to stop myself from running off too.

"Children," Jenny scoffs, "do their parents teach them no respect?"

I chew on my lower lip, and I suspect I'm not going to learn the answer to that hit-and-run style question. Which is really too bad because I am now dying to know as well. I haven't had anyone mark their territory in my dreams but . . . I swallow, and my cheeks heat a little at the memories.

I have come to know a side of Shawn I didn't before. I just didn't recognize him at first because he hadn't shared all of himself with me.

Jenny glances over her shoulder then asks me in an undertone, "Have you met the Carringtons, yet?"

"No, but I'm excited to see the bride. I'm sure she's gorgeous."

Aunt Jenny scoffs. "Sanctimonious bunch. But it's about time someone restored a bit of decorum to the Hayes family name."

She says it with so much venom, I can't imagine she means anyone but Shawn, how he took on being disowned for me. I feel my insides pinch a little. I had no idea they were like this. "I think Deanna's sons have plenty to be proud of. They're all great."

"No, her sister. Went feral in the woods. I can't imagine doing that. So incredibly selfish. And then Dea had the nerve to beg Father Martin to allow her to be buried in the family plot," Jenny says with a derisive noise, waving me off as if this is something I should have known.

I blink, because what am I supposed to reply to that? *"Square up, Aunt Jenny?"*

"If someone else in this family goes feral, it'll ruin the Carringtons as well, to be connected to us," she continues on, and it makes a few more things make sense about Shawn's family, if all werewolves are weird and puritanical like this.

That's such a bummer, too. Werewolves exist and they kinda suck.

"I mean, there's always divorce," I say, because it feels kind of obvious. It's weird to demand people to stay in a relationship just because.

Aunt Jenny's demeanor shifts rapidly away from warm and inviting, and she gives me a withering look. "This generation, I swear. We don't divorce."

"Because . . . wolves mate for life?" I try, stabbing in the dark, wincing internally at myself because some Discovery Channel-esque, and probably outdated, factoid cannot be it.

Jenny rolls her eyes. "It's a sin, darling."

I blink two or three more times. I keep forgetting that people can still be that intensity of Catholic. I don't really know what to reply, because I'm still technically at work right now and it wouldn't be good to express actual thoughts on the clock.

I'm chewing on my lip as I lead her to the table that has her little name card sitting on the bread plate, as she continues, "Besides, there's nothing left to divorce in a feral wolf. They can't change back. They're gone."

One day she didn't come back, I remember Shawn saying.

I hear his voice nearby and let go of Aunt Jenny's arm. I flash her the briefest of parting smiles and depart with an incoherent muttering about being needed somewhere, something like that.

Have I ever seen Shawn fully? In a way where all the inconsistencies and contradictions meet back together, not just a guy who wanted to make me his world, not just a wolf ready to sink his teeth in.

I can see everything that was missing before, the way I was a part of this equation. Our vulnerabilities, the ways we mirrored each other were the things that brought us together initially, and the reasons we pulled back.

I always felt like being married to him was too good to be true, that he couldn't truly love me. That he was out of my league, and I couldn't ever hope to really have him, that I'd have to settle for getting my heart broken bit by bit every month or so. That I was so starved for love of any kind, that I would put up with that.

Every month or so. God. The werewolf thing really does clear up most of my questions, now that I think about it. Not that it changes anything about how his family treated me . . . I mean, maybe it does. I don't know. Maybe we all need one big therapy session.

My heart is thundering in my chest as I return to the kitchen. My head is spinning with my emotions, but I know one thing for certain, I need to find Shawn and talk to him.

24

I am doing my goddamn best, and it's not going to be enough.

The full moon sits high overhead, pale and nearly invisible in the sky, watching every single time I get too close to Elise, apparently. It bristles under my skin every time I so much as hear her voice, and it's always my name on her lips, always asking if anyone knows where I am.

She's been hounding me all morning. I don't know how I'm going to make it through the next few hours, honestly.

The Hayes House has never felt as small, or quite so constricting, as it does right now.

Some of the Carringtons have already started to arrive, and I am hoping to avoid them as much as possible. Too many wolves in one place during the night of the full moon. Not to mention, if any of them remember me from when I still had to attend church over a decade ago, I don't want to have to explain my absence while simultaneously receiving derision for being a lapsed Catholic.

Guests fill the house, meandering in the living room and the foyer, a couple of townies I recognize are dressed in black, button-down shirts carrying trays of hors d'oeuvres around.

When I stand on the other side of the lawn, as far away from her as I can get without leaving the property, I feel a little more like a normal person. I can remember that I'm at my brother's wedding for a moment, that this is what I came home for.

There's been a few people here and there that I've talked to, mostly my more distant cousins. Some of my older relatives have pretty much ignored me, some are confused that I'm here at all. Only two have asked after my excommunication. It doesn't hurt the way I thought I'd have to brace myself for it. Then again, my priorities have been somewhat shuffled by this week's events.

No one's gone feral, we're all here, I remind myself.

All the unrest in my stomach is butterflies for my brother's special day, even if it feels maybe more like termites gnawing at my insides. It still feels like I fucking might. I can't imagine what else is making me want to crawl out of my skin.

My mom planned the dinner area to be closest to the kitchen, so food could go swiftly in and out as needed.

". . . It's mostly a matter of putting things in the oven and then plating them." Elise's voice carries from the kitchen, and I have to dig my heels in the lawn to keep from just gravitating over there. Despite the majority of the prep being finished beforehand, she doesn't seem any amount less stressed about it.

I can barely stand to look at any of the food. Never mind that it's probably Michelin-star-worthy and smells delicious, but the thought of eating anything makes me a little sick right now.

A foreboding lurks something terrible in my gut, an anticipation that won't leave.

I make the mistake of turning around when I get a wisp of her scent on the wind. A loose tendril of her hair drifts on the air, beckoning me over. The wind slows and the curl rests on her shoulder, and all I can think of is putting my mouth there instead. I think I might be salivating over the little droplets of sweat gathered on her neck under her bun.

She looks like utter perfection. The black fabric comes all the way up to her collar, and the straps on her shoulders are only an inch or so wide, nothing for my claws. She looks very professional, and I just want to go over there and run my hands all over her.

I feel like I could shift at any moment, like even after last night's close call, morning never came.

I'm actively unlocking new ways to drool over her that I can barely even comprehend, and all of it sits heavy in my lower jaw. I always want to kiss her, but it's deeper than that, like I need to sink my teeth into her skin.

Oh.

Oh no.

You. Bonehead. I curse myself. *You utter fool.*

Of course it's always been her. She's my mate. I just didn't want to see it, because I didn't want to give her the chance to hurt me again.

The knowledge fits perfectly in my heart, like some kind of sick twist of fate, except for one detail. One moonlit titty-job that would have been one for the record books, if it weren't for me.

She's my mate, and what if I hurt her?

It doesn't matter, ultimately. We're not good together, because we failed the first time. There were all those reasons she explained to me why it didn't work, even if none of them feel like anything at all when I watch the way she moves, and feel an unbidden growl try to rise up in my chest.

The only thing that feels worth letting her go is what pulled us apart initially: we can't make a life that would be good for both of us work. My nature would hurt her again.

I dig my hands in my pockets for maybe the hundredth time today. Stay out of the way, stay far, far away from her. Every time I start pacing, I find myself wandering back to the kitchen, and have to purposefully go somewhere else.

This time, it's out back, near the woods. I'm this close to just disappearing back into them.

This is the first time I have really seen all of it set up. The lawn beside the house looks like something out of a magazine. It is a small wedding, but that does not mean it's any less beautiful than a fairy tale when our mother is planning it. Ten or so small round tables are spread around one side of the lawn, complete with long white tablecloths, floral centerpieces and settings, and two different stemmed glasses for each elaborate place setting. A few dozen fancy wooden folding chairs line an aisle of flower petals, leading up to one of those gorgeous flower arches full of swaths of gauzy fabrics that wave in the slight breeze. Against the backdrop of the mountains and the thick green woods, it is breathtaking.

Our mother always knows how to host a party, I'll give her that.

It was hard not to think about Elise and the day we eloped. The two of us jumping off the Atlantic City boardwalk into the sand and immediately losing a flip flop in the process. Staring out across the ocean, knowing there was an eternity before us and feeling like it would never be enough. That, for a moment, we were the only people in the world. And as excited and giddy as we had been, it was also incredibly lonely.

There are just so many chairs here.

"If it reminds you at all of the wedding from the movie version of Twilight, yes, that is my doing," Laura whispers as she elbows my arm to break me out of my reverie.

I give myself a little shake and try to pull myself back to the present. Unfortunately for me, I do remember having front-row tickets to Laura's Twilight obsession. "Uh, kinda. Maybe if it was actually in the woods instead of next to them."

"Yeah, Deanna shot that down. She didn't think there was going to be room for everything with how close the trees are."

"I didn't realize so many people were going to be here," Elise says, nearly startling me out of my skin as she steps into our conversation.

"Oh, yeah. I heard you ran into my mom." Laura grimaces a little.

"Yeah. She's, uh . . ."

"She's a hater, I know. She's also Logan's godmother though, so it's not like they wouldn't invite her," Laura mutters, rolling her eyes.

Out of the view of my cousin's theatrics, Elise meets my eyes briefly, and I drop the contact the second it happens, burned by it. I immediately take ten steps in a different direction, pretending to examine the place cards on one of the tables.

"It's still pretty small. A lot of Dad's side of the family is gonna show up. They're a little weird and distant. The cousins are cool though," Aiden says, and he starts to go to playfully mess Laura's hair up but stops himself about two inches from impact at the look she gives him.

"Do *not*. I spent all morning on this; there is so much hairspray keeping everything exactly where I want it," she snaps, deadly serious for a moment, her eyes flashing wolfishly.

"Got it, got it," Aiden yips, chased away by her tone.

Laura glances between me and Elise. "What's the matter with you two?

"Nothing," she says at the same time I do.

Laura frowns, likely contemplating whether or not she wants to press her luck with us but decides against it at the sound of cars pulling up. Elise doesn't hear it, but every wolf in and out of the house looks up at the minute sound of tires crunching over the gravel driveway.

Her mouth is set in a stony frown, but her eyes are full of apology.

She's sorry? Even though I'm the one that tore up her arm?

She has to have come to the same conclusion I had: we weren't meant for each other. It's not the conclusion I want our intertwined lives to come to, that we ultimately go our separate ways, never to see each other again. It seems such a waste, that life in all its oddities would find a way to put us in each other's paths again when we've grown.

And still, she is trying to catch my eye.

It happens, that flick of her dark-brown eyes meeting mine, and it lances through me.

I look away and stalk toward the house, hoping to get inside and away from her again. When I glance over my shoulder to make sure she's still across the lawn with Laura, she nearly gives me a heart attack by being only a couple steps behind me. Christ, this woman is going to kill me.

"Oh my god, dude. Your Aunt Jenny? I'm sure she hates me now. I've said like three things to her, and all of it was a mistake."

How is it possible to feel so loved by someone.

I can't answer her. My heart beats too much.

She frowns and moves on. "Um. So, I know the wedding is at five and the reception ends at eight, I figure you'll be busy tonight too. But I want to talk to you about last night."

My throat is too tight.

"Shawn," she repeats, grabbing my arm, as I didn't hear her the first time.

"I'm leaving first thing tomorrow," I say, shrugging her off. "I only wanted to come up for my brother's wedding, anyway."

"You left me in a field, my arm bleeding and cum all over my tits, and you won't even talk to me for a minute now?" she mutters angrily, but it's clear enough for me, and the two members of the Carrington pack that glance over at us looking concerned.

I wince and grumble through my excuse. "I had a pretty good reason, if memory serves, and it was to avoid making the situation even worse."

"I know you're upset after what happened. But can you please not leave until we've had a chance to talk?" she says quietly, worrying her lower lip between her teeth.

I don't want to make that promise. It's already going to be hard to leave, but if I have to say goodbye to her—I don't know if I'll be able to.

She elbows me with the arm I scratched, the sleeve pulling up just enough to show the large Band-Aid that she's covered it up with. "C'mon, I've still got the other nine fingers. Let's try to be present for your brother's day."

I can't quite laugh, but the breath in me feels a little less pinched for a second.

I try to evade and glance around. "Speaking of being present, has anyone checked to make sure there isn't a bedsheet hanging out of Logan's window?"

Elise rolls her eyes, and then her hand is on my arm, pulling me toward the kitchen. It's empty for the moment, unfortunately. "If you're not going to talk to me later, we're just going to do it now."

She lets go of me once she's ushered me into the room, and then stands in the doorway to block me from going back out.

I try to get past her, but getting closer to her makes the back of my neck hot, so I just pace to the other side of the room. "You should stay away from me. I can't be around you."

"What are you talking about?"

"I . . . I hurt you. I can't come back from that."

Her mouth sets in a hard line as she crosses her arms over her chest. A beat passes before she says, "Remember that time I closed the apartment door on your hand? And in a week your fingernail turned blue and fell off?"

The memory of that example makes me grimace. "I . . . what? God, gross."

"Yeah, it was, that's why I remember it. That low-key traumatized me."

"It's not the same thing, Elise. We shouldn't be together because . . . we shouldn't," I finish, a little underwhelmed with my own logic. I had good reasons a minute ago.

"I know you don't believe that." She holds me in her gaze, her warm-brown eyes searching mine. "Is that what's truly in your heart?"

As the seconds tick by without an answer, the vulnerability of the question stretches between us.

That. I can't deal with that. Not when she knows the truth about me and my family. It was so much easier to deal with when the problem was just some boneheaded move on my part, not an unchangeable part of myself.

Like my entire life hasn't been needing to push my worst self away, resist all my impulses, and she has the audacity to be understanding of them. How dare she love me in the way I need to be loved when I am trying my fucking hardest to stay away from her.

I want her to know that someone would choose her first, would choose her over everything.

Even if it can't be me.

I sigh and scrub a hand over my face. "No, dammit. I would do it again in a heartbeat. All of it."

The words spill out, a confession I have been biting my teeth closed on, maybe even since she first arrived.

I don't know if that's what she is looking for, but she blinks in surprise, her posture easing.

"I . . . what?"

"As many times as you gave me, I'd be back again for you. Even if it ended in another divorce."

Her mouth falls open, but she says nothing. My whole being aches to capture that mouth in a desperate kiss.

"I wouldn't change a thing. I'd go through all the heartbreak of you leaving again, if it meant spending any amount of time together again. And I don't care if that makes me a sap or pathetic, I am all of that for you," I say, and it's oddly freeing to just tell her. "Losing you is worth having had you at all."

But she needs to hear it, and maybe I've owed her this the entire time. Maybe I was just so scared of all the worst outcomes that I kept this final sliver of vulnerability to myself.

But the worst came to pass, and I didn't protect myself. I just hurt her.

"You have been worth every minute of it, unfair or not, terrible ending and all. I'd do it again. No changes, no notes. I loved you then, I love you now. Stay. Keep your life here. And if we can't make it work, tell me to leave and I will."

Elise's eyes are glassy. She looks like she wants to say something, like she's on the edge of finding the words she wants, and I lean in to hear them.

Of course, it's the moment Logan chooses to appear, thudding down the stairs.

I love my family, I really do.

Logan looks like he's ready to bite someone's head off, possibly in a very literal way, as he interrupts our little moment. Asshole isn't even fully dressed for the wedding, and it's in what, thirty minutes?

"Is there a reason you two are blocking traffic?" he asks, like the kitchen is currently a high-traffic area.

Elise shuffles out of the way, and he still rolls his eyes like it wasn't fast enough. Her brow furrows as she looks at him, the way he looks a little paler than usual, sweat beading at his scalp. "Dude, are you ok?"

"No, I'm not. I need an ice pack. Where is all the fucking ice in this kitchen? Didn't I just see like twelve bags of ice a minute ago?" He bitches in a way that, to me, is incredibly reminiscent of when he was a hot-headed teen, slamming the lid of one empty cooler after another.

"Logan, jeez, calm down," Elise says, raising her hands in a placating gesture.

She moves to assist, but Logan is already two steps ahead of her, crossing from the empty cooler to the freezer.

"Don't tell me to calm down! When in the history of telling people to calm down has it actually done anything?" he snaps back at her, taking things out haphazardly and discarding most of it aside.

"Hey! Don't talk to her like that," I say, warning in my voice, my claws pressing out of my fingertips territorially.

Logan barely glances in my direction as he digs through the freezer for probably a bag of frozen peas or something.

"It's fine, he's just stressed."

"I don't care, groomzilla over there needs to tone it down."

Logan barks out a hollow, joyless laugh, and exits the kitchen. I hear something like marbles hitting the floor, and more swearing follows him.

Did he just immediately puncture the bag of peas?

I glance at Elise and wave for her to stay back before I follow my brother's barrage through the emptied hallways. Along with some frozen peas scattered across the floor, there are huge gouges scratched down the halls, out to the patio.

I find my brother at the end of the trail of destruction, sitting on the ground next to the glass door, methodically shredding a curtain with his claws. He seems to be struggling to control himself.

His anger lays around him in little tufts of shredded fabric and frozen peas. He clutches the punctured bag to his chest, shuddering, trying not to snarl or transform. His long hair comes loose, scattering across his face, his eyes wild with anger.

"It feels like a panic attack," he mutters, not even looking at me.

I can see the way it hurts to contain.

I also see the way a couple of guests outside have spied us through the glass and know he wouldn't want anyone to see this.

"Hey, man. It's gonna be ok. Let's take a beat. You go back upstairs, I'll go out there and apologize, tell them you're not feeling well," I tell him quietly, taking his arm and helping him stand back up.

"You want to tell me to just do what you did, just drop all my responsibilities, my loyalty, my family, and for what?" Logan growls slowly, his glare burning into me. "Look how shit everything turned out for you. You threw all of us away for a human that left you the moment it got too hard."

His claws press in and take a few slices out of my jacket sleeve. Gritting my teeth I pull back. I'm off balance when he shoves me bodily.

The door bursts open when my shoulder connects with it suddenly, and the two of us spill outside, onto the patio. A rush of murmurs rise when the sky stops spinning. All the guests look at us, frozen.

I stumble, but keep my footing under me, holding him at arm's length the best I can, my hand clawed around his shoulder.

"Yeah, you talked too loud about your little secret," he snarls, tone venomous.

"Shut up. You don't know what you're talking about," I grumble around trying to hold him. I glimpse Elise behind us, eyes wide and terrified.

"No, you shut up. You broke the rules, you don't get to just . . . be happy! I stayed here and picked up the pieces after you left."

Teeth bared and a low rumble in his throat, he shoves me back, forcing me to let go of him. I stumble back and a table cuts into my side, the sound of dishes and glass hitting the ground follows.

"You picked some girl you just met over all of us," Logan seethes, throwing a glare in Elise's direction. "Did it occur to you how it felt for you to throw the rest of us away? Did it even matter?"

His anger is so singular, it's like he doesn't even see anyone else.

The metallic taste of blood creeps into my awareness. My lip is bleeding, I find, rubbing where he struck me. I swear we used to have a no-closed fists rule about hitting each other. Distantly, and perhaps a little unrealistically, I hope he gets grounded to hell for this.

I push off the overturned table at my back, the broken place settings gathered underneath me.

"No, you fuck off. I lost almost everyone who said they loved me. For eight years. Overnight. Don't think that you don't have to make that up to me."

He growls, the sound wrinkling his nose terribly in a snarl, and he begins the shift, even as dusk has barely fallen.

"Logan! Logan, please," Mom says, her eyes wide, and desperate with concern.

I really thought our mom would be on the other side of this. Even though she is outsized by all her children, she has never looked so small, or frail as her expression betrays her, as she reaches a gentle hand toward Logan.

The moment passes in his eyes, they linger on her, considering the peace she reaches out with.

Then his eyes flick to me, a sneer curling under the dark intensity of them.

"So, Shawn gets to break all the rules, and it's just fine?"

Oh, we're *fucked*.

Logan lunges, and I don't honestly see who it's toward. I just move toward him.

25

I was running after them in the woods before it really even set in. Branches and thorns snag on my clothes and skin; I whip past as if they are nothing.

Shawn. Still. Loves. Me.

And he's in pain. And I don't care about whatever feral means or if he is more dangerous under the full moon than he had been any night before.

All my reservations, my hesitations, are gone, along with one of my shoes. Adrenaline pumping through my veins and my heart beating wildly, I'm not even sure where they are anymore. All I know is that I need to be there for him.

This whole time, we were both just hurting over the thought that the other might pull back first, would be the first to give into that fear. This whole time, I had ached for what it meant to be loved by him, to trust him, and let him hold my heart in his hands, and he had been in that same place, needing it from me.

This whole time, I'd been so scared of being hurt by him, I'd never really let him in. And he had never really given me the chance to love all of him. Now that the part he's been afraid to show me is rampaging through the woods, I'm not about to prove his doubt right.

I pant when I get to the top of a hill. Ok, I have not really been building enough stamina for sprinting like this with my rambling hikes. When my other shoe falls off and rolls down to the bottom again, I know I don't have it in me to go back and get it. Hiking up my torn skirt, I force myself on, the pine needles and fallen leaves crunching underfoot.

Now that I am starting to feel out of breath, I'm starting to doubt—not my convictions, but that my physical form can keep up with a werewolf's ability to run cross country.

I start to slow down when I find a half-ripped pair of pants on the ground. I blink at it, wondering if one of them slowed down enough to take his pants off before ruining them.

. . . Weird. Ok. Not going to linger on this, I decide, and keep moving.

I don't recognize this part of the woods; it is deeper than I have ever been in them before. Normally it is easy to glimpse out of the canopy to other hills dotted with houses and know I'm not far from the rest of Mystic Falls. But now all I can see, whenever I reach a patch where the branches clear enough to see the sky, is the bright moon overhead.

Then I hear them, snapping and snarling at one another. I hurry on, following the noise and finding a path of debris, broken branches and tree trunks with large scratches gouged into them.

A loud, vicious growl reverberates through the woods, raising the hair on the back of my neck, followed by a hurt whimper.

"SHAWN!" I yell in response, not knowing which sound had been him.

I skid to a stop, catching myself against a tree when I see them.

They are not truly wolves, but I can see why it would be easy to mistake them as such. They stand as if human, hunched over by their beastly transformations, taller and broader, sharper.

Beastly in every sense of the word.

And yet, with how completely different they look from themselves, I still recognize Shawn from the two of them. I can see him now, even with the tail, ears, and fur.

There are glimpses of his features, his frame, in the beast form.

I know the shape of his hands, the knuckle and bone that protrude in the same way, even with the long claws extended. The shape of his jaw is not so different in a muzzle, even with the fangs.

Shawn turns around and looks at me first, the moonlight reflecting off his eyes as they narrow.

The other wolf, Logan. He turned before he attacked Shawn back in the Hayes' backyard.

The moment Logan notices me, a growl that sounds more annoyed than anything else emanates from him. He moves toward me, slow and menacing, but cuts short as Shawn lunges at us and knocks him onto his back. I dive aside the best I can, but it's obvious that tackle hadn't been meant for me in the slightest.

Shawn stands over Logan, snarling with claws extended. His little brother gets a foot under himself, pushing back across the ground and out from under Shawn's reach.

With a shrug that seems all too familiar, the way brothers are, he runs off, tail between his legs.

And then, Shawn turns his eyes on me.

I thought I knew what fear felt like. But it doesn't feel the way I knew it at all, the involuntary trembling, a dizzy confusion, the hot flush across my skin, the electric wave through me from head to toe. The ache between my legs.

Fear feels oddly exquisite, when I trust him. It's almost like excitement.

He approaches me slowly, smoothly on all four, somehow deft and agile at his greater, lumbering size.

He stops about ten feet back, bringing a knee up to stand. His gaze takes hold of mine as he draws himself up to full height, until he is absolutely towering over me.

God, I'm wet for that.

His nostrils flare, and I know he can tell. I fall back a step, a fleeting urge to do what fear should have told me to; a branch snaps under my foot.

All his fur bristles at the sound, his posture tensing up. My heart beats wildly in my throat.

Now I know what was wrong with all those dreams, that they truly were dreams. He was chasing me in those. I had left hoping he would chase me, hoping he would choose me. What I wanted, what I thought I needed, was for him to show me I mattered to him enough.

But wanting someone to chase you without actually asking for it just looks like walking away. Of course, he wouldn't.

Instead of running, I allow myself to fall.

His body cages over mine as the ground comes up to meet me; a pile of leaves takes the worst of it. I feel the springy bumps of mossy ground underneath me when the world stops spinning so much. My leg is caught between us at an awkward angle, my foot pushes to his clavicle as he leans his body over mine. As much as my leg is what's holding us apart, the position spreads my legs open.

He stops just short of pressing his body to mine, a low growl shivering across my stomach as his claws dig into the ground on either side of me.

Perhaps someone with a better sense of self-preservation would be terrified. Someone with that wouldn't be in this situation at all, but I find tenderness in the way he drags the blunt edge of his fangs against the vulnerable curve between my neck and shoulder.

"Shawn," I breathe, reaching up, finding handfuls of his thick coat, carding my fingers through it. "Shh, it's just us."

His breath clouds hot on my neck and the world slows down; and there is only the two of us here in the dark.

I feel my body shaking, quivering beneath his, despite my deliberate choice to stay, with an instinct to flee I am holding back. But the danger of it wakes something in me, something that has been rousing in my dreams these last few weeks. The needy ache between my thighs, wet enough that even I can smell it.

I truly do not have any kind of plan to work off. I wasn't even sure if he would recognize me like this. And maybe it was crazy to think that he might just turn back into a human the moment I hold him again, or some other equally hare-brained hope.

But I knew Shawn had never hurt me on purpose. And this is still him.

He growls almost imperceptibly low, and at first, I don't recognize my name embedded within it.

"You . . . should go," he says, the words almost lost within the gravelly voice.

"No," I insist, my voice cracking on the single syllable. I swallow, bringing my hands to hold his face. "I want to be here for you. You're hurting."

"I never wanted you to see me like this," he manages to grind out between his clenched, bared teeth.

It breaks my heart to hear him say that. All I can do is offer quietly, "I know."

More emphatically, he growls, almost snarls, a dire plea to keep me at arm's length, "You can't want me like this."

The truth, the silent breaker of all bonds: fear. It is so easy to recognize, now that I have left it behind.

"What?" I breathe. A damn bursts in my chest, I almost sit up with indignation at the injustice that someone I love so fiercely could truly believe this makes him unlovable.

"Did you think you could scare me off with this? God, Shawn, I thought you were cheating on me for most of our relationship."

His whole body stills, not even a breath escapes him. Hot tears start to creep up in my eyes to admit this much to him, to show him how utterly pathetic I'd been for his love once upon a time.

"And the way that broke my heart, that I could never be enough for someone I loved as much as you. And I still stayed and let it chip away at my self-worth because I didn't want to let go of the person I thought I knew and loved. Leaving you was the hardest thing I ever did."

I feel a tear break containment from my lashes, rolling straight back into my hair.

I bury my face in his neck, and exhale deep into his coat. "But staying here, now . . . this will be the easiest. It feels more natural than breathing. I want what you said before. I want to give us another chance, with all of you this time."

He nuzzles my cheek a little, and a sigh escapes me, melts the sorrow in me. It doesn't matter now, not when we're here, and I feel ready to approach who we are to each other with more wisdom.

And . . . well. It's hard to ignore his hardening cock as it bobs in the air, twitching over my wet, needy pussy. I did say *all* of him.

His wolf cock is longer and girthier than I had ever seen his regular dick before, veined and shaped a little differently. The head looks dark pink and lush to the touch, the shaft's skin velvety.

Glinting in the moonlight, a thick, white bead of precum drips onto my leg, and I whimper as I realize we're actually going to do this in the woods, right now.

"Oh, um, actually, maybe I should take this off before anything else," I squeak, and look at Shawn, realizing it's going to involve quite a bit of rolling around in the dirt. He sniffs along my neck, his claws dragging up my legs, scoring my tights and catching on the hem of my dress.

I start fumbling for the annoying tiny zipper. No sooner than I get it open, he realizes what I am doing, and cuts the remaining skirt open with a swipe of his claw.

Ok, I am going to have to yell at him about that later; right now I am too horny to really be concerned with work clothes. I shuffle out of the remaining dress and let my legs fall open, almost whimpering when he dips his head between them.

He flicks his tongue across my clit; my body attunes to even his breath ghosting across my skin. I cry out, my head tipping back at the contact. Next, his wolf snout is nuzzled to my pussy, his hot, soft tongue lapping at my clit, dipping deep in my cunt.

He licks greedily, without the preamble of tender kisses. Each drag of his scorching tongue through my folds makes the most-obscene wet noises. I'm fighting the way my hips need to buck into his mouth for more.

My clit is too quickly over-stimulated from his eager attention, and I have to push him away. No sooner than I pull his snout upwards, he's licking at my tits, finding some other way to pleasure me.

"Sh-Shawn," I gasp, my body shaking, quivering. I need the closeness of his body rutting into mine, to just feel completely embraced. "I need you in me, so bad."

He lets out a sound, hungry and possessive, but holds back.

"Elise, I want you, all of you. I haven't changed in that," he says like it's a warning, but the words only make my cheeks bloom red, my body overcome with a new warmth.

Even lying naked on the ground in the woods. I glance to the side and suddenly I don't know what to do with my hands. All our old problems don't seem so big. Maybe we can solve a decade of feeling like I wasn't enough with just a little possessiveness.

Instead of just letting flustered embarrassment take over, I flourish in how happy his words make me and breathe, "Then take me, I'm yours."

"You don't understand. I want you selfishly, greedily, I want to mark you as mine," he growls, dragging his teeth against the soft, vulnerable flesh of my breast. The blunted edge of one fang grazes against my hardened nipple, teasing me.

"I think I understand that. I'm ready, Shawn."

"You understand that you'd be my mate?" he growls and presses his teeth just hard enough to begin to pinch, but not break the skin, demonstrating what he means by mating me. It's marking me. A bite.

And my hips actually twitch at the thought, and I try not to moan aloud in response.

Saying yes doesn't seem to be getting the message across, so I just roll over onto my stomach, pushing onto my hands and knees.

Face down, ass up.

In response, the low rumbling growl in his chest gutters, becoming almost a snarl. A slight breeze brushes across the wetness of my exposed pussy, making me shiver in anticipation.

I let out a hiss as his cockhead presses at my entrance, a palpable heat difference between his tip and my labia. He drags the head through my folds as he lines his hips up to mine, and I stretch out my arms before me, bracing myself for the way he's about to break my back, hopefully.

Finally, he pushes into me, stretching my cunt to capacity almost immediately. I moan in pleasure, and he gives a few slow, experimental thrusts, wetting his cock in me.

"Mark me, mate me," I pant, begging almost incoherently. I'm not afraid of it hurting.

I want to do this. I crave every sensation adding to everything else I'm feeling.

He hooks his clawed hands under my knees and takes me off the ground, lifting me up. The change in position spreads my legs wider, pinning my back to his chest. I'd never felt so entirely thrown-around-able, if that's a thing. He is just so strong; I had no idea how much he'd been holding himself back from me. It is breathtaking to experience him so entirely. I know in that moment I could never regret him.

"Ah!" I gasp, almost wailing in pleasure. I feel decadent and pornographic, and I need more.

His arms curl under my legs, my jiggly thighs squish around his hard biceps, and he gives a sharp rock of his hips, making me bounce in the air. It's terribly exposed on my part, but it's a very good vantage point to admire his arms from, how tense and big they are from holding me up. Each time he pumps into me, I get a brief vision of my tits wobbling violently, as the collision of his body into mine moves the world, tilts me on an unfamiliar axis, and barrels all the breath out of my body.

Each drive feels less careful than the last, each more frenzied. Just as I'm starting to question if I'll be able to withstand this entirely different field of stamina, I recognize the catch in his breath.

It gives into the throaty groan Shawn always makes moments before he comes. I can feel the beginning of his knot start to swell. It slows his strokes, hindering them each time his growing knot meets my cunt, pushing a little further, cutting off the full swing of the motion each time, leaving it incomplete.

I can feel him coming hot within me, adding a slickness to every stroke.

He falls back upon the wood's leaf-covered floor, his arms closing around me. The world swings wildly, gravity taking me fully down over his knot, essentially suplexing me.

The full length of his wolf cock and knot sink deep inside me, and the breath is almost knocked out of me. I don't even feel the landing, just the impact ringing in my cervix.

His hips pounding into mine quickly comes to a stop as his cock is locked inside of me, only an inch or so of room to make friction. My body is pinned back against his, all I can do is pant and whimper as he drags a clawed hand through my folds, finding my sensitive clit with the pad of a finger.

My pelvis is still numb from the collision of his knot just barely fitting inside me the last time he rammed into me, but the added touch ratchets me to a horizon of sensation I can barely withstand. It is something fast and unwieldy, a pleasure so intense I can't keep it contained. I let out the most-obscene moan, arching back into him. I can't care less how it sounds or if there is anyone at all who can hear me out in the woods.

My voice breaks out into a squeal, until I'm gasping for breaths between whines of pleasure. My inner walls start clenching uncontrollably in my climax. It blooms in me, a warm, soft heat that relaxes every part of my body it spreads to.

I grind my hips back against his, desperate to work what little friction I can and ride my climax out. Each punctuated rut ends on a twitch and a spurt, the aftershocks of my climax squeezing around his knot. He lets out a groan that is almost human again, his wolf cock twitches and spurts again.

I whimper, utterly unable to take any more.

I don't remember Shawn biting me, when he sunk his teeth into the meaty part of my upper arm. It must have happened when I was lost in the throes of pleasure. I just notice the sting of it finally able to be heard as all the other sensations lessen, his teeth dislodging from my arm.

I'm so dizzy and maybe even delirious from that orgasm, I don't even really know how long he was biting me for. I can feel his enormous load in me, oozing through the almost nonexistent space between his knot and my reddened, twitching cunt.

"We could have been doing that for eight years," I mutter, and there's a ghost of a laugh in his breath.

We lie there a long time, just breathing, his knot tying me close to him. Honestly after all that, I don't know that I'd be able to move if I wanted to, even to roll over. I feel like I need a cool down stretch and maybe some Advil.

The pearly white fluid seeps out of me the next time Shawn moves to adjust me against him, the swell of his knot finally starting to go down. He makes no move to pull out, and honestly might have fallen asleep. I'm not far behind on that, so I decide to just make myself comfortable, laying my head against his chest, feeling safe with his arms around me.

Shawn still loves me, and it kicks ass, honestly.

It's like finding my favorite sweatshirt that had been lost for a long, long time; it's like standing in a gorgeous sunbeam; it's like that mystical hazy memory of lying down in the grass before you knew there were so many bugs down there. Cozy. Something I missed.

It's not the same as the first time we got married. It's not a promise to commit to forever, to hold on so tight it leaves no room for healthy doubt. It's a commitment to growing together. It's different because we're different. We know we're flawed, and that makes us able to work with those flaws.

Alright, let's give this another try; see where it goes. Whatever happens, it will be worth every moment.

26

Shawn

Considering how yesterday started out, things are going really well.

Despite previous resolutions against it, I am now pro-waking up in the woods naked, as long as Elise is also there, her body pressed to mine.

She's still fast asleep when the sounds of birds wake me. Her head rests on my arm, the odd leaf or pine needle poking out of her hair.

Elise, here. I still can't believe it.

I draw long, gentle scratches up and down the back of her thighs. She shifts in my embrace, rolling over to give me better access.

Every few scratches or so, I pause to trace the curve of her ass, gently squeezing delicious handfuls of it. Unabashedly, that part is just for me, even if she smiles and makes a little pleased sound as she dozes, tucked perfectly against me.

There are few pleasures greater than jiggling your mate's ass and watching it shake like Jell-O in a minor earthquake. Amazing. I don't know how this never gets old.

We fell asleep before my knot went down enough for us to separate. It must have happened sometime in the night. Probably for the best, considering my morning wood is pressed against her stomach currently.

She finally rolls over, dragging a kiss from my chest to my jaw.

"Oh, your breath is terrible," she mumbles, making a face. She reaches for a blanket that isn't there, and then sits up a little more, frowning. She blinks sleepily, taking in the woods around us.

It's hard not to be afraid it's not really as good as it seems, that everything could feel so perfect and right. I hold off on the knee-jerk need to panic, though.

"So . . . this isn't too much?" I ask, pushing up on an elbow.

"No, not at all. You know, it isn't actually that much more body hair than you have normally." She yawns into a hand, before rubbing the sleep from her eyes.

"I, um. Yeah. I was more concerned with the teeth and claws part," I mumble. Between the Band-Aid covering her shoulder and the dried blood of my bite on her arm, I've scratched her up in the last couple days.

Elise is picking some leaves out of her hair when she turns and catches my stare with her gorgeous doe-eyes.

"How long before I can show it off, you think?" she asks, and glances down at the bitemark, stretching her arm to admire it better.

I didn't even realize I was holding my breath, but a sigh of relief escapes me, and I smile. And then my brain stutters over the image of her actually doing that, and my cheeks and the back of my neck get hot.

I look away and run a hand through my hair and fail to come up with anything resembling a sentence. "Oh. Um, yeah, I, uh—"

"Oh, you're so cute when you're bashful," she giggles, stepping one leg over me and straddling my hips, her soft thighs making my cock twitch underneath her.

No one can fluster me like she does, and I'm happy to just melt in the feeling of it. It's such a pleasure to be bewitched by her.

I twine her fingers with mine. I've missed being able to touch her like this. "And you're sure you could put up with this side of me? It's not exactly as avoidable as I used to think."

"I wouldn't want to avoid it," she says, her expression so soft and sweet, I can't help but reach up to touch her face. She leans her cheek into my palm and bites the corner of her mouth thoughtfully. "But maybe next time, can we like, drag a futon out here?"

Next time. It pings something so optimistic in me, for once without the painful apprehension of hope. Just certainty.

I like that idea. Maybe we can even build a little open-air shelter to keep it off the ground, but still accessible for a wolf with no opposable thumbs.

I can't remember the last time I felt so complete. There's a weight off my chest that I've lived with for so long, I forgot it was there.

I foresee waking up naked in the woods with some regularity in my future. Our future, I remind myself, and can't help but grin at nothing in particular.

After maybe another half hour or so, lingering in the sleepy embrace of morning, breaking a couple more public-indecency laws, we decide it's time to get moving before we die of exposure. The trail of clothes we find scattered through the woods is an improvement, but it's still a little chilly.

We even find both of her shoes.

"You really didn't have to shred my dress," Elise says, frowning at the way her skirt doesn't quite cover everything anymore. Oops.

She wrinkles her nose as she picks it up and shakes some dirt off it, the fabric fluttering where I tore through it.

A bunch of pine needles and other debris from sleeping on the ground had stuck to her, embedding lightly in her skin—a great excuse to keep touching her. I couldn't stop. This morning is like something out of a dream. I don't want it to end.

"Maybe we can just live out here in the woods," I suggest teasingly, but, honestly, I'm willing to commit to that idea if she's down. Sure as hell beats having to go tell my family what happened.

"I'm so hungry, I can't even listen to jokes."

"Your house isn't that far away, y'know."

We could go there, and I could make her breakfast and our world could stay just the two of us.

"My cottage is like seven miles from the Hayes House. We didn't run that far into the woods, and I'm not walking seven miles before breakfast."

"Seven miles if you take the roads," I point out, but don't push it further. "Yeah, we probably have to go back to the scene of the crime. At least for a shower and change of clothes. The others probably want to know that we're alright too."

"And apologize to Logan for ruining his wedding."

"Yeah, even if he did start some of it."

She grimaces, flicking some more pine needles off her legs. "Can we leave out the part where we boned it out in the woods?"

"If we're going to tell them you're my mate, that you know about us . . . I think it might be implied. Or just unavoidable."

Some truths are weird and uncomfortable. It's just another Band-Aid we have to rip off.

Now that I think about it with a little more perspective, actually, this is the last way I'd have thought I'd be bringing Elise home to my family. Re-introducing her as my mate. Being certain that's who she was to me.

Maybe that's what I needed to feel in my heart to find the conviction to tell them before. Or maybe I needed the conviction that this is who she was to me to learn that she was my mate this whole time. I don't know. There's no way to really be certain that the universe decides someone is your person like that. But I know I want that to be who she is to me; and to me, that is more than enough proof.

It's going to be different this time, because my mom's trying to change.

"Are we going to include the fact that we've already been married before?"

I can't contain the grimace that question inspires. Elise makes a similar face as she watches mine. I shrug and hedge, "Maybe not? It might not be totally necessary."

She rolls her eyes and gives me a playful shrug. "So, we're not taking any lessons from this."

"Hell no. I don't care for parables or whatever."

"Oh, ok. Maybe we won't even bother explaining, then. We'll just stop in for a shower and change of clothes." She snorts. God, I love how she does that. It makes me smile instantly.

"And . . . after we shower, and all that. What do you want to do?"

"Then I'll invite you over to the cottage. You can help me unpack some of the things I started boxing up."

I don't even try to hold back the way that makes me grin wider. That's something to look forward to. No matter how telling my family goes, this is what I wanted, and it's going to be worth it.

She holds my hand while we walk back toward the house, her pair of heels in my other hand.

"I gotta go back to Boston, water my plants and stuff." I sigh, already dreading it.

"You have plants?"

"My neighbor has plants. I don't know when they became my responsibility."

I bite down against a joke about just abandoning them and staying here forever. I want to be mindful about how we move forward, deliberate about how we both take up space, and make room for each other in our lives. As much as I would love to dive into the unknown with her, I don't want to trample what she's built for herself.

"So I'm thinking, we can ease into this. I'll rent an apartment up here, so you can invite me over or kick me out whenever you feel like. It's probably going to take a few weeks to get everything squared away."

"I like that plan."

"Cool. Very cool."

"We're doing this with like, a little more thinking than we did the first time, right?"

"Mm. Marginally. But I'm excited for it all, all over again."

She squeezes my hand a little tighter as the house comes into view and the trees part to let us out of the woods.

The grounds of the Hayes House feel haunted by yesterday's disaster, a feeling that lingers heavy and urgent in the air like the smell of something burning.

Everything we set up for the wedding is in shambles. Some of the guest seating and tables are flipped over, there's torn white bunting and battered bunches of flowers everywhere. The dance floor set up on the patio is scattered with clumps of grass and dirt. The big flower arch at the end of the aisle is laying on the ground.

I've done my share of walks of shame, leaving a hookup's apartment the morning after and sneaking home in yesterday's clothes to the teasing of old roommates. I've never actually felt all that embarrassed about it before, but then again, I've never had a whole crowd of spectators.

All the Carrington pack members are gone, from what I can tell. It's just my family.

Some of my extended family that I haven't seen in a decade or more are still here, attempting to help my mom clean up the torn-up backyard. Of course, my mom's too much of a polite host to ask them to leave after things became a disaster.

Well, that's lovely. They all stop what they're doing and look up when Elise and I walk out of the woods together. I try to smile and awkwardly wave.

There isn't really hiding what just happened, I guess. It's clear we've both taken a tumble in the dirt.

Somewhere along the way back I recovered the jacket of my ensemble but I'm still missing my shirt, part of a pant leg and both shoes. I'm carrying Elise's muddy heels, and while she's tied the torn part of her skirt together, her pantyhose is so shredded one side has become a loose sock around her ankle.

Everyone here is a werewolf, and, I have to assume, has either the same or greater amount of knowledge about what being mated means, but maybe they don't necessarily know that I ripped her underwear off her body, or that I donated my shirt to the cleanup effort when it came to all that mess I knotted in her.

I try to resist the urge to check that it's not that bad, as Laura spots us and bounds over. Behind her, a few more family members including Mom and Aiden trickle out across the lawn to us.

"Holy shit, I can't believe you came back, and you're ok? Logan is gone. I don't know how the wedding can go on now—" Laura stops short right before us, cutting herself off with a loud gasp.

Maybe we don't even need to think about it that much. Maybe the crescent of dried blood on Elise's arm is enough.

"Shawn . . ." my mom says, warning in her tone. Her eyes widen when she gets a better look at my mate. "Oh my god, Elise."

"It's really not that bad." Elise shrugs, trying to play it off, but she still winces a little at the movement. Her eyes drift to my relatives staring from the backyard patio, and red scorches her cheeks. She shifts incrementally behind me.

Laura is a lifesaver, and she moves quickly to pluck a white tablecloth off the ground and drape it around Elise like a shawl, or maybe a shock blanket. "What happened?"

Eyes shift back to me, and I glance away, running a hand through my hair.

I don't really know what to say first. Maybe that it's ok, she knows we're all werewolves. We're obviously way past that, but I don't know how far we need to backtrack to get everyone on the same page.

"Oh. Um. Right. Hey, Mom, you've met Elise. Funny story, she's also my ex-wife."

Those are the words that break Elise from her reverie of embarrassment, and her knee-jerk reaction is to elbow me in the side. "Hey! Why are you leading with that?"

"I mean, all of it's bad," I mutter, shrugging and rubbing the spot.

Mom's face drains of all blood. I'm honestly a little worried she'll faint or something. Eyes darting rapidly between us, she just echoes the words, "Ex-wife?"

I try really hard not to glance to the relatives by the patio.

"We got divorced like eight years ago. There's a lot to catch everyone up on," I explain weakly. I try to smile to maybe encourage a more cheerful mood, but it probably comes out as an anxious grimace.

"Oh, you weren't here for that part. So, first, Shawn was all like, put me back in, coach, to Elise," Aiden is recapping for my mother, in what might be the most unhelpful way possible.

Yesterday evening is a little hazy to me at this point, but I swear I did not call my ex-wife "coach" at any point. Sure, most of the details are fuzzy because of full-moon-fuckery, but not that fuzzy.

"Did you really use the words, 'put me back in'?" Laura asks immediately, making a face like she's just barely holding back on a joke too dirty to tell in front of my mother.

"Obviously, because it worked on me," Elise replies dryly before I can tell Laura to can it. She gives me a look that is completely unreserved in how happy she is, and everything else in the world melts away.

"You know what, you can embellish however you like, I'm going to find my mate a change of clothes and a hot shower," I say, and I take the opportunity to tug Elise away.

We make it maybe another ten feet before my mom repeats, "Mate?"

I wince and stop on the stairs up to the patio, glancing over my shoulder. "How much do you really want me to explain?"

"Oh, that's why you asked about . . . ugh, ew." Aiden grimaces.

Deanna has one arm crossed over her chest and the other supporting her head as she processes it all. Or attempts to and just gets stuck somewhere along the way.

"I love you both," she says at last, before shaking her head and waving her hands between the both of us. "But what the fuck?"

Aiden looks like he's never heard Mom swear before, and I can count on one hand how many times I have.

"Mom . . ."

"I need a minute, but I need to figure out what to do with all this mess first," she says, gesturing to the lawn, and looks resigned to that. It's probably easier to tackle things within her power.

She stands still, looking out over all the destruction for a moment, before she steps forward and hugs Elise and me both. "You're both grounded."

"Yeah, I figured."

"Let's take a minute, and sit down, get a glass of wine," Laura offers gently, sliding her arm through my mother's, even though it's probably ten a.m. at best.

"Yeah, Aiden and me will handle the rest of the family," I add, because I know that's probably what she's most worried about right now.

"Aiden and I," my mother corrects me out of sheer rote memory when she pulls back; it doesn't look like she even registers speaking.

"No, I said me, not you." I roll my eyes. Elise snorts, and, when I catch her eye, she breaks out into a wide smile. God, I've never loved anyone so much. I never want to let go of her.

Elise puts a hand on Mom's shoulder. "Everything's ok. We can handle it."

She looks at Elise, and for all the shock still remaining on her face, there is some warmth. "Thank you, dear."

Laura tugs on my mom's arm and leads her back inside. Once they're out of earshot, Aiden sidles forward and says to us in an undertone, "Logan hasn't come back yet."

I grimace. I don't remember everything that happened during our fight, but I don't think either of us did any lasting damage. It was just a bit rougher than our usual tussles.

I shrug, honestly glad that he's not around right now. "He'll be fine. He's just gotta lick his wounds a bit first."

I turn around and find Elise looking curiously at the patio full of distant family. "Is that your whole family?"

"Yeah, pretty much."

Her stare remains on them, as she shifts her weight from one foot to another, considering the overturned chairs, the flower arch that could probably be propped up again. "I mean, we eloped on a crazy whim the first time. And, well, it's no Atlantic City, but . . ."

I watch Elise's gaze sweep across the lawn. I'm pretty sure there's no way I'm catching her drift. Still, the endorphins from the other night give me the unwarranted confidence to catch her eye and ask, "Are you about to suggest we throw taking it slow to the wind?"

Elise rolls her eyes, but she grins. "Well, we're already here. We can always just get divorced again, right?"

This utter madwoman. I love her. I did say I would do it all over again, and I mean it. Marrying her again is going to be such an adventure, and I can't wait for all of it.

"You sure can try," I tease, stepping into her space and cupping my hands around her face. I brush a speckle of dirt off her cheek, and dip down for a kiss that is more grinning against her face than it is anything else. I pull back for just a second.

"You'll still be mated to me though, right?"

She clasps her hand over mine. "You can't get rid of me that easily."

"*Clearly*. It barely worked the first time."

27

I will admit I am far drunker at my second wedding than I was at my first. The evening is a blur.

"Uh, hey, guys," Shawn said as he gathered the remaining guests, his extended family. "So, um, a lot's happened, in the last day or so. I know some of you guys were invited to see my little brother get married; he's a little indisposed at the moment. I guess we're going to have to reschedule that one. But uh . . . we're still going to have a party. There's lots of food, please, enjoy yourselves."

Laura said the Carringtons are upset, to be sure. Apparently, Deanna tried to smooth things over the best she could, but Logan will have to make things right with them when he comes back. But that's something to worry about another day.

We got cleaned up and Laura pre-heated the ovens for the food that never made it out yesterday. Something to do with the caterer sprinting off into the woods, leaving the couple of waitstaff I'd hired for the day to flounder and pass out the hors d'oeuvres that they did have. I'm going to have to email them an apology, but it's going to wait just a bit.

My vows might have consisted of wiggling my eyebrows and giggling, "Round two, baby!"

It was worth it to see Shawn try so hard not to laugh, and ultimately fail.

Not all of his relatives stayed, in fact the older lady who gave me the stink eye earlier made it very clear she was leaving. Everyone who remained at the house is still pretty toasted. Aiden mentioned something about werewolf weddings and funerals, that the aconite consumption does need to be some next level shit to pacify the inner wolves.

Deanna is at least a little wine drunk, but maybe that helped, because she's given me a number of hugs and said that I'm her favorite daughter-in-law. Which, honestly, kicks ass, even if I'm the only one.

I think she and Shawn might even be on somewhat better terms now, because immediately after, she flicked him on the forehead and only said, "Grandbabies."

"Considering that Mom's not giving me shit for the whole ex-wife thing"—Shawn shrugs, rubbing his forehead—"it's an improvement. And you don't need to worry about the grandbabies thing, we don't need to—I'll ask her not to—"

"It's fine, really, Shawn."

Even if it's still rocky between some of us, I'm happier than I've been in such a long time. I have a family with Shawn, Deanna, Laura, Aiden, and, whenever he gets back, Logan too. I've never had such a big family before or felt like I was at the center of it.

Laura has also gotten very wine drunk with me and is apologizing to me for getting carried away at the bar during the stag night that feels so distant now, and in the same breath giggling about the mystical tit-jobs line again. We're never going to hear the end of that.

I look for Ava, but apparently Laura's friend ended up leaving early; it sounds like Logan said something that pissed her off. I'm honestly not surprised, considering what I saw pass between them yesterday.

The only thing that feels amiss tonight is that Logan isn't here. Shawn said it was better that he got some space after that fight. It wasn't just the full moon's frantic energy agitating them, clearly there were some deep-seated issues that they needed to talk about.

But there's going to be time for them to figure it out, now that Shawn's going to stay in Mystic Falls. I'm really happy he's going to have the time.

Shawn drapes an arm around my shoulders, pulling me into his side. He nuzzles and kisses the crook of my neck, and it makes everything in me feel complete.

"We should probably wrap things up soon," he murmurs into my skin.

"Tonight's not going to be like last night, right?" I ask, and, as he starts to shake his head, I have to add on, "You guys weren't going to go feral, were you?"

Everyone I've heard use that word this week has all but whispered it, grimacing around it like the very thought was repulsive.

His expression softens as he sees the trepidation in my expression. He shrugs, as if to say he doesn't really know either.

"I have you, and that is worth making sure it doesn't happen."

I glance at the woods again. Shawn's hand traces soothing shapes along my arm.

"He had enough of himself to choose to stop fighting me, I think he'll be fine. Besides, what you saw wasn't even that bad. Logan and me have done worse to each other before," he says, and I frown at him, because that's not reassuring in the least.

He catches my expression and rolls his eyes a little. "I can tell you didn't grow up with brothers because no one your age tried to murder you constantly throughout your entire childhood."

Before I can point out I do have stepsiblings, Aiden follows up with, "Elise, I can just tell you've never tried to reenact a Dragon Ball Z fight and then been sworn to secrecy about how Shawn broke his nose. It's in your aura."

Huh. I had just assumed it was naturally crooked.

"Yeah, alright, maybe." I nod, briefly glad I didn't grow up with siblings. At least, I'm glad to have siblings-in-pack when they're past the roughhousing stage. I hope.

Shawn shoves lightly at Aiden's shoulder. "Just because the statute of limitations is up, doesn't mean we need to tell people about it."

"The baby picture book is coming out first thing tomorrow morning," is all Aiden bothers to reply, wearing a shit-eating grin.

—

The night is winding down, and most of the relatives have left. Evening creeps in, first with fireflies, cool humid air, and sunset around the horizon's edges. I can see the wolfish shifts starting to light the edges of my new family, Laura's teeth are a little longer, Aiden's ears a little more pointed and tipped with fur. Deanna has started going around to the others and saying her goodnights.

It feels good in an exhausted sort of way. It feels utterly different from yesterday, when the energy of the crowd was tense and on edge. Everyone is much more relaxed.

The full moon lasts only one night technically, but I'm trying to think of an innocuous way to ask if we might have a repeat of last night, or is that only when it's at its peak? Just curious, of course; there's no particular reason.

The follow up question to that is if I can plausibly sneak off into the woods again with my mate, and I think I will never get tired of calling Shawn that. I'm working on figuring out how I want to ask it when Aiden knocks a playful shoulder into Laura's.

"Oh, you wanna do a howl? It's been forever."

My eyes widen as I look at all of them. There's still so much I don't know, but I'm excited to learn. I nudge Shawn and ask, "You guys actually howl?"

"Yeah, I've been practicing too," Aiden says, before taking a few steps back, the fur on his ears bristling before he opens his mouth. It sounds like an actual howl, not a human imitating one, but there's clearly an extra element of control. The effect is almost musical, how smooth it carries his voice on the air.

And then it hits me that I've definitely heard this sound and this song before.

"It was YOU," I blurt out a little too accusatorily, cutting him off. He looks at me in surprise. "I thought I was going crazy this week, hearing a wolf howling Bohemian-FUCKING-Rhapsody. God, I never would have thought the answer to that one was lycanthropy."

Aiden snorts and leans into my side conspiratorially. He takes in a breath, clearly about to explain something else to me, probably about how he likes to freak out hikers with this little talent, when his head jerks towards the woods.

I turn my head too, and after a moment, spot Logan coming out of the woods. His clothes are pretty torn and dirty. He looks a little dazed and vacant as he approaches and stops at the edge of the party.

"Hey, man, what happened?" Laura calls out, pretty much the same time as Aiden yells, "DUDE, YOU WILL NEVER BELIEVE WHO GOT REMARRIED!"

"Well, when you phrase it like that, there's not that many options present," Laura huffs, giving Aiden a shove. "Also, maybe we don't *lead* with that."

Shawn lets go of me, pausing only to press a kiss to my temple. "I'll be right back," he murmurs, and I squeeze his hand before he jogs over to where Logan stands, under the shadow of the woods.

—

Logan barely registers my presence until I get close to him, and he glances up. He's always had a little bit of a gaunt look to him, but it used to be because he wore eyeliner in high school and dyed his hair. Now it looks like it's natural to him.

"You were gone a long while," I say, dropping a hand on his shoulder, and he sways with the impact. Executive decision to not lead with the wedding thing. I'm just glad he came back. We can figure out our differences after the full moon is a little further away in the calendar.

"I . . . couldn't figure out how to turn back. I just kept running, and then it's hazy," he mutters. His words lance through me. I put an arm around his back and try not to show too much of the panic and concern they inspire.

"It's over, the worst of it's passed," I say, scratching his back in a way that probably betrays my frantic thoughts more than it is comforting. "Hey, man. I'm sorry. Things were heated."

It's not the apology he deserves, but it's a start. We have a lot to work on.

"I'm tired. I don't care about it anymore." He sighs, defeated. I know he doesn't mean it. But I know what it is to be so tired you feel like giving up.

It's been an extremely long day and night. I hate to think that he's in for another one.

I bite my tongue on any further comment about our argument. It's too raw right now. We don't need to open that up right away. It's probably best to wait till the moon wanes some more.

I start to lead him back to the house, when he stumbles. Logan puts a hand to his temple, wincing. There's some pretty gnarly bruising on his ribcage too, I notice through the tatters of his shirt.

"Jeez, you pick a fight with someone else?"

"Not that I remember," he says, but as we step into the light and he looks at me, I can see there's blood in his teeth.

I stop abruptly, immediately inspecting and pulling back his cheek. I half-expect to find he's broken a tooth or got a scrap of fur from chewing on a squirrel, but all I see is the blood, the way it coats his teeth in red.

"Dude, stop, stop," he tries to say, but doesn't resist more than that.

"I think you're bleeding in your mouth," I tell him, and he frowns at me.

"It doesn't hurt," he says, batting my hands away. I watch as he massages the other side of his jaw, wincing again. He reaches in and after a moment, pulls a scrap of something out. He holds it out in his palm, staring blankly.

It's one of those little corsage things, or what's left of it. It's really just a knotted bit of bloody lace and a couple leaves still tied together, and another piece of fabric skewered through the pin. I vaguely remember Laura's friend carrying a box of those around, asking if anyone in the wedding party didn't have one yet.

My hand reaches up and pats over my shirt, finding the one I got before. I still have mine, so he must have bitten that off someone else.

"Is that yours?"

He's not wearing one, but I'm not sure if he ever was. He shakes his head a little. He tries at first to put it in his pocket, before realizing that his pockets are pretty slashed up and not great for storage. He shrugs and pins it through part of his sleeve, twisting the end closed, like that's not gross as hell.

"Guess it is now," he mutters, and levels me with that look of, "*We're not going to talk about this.*"

I grit my teeth, but don't push it. Sooner rather than later, we're going to have to confront that Logan definitely bit someone last night.

If you enjoyed this book, you can find updates on future projects, events, content notes, and subscribe to the author's sporadic newsletter at kate-prior.com.

You can follow Kate on socials: Instagram, Threads, or Tiktok @bykateprior, or join her reader's group on Facebook, *Kate's Priory of Paranormal Romance.*

If you enjoy learning about the craft of writing or finding solidarity in the ups and downs of publishing, listen to the podcast *Romance Writer's Therapy*, hosted by Kate Prior and Marty Vee.

More by Kate Prior

Love Laugh Lich (Claws & Cubicles 1)
Lily has been the Lich's secretary ever since his evilness took over the company. She loves her job, but she's got some questions about her boss. Like what's under that cloak of ever-billowing.

Her wondering intensifies when one day the Lich needs something from her that isn't just scheduling appointments-- but a shiver. He needs it for a spell, but it feels like it crosses a line from their usual banter.

After her contributions to his dark rituals become more than OSHA compliant, sex-magic-and-triple-cocks-oh-my, she starts to contemplate whether the Lich Lord returns her feelings, or still only sees her as his secretary.

Lily may have given him her body, but he never asked for her heart.

The Orc from the Office (Claws & Cubicles 2)
Mate-bonding with a co-worker is against company policy... accidentally or not. Janice knows better than anyone that entanglements with co-workers are risky business.
But when Janice accidentally breaks a co-workers nose, she finds herself unexpectedly mated to an orc, and under Monster Resources' scrutiny. Khent from the IT Department is quiet and nerdy, despite the tusks. His emails are overly wordy. He won't stop apologizing even though she's the one who broke his glasses. Clearly, fate got this one wrong.
All Janice has to do is stay away from Khent until the bond dissipates. Easy enough, right? Except...

…Her company laptop chooses this week to need the orc from the IT Department, repeatedly.

…She accidentally clicks on orc porn at work and has to take remedial phishing training with Khent.

…Their bond will keep pulling them back together until it is completed.

The Gargoyle from General Management
(Claws & Cubicles 3)

A siren in heat, a gargoyle who keeps getting under her skin, and an inescapable work trip…

Gwen doesn't want anyone to know she's a siren. She doesn't want anyone to know she's terrible at her job either.

Perhaps least on her list of priorities, Gwen would also like to avoid the gargoyle who saw her vibrator in the TSA check. Except, the very same gargoyle is the new manager she has to work with, and he's going to the same corporate retreat she is. He reminds her too much of her past and exactly the career-driven sort of guy she can't stand from Fortune 666 companies.

When things start to heat up between them, Gwen's afraid he's going to learn all her secrets, but when he offers to help feed her siren appetite, she can't resist mixing business with pleasure.

And They Were Broommates
(A short story included in Hexes and Ohs: A Witch
Paranormal Romance Collection for Charity)

Astrid is breaking her lease. The tower isn't big enough for her and Jason, and the town only needs one resident witch. She's tired of competing with him over every little thing.

Except, the lease-breaking ritual goes wrong, and they end up with a strange bond letting them hear everything the other is thinking. They didn't need a psychic link to know they hated each other, but now they can't hide everything else they think about each other.

Mushrooms, halfling-eating monsters, and orcs, oh my. When Bianca Chanterelle gets lost in the woods, she doesn't expect the orc hunter that finds her to be any help getting back to her traveling party, but with him finds adventure, a secret microbiome, a terrifying monster, and a budding attraction between them.

Tanis, son of Dhane the Bloodthirsty, shouldn't be so curious about the halfling woman who is utterly unsuited to living in the woods, but he can't resist the way his blood calls to her, especially when they find themselves hiding in a tent, sharing his bedroll.

When the rest of the orcish hunting party decides to raid the traveling halfling troupe of actors, however, a staged kidnapping and a monster intervention may not be enough to make sure everyone gets out of the woods.

Meet Me at the Anvil

When Diane faints during her wedding vows, it's expected. Her family thinks almost everything is too stimulating for her because of her fainting condition. Of course they matched her with a man who couldn't make anyone's heart flutter.

When her fiancé tries to make light of the situation by giving her a fainting goat, the ridicule is too much to bear.

Diane wants more than the life before her— she wants to live the passion and adventure she's only ever found in the erotic sketches she creates, and the kind of heart-racing feelings her fiancé's cousin and best man Liam gives her.

The last thing Diane expects as she flees from the church, however, is for the best man to run away with her.